BROTHERLY LOVE

RANDYE LORDON

BROTHERLY LOVE

ST. MARTIN'S PRESS
NEW YORK

DESIGN BY JUDITH A. STAGNITTO

Library of Congress Cataloging-in-Publication Data

Lordon, Randye.
   Brotherly love / Randye Lordon.
      p.   cm.
    ISBN 0-312-09254-7
    I. Title.
    PS3562.O7542B75   1993
    813'.54—dc20   93-15048
                                  CIP

First Edition: July 1993

10 9 8 7 6 5 4 3 2 1

For Shan.
With friends like you,
who needs fairy godmothers?

I would like to thank John and Jean O'Reilly,
Winslow Eliot and Tina Hayward,
Henry Morrison, Keith Kahla,
Maude, Marla, and, of course, Kathe.

BROTHERLY LOVE

O N E

I was the youngest of three children. My first memory of my brother and sister is when I was three years old. David was six, Nora was nine, and they had finally decided, after much debate, that I would be allowed to play cowboys and Indians with the big kids.

It took me two and a half hours to free myself from the dining room chair.

It could have been worse. David was all for "Burnin' the Injun at the stake," but fortunately Nora intervened just as he lighted the first match, which is, in part, why I am here today. I didn't care much for either cowboys or Indians after that, but I continued to play because being able to hang out with the big kids was all that mattered. As a result, I learned how to be the best Injun scout in the whole darned building.

All things considered, I could never figure out why my sister was so chagrined at my career choice.

My name is Sloane, Sydney Jessica Sloane, and I'm a private investigator.

For the past ten years, my partner, Max Cabe, and I have had an office on the Upper West Side of Manhattan near where we both live—which is not to say that we live together. Max has a cozy one-bedroom on Eighty-ninth Street just off Riverside Park. I inherited my parents' three-bedroom apartment on West End Avenue when my father was killed eleven years ago. Max says he likes to see us as "lovers waiting to happen," which is as likely as goats flying or Republicans agreeing to tax the wealthy. I see Max more like the brother I never had in David.

Like Max, Nora has her own agenda for me and hasn't approved of most of the choices I've made since 1972, when I first applied to the Police Academy. Fortunately, she lives far away in Baltimore with her husband, Byron, which, if nothing else, makes the stress level in my life more manageable. Don't get me wrong, I love my sister. It's just that ever since Mom died, Nora's tried to take her place in my life. Nora doesn't seem to understand that I don't need her to be my mother. I need her to be my sister.

Siblings.

It is now mid-March as I attempt to sort out what happened in February.

February was one ugly month.

It started Monday morning after I had taken my neighbor's cat, Charlie, for a few days. Long ago, Charlie found a way to maneuver between our two apartments, but when Carmen leaves town, she officially moves his bowls and litter box from her kitchen to mine. Charlie is an exotic, friendly Abyssinian who, as it turns out, is a perfect companion; independent yet affectionate, his needs are simple, and his demands are few—unlike most of the relationships I've experienced. This doesn't mean, however, that I would own a pet. I will occasionally pet-sit for friends to satiate whatever fleeting needs I have for petlike companionship. Unlike most of the people I know who are either cat or dog owners, bird lovers or even fishophiles, I like to live alone. I don't want to commit myself to anything even as permanent as gold-fish. But I do like Charlie.

Just after 9:00 A.M., when Carmen left and Charlie was scoping things out in the apartment, I went to Nora's and my old bedroom—now the den—with a pot of Zabar's gourmet decaf and the newspapers, prepared for a long morning of hedonistic rest and relaxation. A pre-fab log burned evenly in the small but functional fireplace, and I settled onto the sofa. Max was in the Caribbean with a model whose name I kept forgetting. Kerry Norman, our secretary, was taking care of the office, so I felt comfortable taking a morning for myself.

All was right with the world when I took that first sip of joe and started reading slowly through the A section of the *Times*. By the time I was ready for the *News*, Charlie had joined me and was snuggled in a ball by my feet.

It was page three that caught my eye.

There was an article about a murderer who had accidentally been released from prison while awaiting trial. There had been a mix-up with the bail papers and he managed to slip through the red tape. Now he was back out on the streets.

But it wasn't the story that caught my eye. It was the mug shot printed just above the article. Noah Alexander.

———

3

The name meant nothing to me, but the face was another story. Noah Alexander wore a full beard, long hair, and a glazed-over look. The picture was a bad blurred reprint of his mug shot, but I knew that face as well as I knew my own name.

I hadn't seen it in close to fifteen years, but I would have been willing to bet my teeth—which are near and dear to me—that this was a picture of David, my older brother and onetime nemesis.

A voice in the back of my head suggested I breathe.

David was dead. He had died in a bombing in Israel thirteen years earlier.

I squinted at the photograph. It had to be David. His left eye was slightly off center and his eyelids drooped gently as if he was about to fall asleep. The right corner of his mouth pulled up into the hint of a smile, and though I couldn't see beyond his lips, I'd have been willing to lay any odds that there was a gap between the two front teeth.

Thirteen years ago, my sister had called me ghoulish, among other things, for doubting that David was really dead. Ghoulish, perhaps, but my instinct to doubt David's earthly departure was testimony to his life. Nora, like our mother, had a "pass the peas" approach to life and death. I, like our dad, liked to have proof in hand—especially when it concerned David.

He was a pathological liar who had been rescued from the long arm of the law on more than one occasion by our father. Dad had created a respected place for himself as an attorney and his connections worked as a buffer for David in his blossoming career as a forger. It had worked until David was arrested and charged with stealing, forging the signature and cashing in stocks that belonged to the mother of his girlfriend. No one could persuade the woman to drop the charges, so David, out on bail, decided it was time to leave the country.

I read the article again and again, trying to find something, anything that connected the face I saw with the man I knew.

Noah Alexander had been in prison pending trial for the murder of liquor-store owner Jesse Washburn and one of his clients, Ms. Mildred Keller.

While David and I had never been friends, as kids he had always been devoted to Nora. I decided, with trepidation, to give my big sister a call. I fished my address book out of my purse and hiked my feet up onto the desktop. After dialing the number, which I have a mental block against, I leaned back into the squeaky old swivel chair. Three rings later, Nora's familiar singsongy voice came at me through the receiver, loud and clear.

"Hel-low-oh."

"Hey, stranger, how you doing?"

"Sydney?" She paused. "Are you all right?"

"Yeah. Couldn't be better."

"Really? Then why are you calling? Especially on a weekday."

"I'm just calling to see how you are. How are you, Nora?" I reached for the binoculars I keep on the window ledge in the den. In the last ten years, I have witnessed surprisingly little with the help of my glasses.

"Fine." She sounded wary, as if she was waiting for the other shoe to drop. Which, of course, it would.

"And how's Vicki?" My niece was away for her first year at college and, according to her letters, loving every second of it.

"Oh, puleeze, that child is going to be the death of me. Do you have any idea what she's doing now? She's playing electric violin with an all-women's rock-and-roll band."

"Hey, that sounds great."

There was silence, then a sigh. "Well, it figures you'd think so. Personally, I hate it. I think it's gauche and a waste of time, but then, whenever I say white, you seem honor-bound to say black. I don't know why you always have to be so contrary."

"I am not contrary. I'm just different from you."

"Mmm. And was her playing electric violin your idea? She was perfectly content with classical music until you gave her that horrible album."

"Stephane Grappelli is not horrible music. He's one of the best jazz violinists of our time. He's great. Besides, that was ten years ago, Nor. What is with you?"

She sniffed and cleared her throat. "Ach, I don't know. This house is just so damned stuffy. I'm just . . . hot. I hate being hot."

"It's February. It's cold."

"Well, this house is just unbearable. I turn the heat down, and Byron comes home and turns it right back up. It's enough to drive me crazy."

My brother-in-law, Byron, is an attorney in Maryland who has made a small fortune from saving the hides of political screwups who have been caught with their hands in the till or their pants around their ankles. He looks like a cross between a weasel and a bear, with a tiny little head and beady eyes atop a massive, misshapen body. When Byron hit forty-five, his body changed drastically, and without any apparent warning the large Byron Bradshaw became the massive Mr. Bradshaw, belting his pants just inches under his chest and waddling like a chafed penguin. Though he's noted for being a killer in the courtroom, Byron is one of the gentlest men I have ever known. He has the patience of Job and a heart the size of Texas.

"Well, you know what it sounds like, Nor."

———

"I don't want to talk about it, Sydney, do you understand?" she snapped.

"Hey listen, I have a lot of friends who—"

"I do, too, and I'm too young, all right?"

"Sure, but forty-five isn't—"

"No *buts*. I know what you're going to say and I don't want to hear it, okay?"

"Okay."

"Good." She exhaled loudly. "So what's up? I know you well enough to know there has to be a reason for this call."

"Well, as a matter of fact, I saw the strangest thing this morning. I was reading the paper and there's a story here that caught my eye." I pulled the paper off the file cabinet, set it in my lap, and looked at his picture.

"Oh?" I could hear Nora lighting a cigarette.

"I know this is going to sound crazy, but there's a picture of a guy here—a mug shot, actually—and you'll never guess who he looks like." I tried to make my voice sound light.

"Who?"

"David."

Silence.

"Hello?" I tapped at the mouthpiece.

Big sigh.

"I know you're there—I can hear you smoking."

"Just tell me, are you planning on starting this all over again?"

"Starting what?" My voice went up an octave or two.

"You know perfectly well what." Nora had mastered the tone of sanctimony by the time she was fifteen and made Mom—our family disciplinarian—look like Glinda the Good Witch of Oz. When Mom died, Nora thought her lectures might encourage me to act more in line with what she thought Mom would want, but then, as now, it only turned every muscle in my body to stone.

"I didn't call for a speech. I just wanted to know if you'd heard from him, that's all."

"He's dead, Sydney. If you're so anxious to see him, why don't you call Minnie?" Her throaty laugh turned into a hacking cough.

Aunt Minnie is our father's sister, who connects daily with loved ones who have already passed on to the other side. She is seventy-nine, and apart from her dialogues with the deceased, she still works, meditates, and smokes a pack and a half of Parliaments every day.

I listened as Nora's cough worsened.

I had stopped smoking three years earlier on a bet. My pal Ned, a great trumpet player from Louisiana, was a betting man. One night, when we were out on the town and neither of us was feeling any pain, he bet me that he could give up smoking before I could. If I had a cigarette during a period of five years, I owed him five thousand dollars. If he had a cigarette during that time, he owed me five thousand dollars. Piece of cake. There was only one problem. Ned died of cancer after six months without a cigarette. Being the gentleman that he was, he stayed true to his word even in his will. If I go for five years without a cigarette, I am to be given the five grand and his trumpet. If I have a smoke during that time, the money goes to the cancer society and the trumpet is to be tossed into the Hudson River. I look at it this way: Either way, the money goes to the American Cancer Society, but I'll be damned if the Hudson will get his trumpet.

"Are you all right?" I asked when her coughing had subsided.

She took a deep breath. "Fine. You shouldn't upset me like this."

It wasn't a point worth arguing over.

"I don't mean to upset you, Nora. I just assumed that *if* David was alive and well, he'd contact you before anyone else."

"Why are you so obsessed about David?"

"I'm not."

"Think again, Sydney. I mean it wasn't bad enough that you two hated each other when he was alive, but you insisted on certification when he was dead. You don't think that's sick?"

"Nora, he was a liar and you know as well as I do that—"

"That what? You were being absurd then, and as far as I can tell, nothing's changed. You're still being absurd. And obsessed."

I took a deep breath and counted to eight silently. "If you remember correctly, he was wanted by the law here." It was an old argument and I could feel my heart starting to race.

"My memory is fine, Sydney, it's my patience that's wearing thin. We have been over this a thousand times. David wasn't wanted anymore. He was married and he'd made a clean breast of things. Why do you find that so hard to accept?"

I hadn't felt this sort of friction between us since I'd decided to move back into and renovate the apartment. Nothing had been changed since Mom renovated it in the mid-sixties, and when Dad was killed in 1980, the kitchen wallpaper still had grotesque huge orange and yellow "mod" daisies that made me queasy even when they were hip. When Caryn and I redesigned the place in 1981, the daisies were the first thing to go. It was more an act of survival than anything else. Nora hated the thought of changing the apartment and resisted us every step of the way. To her, it was like erasing our past and our parents from the place. In a way, she was right, I was trying to create a new life in an old space.

But Nora and I always butted heads when it came to family matters, especially David matters. Nora believed in protecting family, right or wrong. But I'd been burned by David enough to know I didn't buy the right-or-wrong bunk.

After David left the States, he'd moved to Israel, where he allegedly came clean by marrying Basha, a well-endowed Israeli citizen whose parents were well connected. Her parents had pull with the government and struck a deal with David. If he promised to stay clean, put in eight-hour days six days a week in their bookstore, and remain faithful to their daughter, they would happily welcome him into their little fold. For this, he would become an Israeli citizen with a clean record. His alternative was a three-year lease on a cozy little jail cell back in the States. However, for the first year after their marriage, David had Basha convinced that he was a bona fide surgeon, though he had gotten his high school diploma by the skin of his teeth.

"If he thought this was a way to get out of Israel, do you honestly think he wouldn't have at least tried to fake his own death?" I paused. "I'm telling you, if you saw this picture . . ."

"I'd probably say that he looks a lot like David. Big deal." There was a sharp edge to her voice that struck me like nails on slate.

"Why is it, Nora, that it couldn't *possibly* be David? Stranger things have happened."

There was a long pause. Finally, she exhaled. "And you don't think you're obsessed?" She snickered.

"I'm sorry I brought it up." I tossed the paper onto the desktop.

"Well, that's all right. I understand these things."

I resisted the urge to dump the phone into the garbage.

"So have you heard from your . . . friend?" Nora struggled to be oblique.

"Which friend?" Squirm, worm.

"You know, what's her name, the girl who went to Europe," she said impatiently.

"Caryn?"

"Yes, her."

"Caryn's not a girl, Nora. As a matter of fact, she's still older than you by five years."

"Whatever. Now please, don't go getting defensive."

Conversations with Nora can be exhausting. By the time we hung up, I felt as if I had done a long hour on the rowing machine.

I started pacing and wound up in the living room. Above the fireplace was the only piece of artwork in the room. A portrait Caryn had painted of the two of us nine years earlier. In the painting, I was sitting on an armchair, with my hands folded in my lap, looking straight at the artist. Caryn was squatting at my left side. Her right arm rested on the arm of the chair and her feet were bare.

When Caryn decided to move to Ireland and study sculpting with Liam Greene, it hurt to look at the portrait. But as the days turned into months, and now years, I have discovered that whenever I need to lighten up, I look at that painting.

I felt Charlie rub against my leg. His touch brought me back to the moment.

"Yeah, pal, maybe you're right. Maybe I should have called Gilbert in the first place."

T W O

When I first met Gilbert Jackson, I was ten years old. My father and Gil (who was then a new detective with the NYPD) had been working together. He and his wife, Jane, came to our house for Christmas, and my brother, sister, and I had to dress in our Sunday best and remain as clean as possible at least until dinner. By the time they arrived, I was already stained with grease from trying to disassemble a brand-new bicycle. Gil had come into the bedroom, introduced himself, and when we heard my mother call out that dinner was ready, I must have panicked. Without missing a beat, Gil smeared grease on his shirt and forehead, rolled up his sleeves, loosened his tie, and offered me his hand. Together, we walked into Christmas dinner looking like two mechanics.

It's been a love affair ever since.

I knew if anyone other than Max would listen to me, it would be Gil. Not only did he know David but we had shared the same suspicions thirteen years earlier. I went back into the den and called him. It rang three times before he answered.

"Jackson," he barked into the receiver.

"Guess again."

"What do you want?" I could hear him unwrapping the Rolaids.

"I want to take you away from all this, how's that? What's got you so upset this morning?"

"What's got— You wanna know what's got me upset? I got a lady claiming that one of my officers is a racist and ready to press charges. I got a rapist out there who's attacking ten-year-old girls and I can't get a line on the son of a bitch. Jane is steamrollering me with the bullshit to stop smoking. And here it is twenty below bullshit and some asshole stole my car. All in all, this has not been one of my better days."

"Did you see the paper this morning?"

"No, why?"

"Well"—I took a brass poker and jabbed at the pretend log—"I was looking at the *News*. There's a story about a guy, Noah Alexander, who was mistakenly released from prison pending trial."

"Yeah? What about him?"

"There's a picture of him in the paper. He bears an uncanny resemblance to David." The log sparked and sputtered as it splintered into three pieces.

"David? David who?" he asked. This was followed by a stunned silence on his end of the line. "Hang on a second, lemme get a paper." Gilbert never puts anyone on hold. He usually throws the receiver down on the desk or the chair or the floor.

After a few minutes, he picked up the receiver and sighed into the mouthpiece. "I dunno."

"It looks exactly like him." I paused. "Look, I know it sounds crazy, but it couldn't hurt to run a trace on the fingerprints. That'll tell us for certain if it is or isn't David."

Gilbert sighed. "It's been a long time. I mean, there's a resemblance between the two of 'em, but this is a shitty picture. Hell, I was constantly mistaken for Ernest Borgnine when I was younger. People look like other people." He exhaled.

"That's right, but everyone has their own distinct set of prints." I paused. "I might be wrong. As a matter of fact, I *hope* I'm wrong, but I have to check this out. Remember, there was a time when you didn't believe David was dead, either."

"That was a long time ago."

"Right, but it was a possibility then, and you can't just conveniently forget about it now. Look, I don't want it to be David, but the resemblance is just too close. You know as well as I do that if he wanted out of a bad situation, he would have done anything, and he wanted out of Israel. Remember the lies he told Dad just to get money?" David liked to fabricate tragedies and then ask Dad to pay him for his troubles. If nothing else, his lies were colorful. Once his foot had been blown off in an explosion, once his wife had a radical mastectomy, and one time he needed dentures.

"Gil, I just can't sit here idly doing nothing." I downed the last sip of cold coffee.

"We're talking thirteen years, kiddo. This Alexander is a nothing, he's a junkie who killed two people during a robbery."

"*Allegedly* killed two people. How do you know he's a junkie?" I grabbed the paper and scanned the article. There was no mention of drug abuse.

"I remember the arrest. The evidence was pretty cut-and-dry." I could hear papers rattling on his end of the line.

"Will you just run a check? If you're so certain it's not David, then what harm can it do?"

"If you're so certain it is David, what good can it do?"

As far back as I can remember, the rivalry between David and me went deeper than simple sibling rivalry. The open hostilities really started when I was seven and he was ten (he thought it would be funny to freeze my pet turtles into ice cubes) and didn't end for me until I was seventeen and discovered that he had used his forgery skills to wipe out a checking account I had opened for college. I didn't press charges out of respect for my folks, but I made it clear that there would be no further contact between the two of us. That same year, he left the country.

The next time I saw him was six years later, when he had surreptitiously slipped into the country and caught me off guard with a late-night visit. I was living in Brooklyn with Caryn then and I tried to see that all her valuables were hidden before I agreed to let him spend the night with us. She had been upset that I was so openly suspicious of my brother, but after his departure, the diamond earrings I had given her for her birthday were missing. Years later, after David's death, I saw the same earrings on his wife.

So David and I never liked each other, but I knew I wasn't out for vengeance. At least I didn't want to think I was.

No one in the family could have known what the

thought of his death ultimately meant to me. Maybe I needed to tie up loose ends, but after Dad died, I went into a long period of actually mourning David's death. Somewhere along the line, I thought I had learned, perhaps in an abstract way, to love him. It's amazing how death can improve some relationships.

But the idea of vengeance taunted me. I didn't want David to be dead, but at the same time I always hated the way he used and abused people. I wondered, If I had the chance to confront him face-to-face, without our family protecting either one of us . . .

"Yo, Sydney, where the hell are you?" Gilbert yelled into the receiver. "You hear what I said?"

"I'm here. Please, I need your help, Gil. I just have to know."

He finally promised to check Alexander's fingerprints against David's and get back to me as soon as possible.

Before I could go to my office, I had unfinished business to complete for a client. The curator of a small museum had neglected to report the theft of a priceless small statue, and we had been hired by the owner to find it. As it turned out, the curator insisted the artifact hadn't ever been missing. His sister-in-law, a mystery writer, had "stolen it for research for a book but had every intention of returning the damned thing." Without much prompting from the museum board, the curator, a rather homely man whose nose could have been a prototype for Fred Flintstone's, decided it would be prudent to change careers at this point in his life.

I had to return the statue to its rightful owner, a feisty old lady on Fifth Avenue. With that done, I decided to treat myself to a tour through the Impressionist collection at the Metropolitian Museum before going to work.

———

Our office is on the second floor of a three-story building, which in itself has become a rarity for the Upper West Side of New York. The landlord, Hershel Schwartzman, has promised us that while he's alive he has no intention of evicting us in order to raze the building and build another thirty-story eyesore—unlike most of his peers between Seventy-second and Ninety-sixth streets. If his greedy children had had their way, we would have been history a long time ago, but Hershel, a handsome, dignified man in his late sixties, once confided in me that he has a special attachment to this particular building. I was led to believe that matters of the heart were involved, but being the circumspect kind of gal I am, I didn't pursue it. He'd given us a good deal on the space and a long-term lease. Though it's old, it's well run by Lyle Kelling, the super who works three of Hershel's buildings in the neighborhood.

The outer office is simple. Kerry's pine desk is at the right as you walk in, angled to face both the outer and inner doors. Directly across from the outer door are our offices. The one on the left is Max's, the one on the right is mine. My office faces Broadway, and his the side street.

Three huge arched windows look out onto Broadway, which was why I chose the front office in the first place. My desk faces the windows.

Whereas my office is bright, Max's is cozy. One wall is covered with memorabilia: photos, newspaper clippings, awards, trophies, and framed finger paintings by his niece. He likes organized clutter and he collects toys, so there's always something to play with: darts, windup games, battery-operated cows and pigs, chickens that lay eggs, and two basketball hoops—one above the door between our offices and the other attached to the side of his garbage can.

The staircase leading from the ground floor to our

office is unimpressive, but it was warm. Having just walked half a mile in the bone-chilling cold, the warmth was all I cared about.

When I reached my office, I could hear raised voices from behind the oak door. It's times like this I wish I hadn't let Max talk me into getting an oak door. However, the three other doors we had had, all of varying degrees of frosted glass, had each been shattered either by Max's friends or foes. He has that sort of effect on people.

I pressed my ear to the cold wood and listened.

"If you think I'm afraid, then you don't know me very well." I heard Kerry's deep voice quite clearly.

"You don't know me, either, lady. I like to watch people suffer. It's what you might call a hobby." I didn't recognize the voice, but the laugh that followed sounded greasy and dirty.

Kerry said something I couldn't catch and then I heard her say, ". . . people like you who would be better off left in the gutter." A loud smack sounded and then Kerry cried out in pain.

It felt like all the blood in my veins stopped cold. I slid my gun, a Walther compact, out from my bag, flung open the door, and aimed in his direction.

"Okay, pal, up." I motioned for him to raise his hands. He had been kneeling next to the desk and complied. "Kerry, are you okay?" She was sitting on the floor, with her back against her desk. Her thick red hair fell gently over her shoulders.

She smiled.

"Oh my God, this is great. Did you think he was trying to hurt me?" She pointed to the young man who had his thick-lashed hazel eyes trained on the barrel of my gun. "Can you believe it, Bo?" Her voice rose with excitement. She slowly got to her knees and introduced me to her acting partner, Bo. "We're doing a scene together for class next week. Do you have any idea how fantastic this is? You believed us!'' Kerry's euphoria was not contagious. I was angry and Bo seemed, at best, relieved to know that a crazy lady was not going to shoot him, after all.

"How do you do, ma'am?" He nodded his loosely curled head of dredlocks and tried to smile.

Ma'am. I swallowed my consternation, slipped the gun back into my bag, and smiled at Bo's very young, very unlined face. Ma'am.

"Sorry if I scared you." I glanced over at Kerry. By now, the image of me flinging myself into a room, my gun in hand, had apparently struck her funny bone and she was laughing so hard, she could hardly catch her breath. "You're fired," I said to her as I closed my office door.

I slipped out of my brown leather jacket, threw it and my scarf and gloves into a heap on the sofa, and went to the window. On the west side of Broadway, even the second-floor offices get plenty of sunlight, so even on the gloomiest of days I don't have to turn on the lamps.

I looked through the mail—a pile of junk, two checks, and a postcard from Caryn that had gotten chewed in transport. All I could make out was that she had taken two weeks to travel to London for a show. There were five telephone messages, the most interesting being from Max, and one from Minnie confirming our dinner date for that night.

As I was about to open a sweepstakes envelope boasting $12 million up for grabs, the phone rang.

It was Gilbert. He had pulled the Alexander file and was able to give me some information. For starters, Alexander had a girlfriend, Shelley Gomes. Apparently, they had been living together when Alexander was arrested six months earlier. I took down her address.

"I want you to know I feel funny giving you this information." Gil sighed.

"And I want you to know I really appreciate it."

After our call, I looked up Shelley's number in the telephone book and then dialed the Circle exchange. There was no answer. I let it ring ten times before giving up.

I considered my options. I could go to her apartment, see whether she was home, and enter with or without her permission. I could stake out her place, along with, no doubt, a host of plainclothes policemen. However, seeing as though I didn't really know what I hoped to learn from her, I widened my scope of possibilities. I could run a few errands, go for a swim at the club or even to Tina's Gym for a round of boxing with Zuri. As I weighed my alternatives, Kerry came barging through the door.

"You're supposed to knock first," I said.

"I never knock," she reminded me.

"On the rare occasion when I'm pissed at you, it's a good idea at least to tread lightly."

"Sydola, you're pissed at me?" She flipped her mane of hair with the back of her hands and perched herself on the edge of my desk. "But why?" She pressed her palms to her chest. "You were not only willing to scare some schmuck for hurting me but, more important, you really believed our scene. I don't want you to be upset, because, let me tell you, I'm a very happy woman. I mean, I'm walkin' on air here because you've made me feel like a true performer. Call the *Voice* and tell 'em to polish up an Obie for me."

Kerry is about five four in two-inch heels, which I suspect she even wears to bed. She has a voluptuous body that women would have killed for in the fifties. We met three years earlier when Max and I decided to use an agency to find a secretary. Kerry had come in wearing a trench coat, seamed black sheer stockings, and ruby red patent-leather heels. She told us that she was actually looking for part-time work, as she was a full-time actress. She wanted something more exciting than word processing on Wall Street and less taxing than waitressing in midtown, and she figured that working with detectives might be just the thing for her. As I was explaining to her that her job was strictly clerical, Max suggested she help him gather some information for a case he had been working on. She's been our right arm ever since, managing to balance her acting career and our office.

"I didn't think you'd mind if we rehearsed here." Kerry softened her tone and her expression. One of the things I like best about Kerry is that she lets you see her changing gears, allows you to watch her thinking process. It's a method of manipulation I admire.

"So tell me, what's got you all jittery?" she asked.

I slid the newspaper toward her and pointed to Noah Alexander's picture. "That man bears a striking resemblance to my brother, David, who allegedly died in Israel several years ago."

She peered at the picture. "Wow. I never knew you had a brother."

"I did, and if I'm right, I still do. I'd like you to try to get as much information on Noah Alexander as possible. Date of birth, schools he went to, Social Security number, driver's license—everything."

"Okay. Do you have anything I can start with?"

"Gil said Jersey City was his place of birth. That's all I have."

"Jersey City? Yuckolamotsky. Have you ever been there?" She made a face. "I went there for an audition a month ago." She shuddered and slid off the desk. "Here"—she tossed the paper at me—"I'll get on it right away." She started toward the door and stopped. "Sydney? This Noah Alexander's wanted for murder."

"Yeah, I know."

She seemed ready to pursue the idea but then apparently thought better of it.

Thinking about David had me feeling scattered—a sensation for me that's like having an itch I can't quite locate. I tried Shelley Gomes's number again. No machine picked up with a message telling me Shelley would call back if I left my name and number. I called Minnie, got her machine, and told her I would be at the restaurant at seven. I then placed the receiver back in its cradle and decided to go to Tina's.

I actually hate exercising, but I work out three times a week at the gym, swim once or twice a week, and occasionally do an hour on the rowing machine. I do at least half an hour of yoga a day. I like to think that I need to keep in shape for my work, but who knows? I was the only kid in my class to fail gym in the seventh grade. Maybe this is my way of exorcizing that ugly memory. However, I haven't had a lover—or even a fling—in well over a year, which is just enough time to drive me up the wall with frustration. At that moment, the gym felt like just the thing I needed.

By the time I left, Kerry was already tracing Noah Alexander's past. Knowing the contacts Kerry had made in three years, I felt confident that by the next morning I would have something more solid to work with.

Tina's Gym is located in the heart of the Garment District, right above a kosher pizzeria. It's a small, stale place with windows that would look out onto Seventh Avenue if they weren't caked with a good twenty years of city dirt. I like Tina's. Unlike the trendy spas that are filled to the rafters with men and women in the latest color-coordinated spandex exercise outfits, Tina's is basically for women who are serious about working out. The membership is about 85 percent women, which suits me fine. Once upon a time, this place was strictly for jocks, bodybuilders, and women who had been victimized in some way. Now there are more and more women who are taking up boxing as an alternative exercise because it's the best aerobic workout you can get. There are still no blow dryers or special makeup lights and it has so little ventilation that the place can smell like a jungle whorehouse, but Tina has no intention of changing it.

Tina was standing at the front desk when I got there. "Speakin' of the devil. We were just talking about you, kid." She talked through her nose and held out her hand to me. I had never seen Tina hug anyone during the twelve years that I had known her, not even her late husband, Victor, who ran the place with her. Whenever Victor would enter a room, she would slap his back and give it a quick rub, but that's about as close as she would ever get to showing affection in public. Victor had once told me, "A woman like Tina just can't show her feelings physically, at least not in public. She's too much of a tiger." Then he had winked.

She was wearing black sweatpants and a powder blue sweatshirt that was ripped just under the right armpit. Her white hair was piled up in a messy bun and her eyes were sparkling. I took her right hand and sandwiched it between both of mine.

"You don't have better things to talk about?"

"I do, but they don't." Tina's wheezing laugh filled her chest.

"Very nice. A fine how do you do." I glanced up and saw Zuri approaching us. She looked more like a twenty-five-year-old model than a thirty-nine-year-old boxing coach. Zuri is one of the few women I know who looks about the same as, if not better than, she did when we met fifteen years earlier when she and her now ex-husband were our upstairs neighbors in Brooklyn. Zuri and Caryn shared an interest in gardening and together they grew everything from arugula to zucchini in the backyard.

"I was hoping you'd be here today." Her cocoa skin was glistening with sweat. "After you warm up, you up for a few?"

"That's why I'm here." I followed Tina into the locker room and caught up on the latest gossip while I changed.

By the time we hit the ring, I was ready for Zuri.

T H R E E

Minnie had arranged for us to have dinner at a small out-of-the-way corner restaurant in the far West Village. The Lone Dove, which had been there for years, was one of the few restaurants in the city that Minnie really liked.

I had arrived early and was nursing a glass of red wine at the bar when a thickset, casually dressed man sat beside me.

"Sydney?" He arched his thick eyebrows up and pushed his chins down.

"Yes?"

"My name is Maurice." Though we'd never met, I knew Maurice was the owner of The Lone Dove. "Minnie

---

just called and asked me to tell you that she's running a little late. She says you're her niece?" His dark brown eyes widened and his head jutted almost imperceptibly forward, bringing to mind a tortoise stretching from the safety of its shell.

"Yes." I nodded and cleared my throat.

"Then *you* are a very lucky woman. There is no one quite like Minnie." He smiled warmly. Despite his bulk, Maurice was very attractive. "Peter," he called over his shoulder to the wistful, pale bartender. Peter pivoted toward us. "Refill Sydney's drink, please."

"Thank you, but that's not necessary." My stomach was running on empty and I could already feel the warming effects of my first wine. Before I could object, Peter had placed a thin-stemmed glass before me and opened his palms like a model on a game show pointing to the dinette set.

"Some crudités to soak it up?" Peter's sibilant *s* seemed to complement his gestures but conflicted with his brooding young face.

"That would be great, thanks."

"So"—Maurice slapped his hands on the bar rail—"have you been here before?"

"Several times." I cupped my new glass in my hand and said, "Thank you."

Maurice shrugged and smiled. A small, deep dimple graced his right cheek. "My pleasure. I'm surprised we've not met before. As you can tell, I'm quite fond of your aunt."

"Well, I can tell you it's mutual. Minnie is a great fan of yours."

A classical guitarist started playing softly at the other end of the bar just as the door to the restaurant banged open and let in a gust of freezing air along with three new customers. Maurice slid off his bar stool and welcomed the newcomers. He greeted them warmly and then led them into an adjoining room where there were about twenty more tables, a superb art collection, and a large fireplace. The walls in the front room, where I sat at the bar waiting for Minnie, were brick and mostly bare. A large oak-framed mirror hung behind the bar and one overlarge unframed painting of an iridescent pink female nude hung dead center on the back wall. The short front wall was mostly lace-covered windows and a door.

Peter placed the crudités in front of me and smiled for the first time. It made him look boyish and full of mischief.

Maurice returned and we spent the next half hour polishing off the crudités and talking about food. To my surprise, several of his recipes were from Minnie's cookbook. He promised to give me his recipe for mahimahi with thyme cream sauce.

Minnie came pushing into The Lone Dove forty-five minutes late, complaining, "In the old days, cabdrivers not only spoke English but they knew the streets of the goddamned city." Then she smiled. "Maurice dear, have you been treating my niece well?" She took Maurice's round face into her red-gloved hands, pulled him down to her, gave him a kiss on the lips, and winked at me.

"I'm so hungry, my stomach thinks my throat was slit." Several tables turned to see where the ruckus was coming from. Minnie pulled her thick red coat tighter around her small frame as she was escorted by Maurice into the other room. "How are ya?" she said à la George Gobel as she passed a table of four women who were gawking.

Our table was right beside the fireplace. Minnie complained that since it was a table for two, it would be more difficult for Maurice to join us. "I was hoping you and Sydney would get acquainted," she added.

"Later, my love. Tonight I have to do liquor inventory. Besides, I had the distinct pleasure of getting to know Sydney while we were waiting for you. But now I must sneak downstairs to do my work." He kissed her hand and left, but only after agreeing to join us after dinner for a nightcap.

Once settled into her seat, Minnie let out a long sigh.

"That's a mighty big sigh for a little thing like you," I said.

The waitress brought the menus to the table and Minnie ordered an extra-dry vodka martini up, with a twist.

It was going to be one of those nights.

"What's up?" I asked. The candlelight softened the tension around her lively gray eyes.

"I don't know. I've been having odd feelings all day. Something's just not right. Have you ever known me to be *this* late?" She looked me straight in the eyes for the first time that night and then answered for herself. "No. Never. I loathe unpunctuality. How many times have I told you about Howie LeClere, the one who wanted to marry me? Wealthy, handsome, affectionate, everything a woman could possibly want, but habitually late." She tapped the table twice as she said "habitually late." "Think I would marry a man with that sort of ego? Absolutely not. Howie was an egomaniac and it showed in his constant tardiness." Minnie smiled sweetly at the waitress, who carefully placed her drink before her. "Thank you, dear. Now I'm famished. Are you ready to order, Sydney?"

I was and we did.

"So"—she took a long sip from her glass—"mine's been a perfectly dreadful day. What about you?"

"How has it been dreadful?" I asked.

"Well, dear, the last thing you need to hear is a list

of complaints from an old lady, but first, I overslept. Now, God knows at my age I don't have to be up at any given time, but I have gotten up at seven-thirty without fail and without a clock for the last sixty years. Today, I slept until nine."

"You probably needed it." I dipped a spoon into my warm carrot-tomato soup. "When it's this cold, people hibernate. I know I stayed in all morning. And who knows? You could be getting a touch of the flu or something."

"Nonsense, I've never been fitter in my life. I'm convinced I slept until nine because there was something psychic *keeping* me asleep." She nodded once for punctuation. "There's activity, Sydney, activity I don't understand, and that bothers me. Believe you me, I didn't oversleep because I was tired." She reached for her glass. "Either way, it was unsettling not only to get up so late but to feel an underlying sense of . . ." She pressed her lips tightly together and stared at the candle.

"What?"

"That's just it." Her eyes met mine. "I don't know what. You know me better than just about anyone; it's not like me to be so out of touch with my feelings."

Minnie suddenly looked smaller than she ever had before. Under five feet three inches, she has never been a big woman, but there has always been something larger than life about her. For a fleeting instant, I was looking across the table at a frail old lady.

She thrust a forkful of food toward me. "Would you like some? It's quite tasty." She offered me her appetizer of gingered quail and picked up where she'd left off.

"I assumed that after I showered and had my coffee I'd be feeling more clearheaded, but I'll be damned, I still felt that nagging. So I meditated because it always makes me feel so centered. But today it only heightened the sensation of being out of focus."

She downed her drink, motioned for the waitress, and ordered two glasses and a half bottle of Perrier-Jouët. After the waitress was out of earshot, Minnie leaned toward me and whispered, "Something, I don't know what it is, but something is very wrong." Her face grew somber, almost downcast, as she added, "I tried reaching your folks tonight. That's one of the reasons why I was late. I couldn't get through to them."

Whether or not Minnie actually speaks to Mom and Dad—or, for that matter, any of her deceased friends and family members—is irrelevant as far as I'm concerned. I figure the important thing is what she gets from her sessions. She always seems so peaceful after chatting it up with the dearly departed, so who am I to question it?

"What does that mean?" I asked.

"I don't know. I've never had trouble connecting with them before, especially Nathan." She pushed her plate away. "I don't know why I order quail. It's all bones and no meat on the damned things."

"Maybe Dad's on vacation. He always wanted to see Russia," I suggested.

"Ha-ha. You're sounding more and more like your stuffy sister." She offered me a half smile and shook her head. "I just don't know what to think." Minnie's body seemed to sink down, as if a weight had been placed on her shoulders.

"I had something weird happen today, too." During dinner, I told Minnie about the picture in the paper, my conversation with Nora, and my call to Gilbert. She listened carefully as she savored her dinner of scallops and shiitake mushrooms with scallions and peppers. I barely touched my grilled swordfish. When I had finished recounting everything, she nodded thoughtfully and fished a cigarette out of her bag.

"Did you bring the picture?" she asked.

"No."

She called the waitress over and asked whether she had a newspaper. The waitress went to check.

"What if it is him?" she asked as she exhaled a steady stream of blue smoke away from my face.

"This man's wanted for murder."

"So?"

"Do you think David's capable of murder?" I asked.

"Maybe. Certainly if the stakes were high enough. Hell, aren't we all?"

"No, I don't think so." I stared at the fireplace. Orange flames jumped unevenly behind the ornate antique screen. For the first time that day, my feet were warm, and it felt great. "For instance, I don't think Mom could have hurt a fly."

"Don't kid yourself. Given a set of circumstances where she might have felt that any member of her family was in danger, Eleanor would have killed all right." She took another greedy drag off her cigarette. "Look, David may have been more passive than aggressive, but I could see him killing someone."

"If it was life and death?"

"Not necessarily. Besides, what is life and death? Given what I read in the newspapers, I have to assume that it's different for each and every one of us." She stubbed out her cigarette in the small glass ashtray and reached for the last of her champagne. "Look, as far back as I can remember, David was a troubled boy. Eleanor always said he'd grow out of it, this penchant for mischief, as she liked to call it. But by the time he stole all your money and then jumped bail, well, none of us felt like we knew him anymore. He was unreachable and so angry."

She paused, lost in thought. I waited.

"I know Nora gave you a hard time after David died, but you should know that your father had a hunch that you were right."

"Dad told me."

Minnie seemed to be gazing at the past as she stared at the lipstick-stained filter in the ashtray. "Now that your parents are dead, who knows? David might think it's safe for him to surface."

"I don't think he surfaced intentionally."

"Regardless." She pulled a fresh cigarette from the pack and tapped the filter against the tabletop. "You still think David's alive?"

"I don't know what to think."

"But do you think David's alive?"

"Yes."

"Then what do you plan to do?"

"That's a loaded question and you know it." It felt as if there were an elephant sitting on my chest.

She took her time lighting her cigarette, apparently enjoying the ritual. In a flash, the busboy was there with a fresh ashtray. Though she'd smoked at least a pack and a half a day for the last fifty-two years, Minnie loathed the smell of stale cigarettes. The staff at The Lone Dove seemed to be aware of this and responded well to her needs. I liked knowing that there was a place where Minnie was treated like royalty.

"Well, here comes the waitress. Let's see what this picture looks like." She flipped past the first few pages and squinted at the blurred newspaper photo.

"You know, I've never been able to connect with David. Your father once told me that they've not connected there. Who knows"—she ran her arthritic hand through her very white hair—"maybe that's what *I* was feeling today. Maybe that's why Nathan was unreachable."

"Maybe." I paused. "Min, let's say that it is David and I investigate and I find him. I could be sending him to prison for a very long time."

"There's a flip side to the coin, my dear. Let's say it is David and you investigate. You could be saving him from a bogus murder charge."

"That's what I tell myself, but I don't know. You know we didn't like each other. Hell, until recently I hated David. To be honest with you, I don't know if I can trust why I'm investigating. I don't know if I want to find him to help him or to get even." My face felt hot.

"What do you mean?" She waved the approaching waitress away with a small birdlike gesture.

"I just wonder how much of me, if any, wants him to get caught."

Minnie laughed softly. "Good God, you are your mother's daughter." She shook her head and wiped the corner of her mouth with her napkin. "Eleanor was always trying to second-guess herself, trying to find out the real motivation behind why she did things. One year—it was during the war—Ellie and I spent a lot of time volunteering at the hospital. Well, one night we were coming home and Ellie just started crying. It was freezing and I couldn't get her to budge from this street corner, which I'll never forget was Broadway and Fifty-eighth. I must have asked her ten times, 'What is it?' before she finally looked up at me and cried, 'Oh Minnie, I'm so ashamed. These boys are suffering, and every time I leave there, I ask myself, Am I doing this just to make myself feel good?' I asked her what difference did it make. But to her, it was important. Not only that she understood her motives but that she was motivated by the 'right' thing." Minnie paused and looked at me.

"Chances are it's David." She continued. "Given the circumstances, it's more than likely that he needs your help. Whatever your history is with him, I know you. You see"—she played with the wax dripping from the candlestick—"like your mother, you may feel compelled for what you consider to be the wrong reason, but you mustn't forget what might result from your actions." She motioned for the waitress. "David might kill, but he wouldn't murder two defenseless people, and you know that. Trust your instincts, my dear. If it turns out not to be David, then it's nothing more than a few moments from your life. If it is David . . ." She shrugged.

The waitress arrived and I was grateful when Minnie changed the subject and suggested a fattening chocolate dessert, which she guaranteed would induce sugar shock. Maurice joined us for an after-dinner drink.

After dinner, we stopped at Gertie's, a small women's bar in the Village that caters to a slightly older, quieter crowd. Minnie always prefaced suggesting we stop there for one last nightcap by saying, "You don't have to worry about men making passes."

Inevitably, I would always ask, "What if a woman makes a pass, Minnie?"

Her response varied. Sometimes she would get a gleam in her eye and wink suggestively, while other times she would simply tut-tut at the thought. Either way, Minnie loved Gertie's and the women at Gertie's loved Minnie.

By the time I got home, I decided a hot bath, a cup of decaf, and a novel were just what I needed to help me relax. My mind was racing and there was too much alcohol in my system. Unlike Minnie, who seems to have a hollow leg, I have a limit on how much I can drink. That night, I had stopped just one drink ahead of a hangover.

The decaf was weak, the bath tepid, and the novel not so novel. I fell into a fitful sleep and dreamed about David and a ferryboat that was taking passengers, even though it was submerged in four feet of beautiful opaque turquoise water. David and I were working together on a project with a scientist and our mother. The first ferryboat left teeming with people and I was worried that they would all drown. The water was warm. I jumped in and came out dry. David, Mom, and I boarded the last ferry because we had a very important meeting on board, but then it turned out to be nothing more than an amusement-park ride.

I awoke at 7:30 in a cold sweat. The bedroom was dark and cocoonlike. I reached out from the warmth of the covers and pulled the phone toward me. Charlie looked up sleepily from the foot of the bed, licked his neck, and pushed his face back into the comforter.

By now, I knew Shelley Gomes's number by heart. She picked up on the first ring and sounded very much awake. I didn't give her a chance to say no, and after five minutes we agreed to meet at her apartment at 11:30. That gave me enough time for yoga, coffee, and a quick visit with Gilbert.

F O U R

I took the number three train to Gilbert's office. I love the subways in New York because, apart from the fact that there is no faster way to get around this city, it's like stepping into another dimension. Max contends that being underground here is as close to the netherworld as you can get. When I go down there, I don't see it as Hades or a war zone. Here is a place where people have been known to live, quite happily, for years on end without ever having to surface. Mind you, this isn't a lifestyle I could handle, but just knowing that it exists updates fairy tales my mother would read to us when we were small. All the characters are there, from gnomes and trolls to toothless beggars, but instead of a tree stump, they live in abandoned stops and cardboard boxes.

Then again, most of the time I carry a 9-mm pistol, which makes subway travel feel infinitely safer.

No matter how you see it, if you're headed from the north end of Manhattan to the southern tip, there is no quicker way to travel.

In less than half an hour, I was sitting in Gilbert's small institutional-green office, studying the posters tacked to the walls. There was a museum poster by Monet of three women in a rowboat, their reflections mirrored in the water; one framed poster of Seurat's *Sunday Afternoon on the Island of La Grande Jatte;* and a large multicolored map of the world that depicted countries in vivid blues, reds, purples, and oranges.

Gilbert had been on the phone when I arrived. He motioned for me to sit. "Yeah, I know 'em; he's a scum-bag." He squinted as he lighted a cigarette. "Let me tell you something, Hank; you make a deal with that little shit and you're making a deal with the devil. Get the goods on this other schmuck a different way. How? How. How the hell should I know? That's what they pay you to figure out, right? Right. Look, I got to go. You'll do what you have to do. Whatever you do, don't be stupid."

He exhaled a burst of bluish gray smoke into the center of the room, away from my face. He held up the cigarette. "This bother you?"

"No. I still like the smell." I inhaled deeply. The vicarious thrill of inhaling secondhand smoke still gives me a charge.

"God, I wish I lived with you instead of Jane. She gave up smoking and all of a sudden her right hand becomes a fan." Gilbert waved his hand furiously in front of his face and blew puffs of air. "Like this. She looks like a moron. But what can I tell you—I'm crazy about her, so

———

40

I agree to go to this friggin' smoke-ending class. I'm not up for this shit, Sydney. I'm too old to change my ways."

"I think it's great, Gil. When do you start?"

"Some detective you are. Tonight, for God's sake." He let out a loud sigh and leaned back in his chair. "So I know you're not here to exchange pleasantries, right?" Gilbert's smile is a gentle gift that transforms his hound-dog face into that of a choirboy. The lines around his heavy brown eyes always seem to disappear when he smiles. It's probably high blood pressure that accounts for the red splotches of color on his pale, sagging cheeks, but if only for an instant, when Gilbert smiles, he becomes a boy again.

"Anything on the fingerprints?"

"I've got someone working on it. Out of respect to your folks, I don't want them to cross-reference David and Noah's prints, get it? So for the time being, they're just looking for David's." He rubbed his eyes. "However, I was able to get some more background on Alexander." He leaned forward, planted his feet firmly on the ground, and pulled his chair up to his desk. He then pulled a sheet of paper out of the top drawer and slid a pair of reading glasses onto the bridge of his wide nose.

"Alexander, Noah. No prior record. Born in Jersey, Jersey City. I told you all that before, right?" He glanced at me over the rim of his glasses. "Okay, so six months ago—it was late August—Alexander goes into the Beverly Liquor Store on the Upper East Side, tries to rob the joint, winds up killing the owner, Jesse Washburn, and a customer, Mildred Keller. Naturally, Alexander insists he had nothing to do with it, but he was seen in the area and a pair of sneakers stained with blood matching one of the victims' blood types was recovered from his apartment.

"His release from prison has caused more problems

internally than anything else. Shit hit the fan because they think someone inside had something to do with it. I mean, forging bail papers isn't what you'd call the norm, you know what I mean? They're looking for him, but nobody seems too concerned about it. Fact is, we know we're going to find him, it's just a matter of when." He scratched the back of his head.

"The bail papers were forged?"

"Yeah."

"That's not what the papers said. They said there was a mix-up."

"Really?" Gil shrugged and then a light seemed to flash on overhead. "No, no, no. I know what you're thinking and you can poke that thought right out of your skull. There's no way this guy Alexander, or anyone for that matter, can forge their own bail papers. Believe me."

"Why not?"

"Because it's impossible, that's why." He brought the cigarette to his mouth and took three quick drags. "I know you, kiddo. You're thinking forgery means a definite connection and I'm telling you it doesn't mean shit."

"How many people know you're checking prints?"

"Just Marcus, I asked him to check it out for me." Robert Marcus is Gil's best friend and a sergeant out of the Thirty-fourth Precinct.

"Any information on Alexander's past? Education? Family? Previous employment? Social Security number? Anything?"

"Not much. Says he went to high school, but he dropped out second year. There's a driver's license and I got a Social Security number here."

"How could an uneducated nobody arrange such an intricate escape? I mean, I could understand it if his girlfriend tried to slip him a gun—something like that—but forged bail papers is another class altogether."

"He doesn't have a diploma, Sydney. No one said he didn't have brains or connections."

"Was Alexander planning on pleading guilty or not guilty?"

Gilbert shrugged. "Here's his attorney's name. Court-appointed. Been around some. Not real bright . . . off the record, of course."

"What about Washburn and Keller?"

"What about them? They're dead. Each of 'em took two slugs to the back of the head. Only one was necessary."

"Is this for me?" I held up the sheet of paper.

Gilbert rubbed his neck with his left hand and extinguished what was left of his cigarette with his right. "Discretion, Sydney. Stick it in your pocket."

"One other thing. How come this guy spent six months in jail without going to trial?"

"Judge refused him bail. He was a high risk."

I folded the paper and slipped it in my pocket. "I appreciate it, Gil."

"Yeah, yeah. Listen, just for the record, I want you to know that I've thought about it and I don't believe for one second that it's David. The man who killed these people has no regard for human life. That's not David."

I nodded once.

"So how's that no-goodnick you work with?"

"He's on an island with a very pretty model."

"Figures. That SOB always had luck with women. How 'bout you?"

"I'm too busy to think about it."

Gilbert's laughter filled the small room. "Too busy, my foot. You can't bullshit a bullshitter." We were standing at the door and he gave me a hug. "You'll meet someone again, don't you worry, kiddo. You're just too goddamned picky. Now, be careful. You need anything, you call.''

''Give Jane my love.'' I opened the door and stepped out into the hallway and chaos.

I had spent more time with Gilbert than I'd planned, which meant I had to hurry to Shelley Gomes's apartment without stopping at the office.

By the time I reached the street, it had started snowing. A wet rainlike snow that would probably be great for packing snowballs. Forgoing the speed of the subway, I hailed a cab. I needed to be alone to try to sort out the information I'd just received. The thing I like most about my line of work is that it's all a jigsaw puzzle. Thanks to Gilbert, at least now I had a few pieces to work with.

I settled into the backseat of the taxi and watched the New Jersey skyline become a blur as we sped north on the Westside Highway.

Shelley's fourth-floor walk-up in Hell's Kitchen faced the back of the building, which meant that though there was no sunlight, there was also no noise from Ninth Avenue—a fair trade.

Unlike most of the other buildings on the block, this one was apparently well kept. The locks were intact, the buzzers worked, and the walls were almost graffiti-free. Just under the staircase, across from the mailboxes, a stroller was chained to the radiator.

The walls were painted custard yellow and accented with dull brown paint on the banister and moldings that reminded me of a midwestern diner, circa 1950. The swirled green linoleum metal-lipped steps creaked as I made my way up to the top floor. Tubular fluorescent lights—two to each floor—lighted the way. There were six doors on each floor—four apartments and two toilets. Shelley's apartment was to the left of the staircase, at the far end of the hall. The round fluorescent light farthest from her apartment was sputtering and buzzing. Someone was watching me through the peephole of apartment 4B, my destination. I walked up to the door, smiled at the eyeball, and knocked. I held up my identification. "Shelley? I'm Sydney Sloane."

There were a series of locks to be unlatched. Finally, I saw half a face appear in the space created by the last remaining lock, an inexpensive chain lock. It was a pretty half face. The eye was large, brown, and almond-shaped.

"Yeah?" Through the inch-wide opening, I could see that she was slightly shorter than I, no more than five five, slender, dark-complexioned, and younger than I had anticipated.

"I won't take a lot of your time." I slipped my ID through the crack in the door, which she took and glanced at only briefly. Either people stare at your ID card as if they know what they're looking at or they ignore it. She slid the card back to me, shut her eyes, and leaned her forehead against the door frame. She closed the door.

I considered knocking again when finally, after about thirty seconds, she unchained and opened the door. She stood to the side and motioned me in.

The hallway in which we stood was no more than two and a half feet wide and ran the length of the apartment. A four-foot-long coatrack was nailed to the left and on it hung an assortment of coats, scarfs, umbrellas, bags, and bungie cords. Across from that was a door that seemed to be swollen too wide for the frame. She motioned toward that door and placed her index finger to her lips. I nodded that I understood I was supposed to be quiet. I then followed her down the hallway.

It was a railroad apartment, which means that it was set up like a train—one straight line of rooms, with the last one receiving the only direct light and air. These tenement apartments were put up in the 1800s to accommodate the ever-growing population. By the early 1900s, many of them were declared substandard. Compared to today's buildings, the tenements are a reminder of the good old days when costs were lower and standards were higher.

First we passed through the kitchen, which was small and very yellow. A claw-footed tub covered with what I guessed was a sheet of plywood and a checkered yellow and white plastic tablecloth doubled as a table. Above the sink was a medicine cabinet and a toothbrush holder. In the corner of the room, someone had erected two walls and a door, where I assumed a toilet was hidden. It wasn't a great job, but it was a damned sight better than I could have done, and gauging the length of Shelley's nails, I had my doubts that she took an active interest in carpentry. On the outer wall of the water closet, there were about thirteen shelves, mostly with bottles of baby food and juices.

The next and last room was larger and darker than the kitchen. The brick was exposed on the right and far walls. There were two windows on the far wall, which faced a modern apartment building. They were living in the shadow of the building behind them, which accounted for the lack of light in the room. A futon sat crumpled along the brick wall and signs of a child at play were scattered all over the floor. Brightly colored plastic toys, a stuffed purple bunny, and a teething ring littered the floor. There was an oval rag rug centered in the middle of the room. The colors were faded beyond recognition but left the dull impression that it might once have been black and red or blue and cranberry.

She had placed a square table between the windows and on top of that a small brass lamp. The light was on and splashing a soft glow onto the walls and wooden floor. I looked down at my feet and tried to will my boots to stop dripping. In the far-left corner, a nineteen-inch color television sat atop a rolling stand made for such things—a part of American culture I've never really been able to take seriously. The need to roll one's television throughout a house or apartment has never made sense to me. ("Why, come on, hon, let's take the old tube for a stroll.") There was a cable box prominently displayed on top of the television, and under it sat the toy of the eighties, a video player. Green digital numbers displayed the time. Without thinking, I checked my watch against it. It was correct. I like that.

Despite the lack of furniture and the peeling paint, the darkness and the leaking radiator, Shelley Gomes's home was cozy and inviting. It brought back memories of college and Peggy Dexter, my radical-feminist roommate who read Superman comics and drank Pernod.

On the left wall, the one that ran the length of the apartment, she had hung a collage of photos. As I neared it, I saw that she had taken a bulletin board and thumb-tacked to it about seventy pictures. Most of the pictures were of a baby—the one I assumed was napping in the first room with the swollen door.

"That's my son."

It wasn't until Shelley spoke that I realized how quiet it was.

She was standing in the doorway, leaning against a kitchen cabinet. Her arms were crossed protectively over her small chest. I smiled.

"He's so handsome. How old is he?" Unlike some babies who look either like old men or coneheads, this little guy had a cleft chin, a devilish smile, and already-muscular legs.

"Ten months." She shrugged and smiled, pushing the corners of her mouth slightly downward. "He was a little premature, gave me one hell of a scare, you know? But boy, he's turning into a handful, just like his dad." She suddenly looked uncomfortable and reached for something in the kitchen. It was a pack of cigarettes. Kools. She offered me one.

I said no and turned my attention to the pictures.

"His name is Andrew." Her voice seemed to relax a little now that she had her prop in hand.

In almost every photo of him, he was staring up at the camera and reaching out for the photographer. His smile, broad and goofy, was accented by his little dark eyebrows, arched into what looked to be a mix of surprise and delight. Looking at that face, I couldn't suppress my own smile. "He's adorable."

"Yeah. I think so, too."

"Listen, I appreciate your taking the time to see me." I turned to her.

"It's okay." She couldn't have been more than twenty-five, and though I could understand what David would have been attracted to in her, I couldn't imagine her being drawn to him. David, however, had always been a magnet for women. He had a knack for making plain women feel like goddesses. However, Shelley was no plain Jane.

It always bothered me that David could make his girlfriends feel special, because I knew that in the end he would use them only to promote himself. He invariably attached himself to women who were obviously insecure, either about their weight or their not being Madison Avenue's concept of beautiful, and he would steal from them, cheat on them, and lie to them. But each and every one of his girlfriends would have taken him back in a flash. Even the girl whose mother pressed charges back in 1969.

"I won't keep you long. As I told you on the phone, I'm looking for my brother."

She nodded. Eye contact seemed almost painful for her.

"I saw Noah's picture in the paper. He looks almost identical to my brother, David. Has he ever mentioned that name to you?"

She shrugged. "No. Not to me." She moved to the futon and reached for an ashtray made of one large shell with a plastic mermaid lying on a series of tiny pink shells that spelled out *Florida.*

I sat beside her and unzipped my jacket. "How did you meet Noah?"

Her face softened. "I was waitressing at my Uncle Albert's place on Forty-fourth Street about a year and a half ago and one day Noah came in. I could tell right away that he liked me, but I'd just been burned and I wasn't gonna let anyone near me. You know what I mean?" She stretched her legs out in front of her and balanced the ashtray on her thigh. Her blue jeans were worn through at the knees, revealing smooth skin. She wore thick pink socks and white high-topped leather sneakers.

I nodded.

"Besides, Noah was too old for me." She scratched the ash of her cigarette along the mermaid's tail, staring at the orange and gray tip. "But he was smooth, you know? He never asked me out. Not even once. He just started bringing me flowers and candy and books—can you believe that? *Books!* I nearly died when he brought me a book. It was called *One Hundred Years of Solitude,* by this guy on some serious drugs, but Noah gave it to me and said, 'Read this, it's my life story.' So I read it. Now I'm thinking he's a serious weirdo, but his approach was different, you know? Besides, he made me laugh. So less than a month after we meet, Noah walks me home from work." She folded the filter of the half-smoked cigarette

---

over the tip and put it out in one quick movement. She put the ashtray on the floor and leaned forward on her knees.

The more she talked about Noah, the more relaxed she grew. "He never left after that. At first, my family went nuts because they didn't like him and they thought he was too old for me, but they got used to him. He was . . ." She paused. "He's a nice guy, you know? Like he may be goofy, or a little exha—" She scrunched up her face and shook her head. "I can't think of the word, but he likes to show off for people, ya know? But that doesn't make him not a nice guy."

"No, you're right, it doesn't."

She shook her head emphatically. "I mean, I can't tell you where he was that night, but I'm telling you there's no way Noah coulda killed someone. And for drugs?" Her voice went up. "They gotta be joking. He liked his bourbon all right, but he never touched drugs."

"The police peg him as a junkie."

"That's their problem. Just look at him. Any dummy could see he's not into drugs. All you have to do is look at him."

All I had to go on at this point was a mug shot in the newspaper, and as far as I'm concerned, anyone will look like a junkie in one of those. However, I kept my opinion to myself.

"Where were you the day of the murder?"

"First, I worked at Albert's and then I picked up Andrew from my mother's. I stayed there for a couple of hours."

"What did Noah do for a living?"

She pressed her lips together, puffed out her cheeks, and shrugged. "I don't know. I mean, he told me he was into imports and exports, but he never really explained it. He was funny that way—he never told me about his private life. That's why I said you could come over here today. I'm just as curious as you are, lady."

"So he never told you what he did for a living?"

"Nope."

"And he never mentioned having any family?"

"Only once. I'd been busting his chops about not sharing with me—this was when I was pregnant with Andrew—and he borrows my cousin's car and we drive out to Jersey City. He said, 'You wanna see where I was raised? I'll show you. No big deal. I just want you to be happy.' So he gives me a deluxe tour, complete with a burger at his favorite hangout when he was a kid. But no family. Nothing. He said his parents were killed in a car accident when he was little and this aunt who raised him died a few years ago." She sighed. "That was a great day. I figured it was probably bullshit, but I didn't care, 'cause I was pregnant, you know?" She pulled at the loose strings of her jeans. "Noah and me had something pretty good. I mean, we liked each other, you know? So we treated each other really good. I just wanted some kind of order to things. I guess it didn't even matter if it was a lie. See, I knew that Noah lied to me all the time, but I also knew that it wasn't because he was dishonest. It wasn't like he had other women, and believe me, he wasn't out robbing liquor stores—I know that as sure as I know my own name."

"How do you know that?"

"I don't know how I know, I just do." She pushed the corners of her mouth into a pout.

"Why did he lie to you?"

She gave me a blank look.

"How did he lie?" I rephrased the question, curious as to why she would stay with a partner who lied.

She slid her finger under the tear in her jeans and

gently tugged at the material. "Stupid lies, little lies, like what he did and who he hung with."

Little lies? What was her problem? Couldn't she see she was living with a veritable stranger? I bit my tongue.

"I don't think he could help it, you know, lying? But that doesn't mean he's not a good man." She paused and looked at me as if deciding whether or not to continue. Her eyes were like candy, almond-covered milk chocolate. "Noah really loves me."

Love. It's always the same answer. "I don't doubt that for a minute." There was something immediately endearing about Shelley, something that made you want to believe right along with her, but I couldn't. As far as I could see, she'd painted a picture of a putz, not a prince. "How long did you live together?"

"Just under a year. We met a year and a half ago and we lived together for about eleven months, then he was arrested."

"So what about the evidence against him?"

She sighed. "They got blood on his shoes and not much else. Look, why would Noah practically point arrows at himself? He told me that the blood was someone else's, and I believe him. He swore he was in Brooklyn, but the police won't even check it out. They're convinced they got the right guy, so they won't bother to see if he's telling the truth or not." She unlaced and retied her sneakers as she continued. "See, these guys got into a fight and he helped break it up. He didn't know them, but that's like Noah, to try and make peace with people. Anyway, it's a shitty coincidence that the blood from the guy in Brooklyn matched one of the people that was killed, but that's all it was, a coincidence." She tugged at the laces of her shoe and rested her chin on her knee. "God, I hope he's okay."

"Did you visit him in jail?"

"Once." She took a deep breath. "My family made me promise not to, but I had to see him. It wasn't good." She paused. "Noah agreed with my mom. He told me to stay away from there, too. So I did."

"Have you seen him since he was released?"

"No." Her eyes met mine. They were now clear and defensive.

"And he hasn't contacted you?"

"I already told you, no."

"When you lived together, did he have many friends?"

"You mean his own friends, or friends we had to-gether?"

"Both."

"Well, most of our friends were my friends, or my family. We hang out a lot with my family. But no. He'd see a few people, but not with me. Like he'd see his friends when I was at work or visiting my mom."

"Do you have any pictures of him?"

She screwed up her face as though she was trying to remember something. "Yeah, there should be. He didn't like having his picture took. Even with Andrew. One time, he said he'd break the camera if my stepfather took a picture of him." She jumped up from the sofa and walked to the square table between the windows.

After a brief struggle with the drawer, she rifled through its contents and pulled out a handful of pictures. She came back to the sofa and leafed through them.

"Here's one." She held it out for me.

My heart skipped a beat. It was David all right. He was older and his face had both filled out and fallen slightly, but there was no doubt in my mind that this was my brother. He was alone in the picture. He had his hands locked behind his head and his elbows were pointing out. His eyes were leveled at the photographer and his lips were curled as if he'd been caught midsentence. "When was this taken?" I asked.

"About four months before he was arrested."

That meant the picture had been taken ten months earlier.

I felt light-headed. She continued leafing through more pictures. I stared at the picture until I realized my hand was trembling.

"Here's one that was taken before we met. It fell out of one of his books once. I took it 'cause I like the way he looks in it, but he doesn't know I have it, you know?" She handed me a snapshot that had been torn in half.

It was an old picture, but it was David all right, David with long bushy sideburns and wire-rimmed glasses. Just as he had looked during his surprise visit during the mid-seventies. He was sitting on a chair covered with a brown and orange floral sheet and someone's arm was draped over his shoulders. It was a man's arm. A tanned, hairy arm with a thick gold bracelet and what looked to be a diamond and gold ring. There was only a bare wall behind him.

"What happened to the other half?"

"I don't know." She lighted a fresh cigarette. "So, what? You think Noah's your brother?"

"It's hard to tell. I haven't seen my brother in a long time. It looks a little like him, but I have to check out a few other leads before I can be certain." I knew it was David as sure as I knew my own name, but I wasn't prepared to share that with her just yet. Ignorance can be helpful sometimes.

"I have as much right to know about Noah as you do."

"I know that."

"What was your brother like as a kid?"

"Oh." The question took me by surprise. "He was funny and he liked trouble."

"Do you think Noah killed those two people?" She sounded like a little girl.

"No."

"Good, 'cause neither do I."

She gathered the pictures and tossed them on top of the desk. "You know, I really thought because of Andrew things were gonna settle down with us." She kept her back to me. "I mean I know that kids don't keep people together who don't wanna be together, but we were happy together. I just wish that son of a bitch would call." She held on to the table and inhaled sharply. "He always said, 'I can't make promises I won't be able to keep.' " She sighed and shook her head. "I thought I could break him of that habit. Right, like I can fly to Mars."

"Shelley, do you have any idea where he might be?"

When she turned back to me, her eyes were red. "I don't know anything. I wish I did, then I wouldn't feel so stupid, but I don't know shit." From the other end of the apartment, we could hear that Andrew had awakened and was either hungry, lonely, or in need of a change. She wrapped her arms around herself and said, "Look, I got things to do."

I promised to keep her updated, and as the door closed behind me, I could hear Andrew crying. It was on the third-floor landing I realized that technically Andrew was my nephew. On the second-floor landing, I wondered how Nora would react to a nephew. And by the time I got to the first floor, I was actually getting excited at the prospect of seeing my brother.

F I V E

By the time I reached my of-
fice, it had stopped snowing. I stood at the window and
stared down at the street. Blanketed by the snow, the city
was quieter and almost soft.

I thought about David. I was convinced that he was
Noah Alexander, but it didn't make sense that he should
rise from the dead a junkie and a murderer.

The damp cold had chilled me through and I didn't
realize I was standing there in my jacket, scarf, and
gloves until Kerry mentioned it.

"I haven't had any luck getting information on
Alexander yet, but I am expecting a call from a friend at
the Records Bureau." Kerry leaned against the doorway,

looking radiant in a scarlet jumpsuit and white cashmere cowl-necked sweater.

As I told her about my meeting with Shelley Gomes, I hung up my jacket and sat on the hissing radiator. Its bark was worse than its bite and the heat just warmed my backside.

"Do you want me to continue the paper chase on Alexander?"

"Yeah. Chances are you won't find much, but I'd like to know what you get. David would use an alias or even a stolen passport, but I wondered whether he would go to the trouble to create valid documents. Check out death certificates, as well."

"Death certificates? For whom?"

"Alexander. By the way, any more calls from Max?"

"Yeah. I'll get his number for you."

"Thanks." I settled behind my desk and glanced at the newspaper Kerry left for me. Just as I was reaching for the phone, it rang. "CSI, can I help you?"

"Any news?"

"Hello, Minnie, I was just thinking about you."

"I was thinking about you, too. That's why I called."

I laughed.

"So?"

"So, I'm looking for David."

"Then you know for sure?"

"As sure as I can be without having him sit on my lap."

"You should be careful. These are unsettling times."

"I'm always careful." I leafed through the small pile of mail Kerry placed on my desk along with Max's number.

"I hope David's not in trouble," Minnie sighed.

"Minnie, he's wanted for a double homicide. I'd say that's trouble."

"Well, what are you going to do?"

"I'll think of something." Apparently, it was the season for sweepstakes. I tossed my latest offer into the garbage. Ed McMahon's face smiled up at me from the bottom of the wastebasket.

"Well, just be careful."

"Yes, Minnie. I have to go now. Bye."

I wanted to talk to Max, who was vacationing on a deserted island with a woman he had met two days before they left.

The phone rang several times before he answered. "I knew you couldn't live without me," he said when he heard my voice.

"Got me pegged. Actually, I'm returning your call. Perchance, do you need my help?"

"I called you?"

"I have the message right here in my hand. 'Call Max.' "

"Well, I'll be damned."

"That's beside the point. Are you having fun in the sun?"

"In and out."

"Mmm, sounds like a perfect vacation."

"If you had joined me like I asked, it would have been perfect."

"You're not my type."

He sighed long and steady. "Sloane, you don't know what you're missing."

"I can imagine. What's her name again?"

"That's not what I meant and you know it." He paused. "Her name is Glenna."

"Glenna?"

"Yes, Glenna, and she's crazy about me."

"Who can blame her? You're adorable."

"And don't you forget it."

"I won't. By the way, do you remember my brother, David?"

"Yes."

"Well, I just found out he's alive."

There was a short pause. "Where is he?"

"Maybe New York, maybe not. I was reading the newspaper yesterday when I came across a picture of this guy, goes by the name of Noah Alexander, who was accidentally released from prison."

"What was he in for?"

"Double homicide. No priors. I have Gil checking prints and Kerry tracing this Noah Alexander's history on paper. In the meantime, Gil tells me the release wasn't accidental. Someone forged the bail papers. Then I met his girlfriend and she showed me a snapshot that is about a year old. It's David all right."

"What are you going to do?"

"Start at the beginning. David may have been a pain in the ass, but I can't believe he would kill anyone. Annoy them to death, maybe, but not deliberately blow their brains out."

"Ouch."

"Right. So I'll start with the murders. Who knows, that might lead me to him. It happened in a liquor store on Lexington in the upper Nineties—the owner and one of his customers. I'll start there."

"Are you okay about this?" Max asked.

"I'm adjusting to the fact that he's alive."

"And looking forward to greeting him with open arms?"

"Actually, part of me is, which surprises the hell out of me. You know how I feel about him. If you'd told me ten years ago that he was alive, I probably would have called the FBI." I pulled a number-two pencil out of the desk drawer and started doodling on a pad of clean white paper. "But I tell you, when I left his girlfriend's apartment . . . I don't know, I'm just numb with mixed feelings. I mean, part of me really wants to help him out. I mean, he's really in a bind here."

"Have you told Minnie?"

"Yes."

"And did she say your folks have bleacher seats for this, so you better behave?"

"Minnie thinks David's alive, too." I said this as if it was a validation of some sort. On the paper in front of me, there were now two scowling eyes and a large nose.

"Sydney, not to burst your bubble, but as far as Minnie's concerned, no one ever dies."

He had a point. "On that note, I have to go. Have fun with Gretchen and don't get burned."

"Glenna."

"Sorry, Glenna. Nice name."

"You want some help with this David deal?"

"Nah, this will be a piece of cake." I drew a piece of cake next to the angry face that was now hiding behind several clouds. There was a lot of work to do and sitting here doodling wasn't going to solve anything.

My next call was to Alexander's court-appointed attorney, Brian Cermack. I left a message with his secretary and gave him both my office and home numbers.

I slipped back into my jacket, which was barely warm from before, and rummaged through my desk for a beret. I'm not big on hats, but when the mercury goes below thirty, I like to keep as much heat inside as I can. All I could come up with was a black knit headband that covered my ears. Chic detecting by Sloane. By the time I was ready to leave, Bo had joined Kerry for another rehearsal. He smiled shyly and looked down when I went through the room. I promised not to shoot him when I got back.

The Beverly Liquor Store is located on one of those corners on Lexington Avenue that invisibly divide Spanish Harlem and the fashionable Upper East Side. Ever since crack was introduced to the streets, the dividing lines aren't as clearly defined as they once were.

The rusting gray gates were pulled over the two storefront windows, but the sign hanging crooked on the door read, OPEN. Despite the cold, there was a stench of human urine in the doorway. I shoved the door with my shoulder.

Little bells attached to the top of the door rang as I stepped over the threshold into the dimly lighted store. It was a small space with an L-shaped counter that was protected by bulletproof paneling. Unlike liquor stores in most parts of the city, where a customer can examine a bottle of wine or choose the scotch they prefer, this store kept everything behind the thick plastic wall—the liquor, the money, the workers. A door without a handle was positioned just to the left of the counterman. In front of him, there was a square opening through which money and bottles went back and forth. This opening was backed by another piece of bulletproofing so that if an overzealous customer tried to grab at anything, he or she would have to snake past the two plastic dividers. Definitely a place to make you give up drinking.

There was a light-skinned black man with freckles behind the counter, shaking his head. Another man in front of the counter was whining, "Hell, man, I'm good for it. You know that. Jus' until tonight, man." The man in front of the counter leaned heavily onto a stubby cane; his deformed legs seemed to wave to the right at the knees and then to the left at the shins. He pulled himself closer to the divider and hissed, "It's cold out there, Joey. I need something to warm me up."

"Goddamn it, man, I am not the Salvation Army." Joey impatiently motioned to the door with his hand. "Now get out of here before I have Tiny throw you out."

The would-be customer limped from the counter to the front door, which I opened for him. "God bless you, gal." He turned to Joey, stuck out his tongue, and said, "You ought to be ashamed of your ugly old self, man."

"Can I help you, miss?" Joey pushed up his chin and gave me the once-over.

"I hope so. Are you the owner?" I pulled my ID from my pocket and pressed it against the plastic divider.

"Hell no. Do I look like a fool?" His hazel eyes revealed a sense of humor buried beneath his protective shell. "Tiny!" he called out without taking his eyes off me. There was the sound of movement behind him, but I couldn't see anything beyond the boxes piled up four or five high. "Go get Ray. There's a lady here wants to talk to him." Again there was the sound of movement, but no sight of Tiny.

"Have you worked here long?" I asked Joey.

" 'Bout a year now." He crossed his arms over his chest.

"Then you knew the previous owner, Mr. Washburn?"

Joey's face relaxed when he heard Washburn's name. Body language can say almost as much as words, sometimes more. He uncrossed his arms and leaned on a paint-splattered metal stool. I was obviously not here to discuss whatever it was he wanted to protect. I doubted that a store like this could pay its rent exclusively with liquor sales, and I didn't care. My only interest was Washburn and his date with death a half a year earlier.

"Yeah, I worked as a delivery man for him when he and that lady was killed."

"Did you know her?"

"Seen her once or twice. She was a regular."

"Did the store look like this then?" A flickering fluorescent dangled precariously above me.

"Hell no, lady, this was a real pretty shop. It was all opened and there was display cases, nice oak floor. Can't do that now. Not around here. It's getting like old Avenue A. Times change and they change fast."

A buzzer went off and Joey picked up the receiver of a black phone. "Yeah," he answered. "A lady here wants to talk to you about Mr. Washburn. She's private. Yeah." He winked at me. "Okay, I'll send her down."

He pressed a button under the counter, which unlocked the door without a handle. I pushed it opened and waited. I could hear Tiny making his way back to us.

"You carrying anything?" Joey asked.

"Do I need to?" I smiled.

"Nowadays, lady, everybody needs something. Tiny'll take you to Ray."

I turned and there he was. Tiny was about six three, over three hundred pounds, with extraordinarily thick hands. His hairless belly was peeking out between his Grateful Dead T-shirt and dirty worn jeans. "Hi." I nodded. He didn't say a word. He looked at Joey and turned, leading the way through the cluttered maze of unopened liquor boxes to a peeling linoleum staircase. Tiny laboriously made his way down the steps, his arms and hips brushing the brick walls on either side of the staircase. At the foot of the stairs, he ducked under a bare light bulb hanging from the low ceiling and made a left. He stepped to the side and motioned me forward.

A closed metal door had been painted brown and a

GO METS bumper sticker that had seen better days was pasted in the center. I knocked.

"Come in."

The base of the door scraped against the concrete floor. "Ray?" I peered into the smoke-filled cubicle. Considering Tiny's winning impersonation of Igor, I half-expected to see Dr. Frankenstein behind the door. However, sitting behind a large mahogany desk overflowing with papers was a small, wiry guy with one cigarette dangling from his mouth and another burning in the ashtray.

"Yeah, yeah, come on in, Miss . . . ah?" He waved me in like a flagman waving in an airplane.

"Sloane. Sydney Sloane." I handed him a card and took a seat on the folding chair in front of his desk.

He scratched the side of his nose and glanced at my card. "Private investigator, huh? Isn't that a little wild for a classy number like you?"

After seventeen years, I've gotten over my initial desire to educate people—both men and women—who are still startled to see a woman in my line of work, and a "classy number" at that. When I first told my folks I wanted to be a cop, my mother forbade it. She told me that I was "too pretty to be a police officer." Out of deference to her illness (she was in the last throes of cancer at the time), I stayed in college and waited. But when I made the move and left college to enter the Police Academy, my sister's reaction echoed Mom's. She added another dimension, though: No one would take me seriously.

"No. I'm here regarding the deaths of Jesse Washburn and Mildred Keller. I'd like to ask you a few questions, Mr . . ."

"Ray's fine. Go ahead, shoot." He tucked his hands

behind his head, leaned into the chair, and put his feet on the desk.

Ray was thin and pasty white, with dull red hair going gray. He wore a soiled white shirt, black baggy pants, and he hadn't shaved in several days. In the harsh light, his skin was almost translucent. He was the perfect size for a jockey.

"Did you know Mr. Washburn?"

"Hell yes, Jesse and me go way back." He was going to enjoy this.

"Did you work with him?"

"Only when he was in a bind, you know? Christmas, New Year's Eve, when things would start jumping and honest help was hard to find. You know what I mean?"

"How did you know each other?"

"We met in the army. Why?" He lighted a third cigarette and sniffed.

"I'm curious as to how you came to own the business."

"Jesse was a pal, you know what I mean? I mean, he knew I had shitty luck with my own business. I once tried my hand at dry cleaning in Brooklyn." He let out a short laugh. "Lemme tell you, I was the only thing taken to the cleaners." He brushed a fallen ash off his chest. "You see, I had a slight problem back then. I liked the horses and women more than I liked working or my wife. You know what I mean?"

I didn't say anything.

"So Jesse tells me, 'One of these days, hotshot, yer gonna wanna settle down. I'll give ya this joint.' He loved coming here, but he knew his family didn't like it, you know what I mean? A year later, that son of a bitch is dead. Lemme tell ya, you could have knocked me over with a feather when his lawyer tells me he left the place to me. You know what I mean?"

"What do you think happened here that day?"

"I think he got shot in the back of the head about two feet from where you're sitting right now, that's what I think." He looked two feet to my left. A dented yellow filing cabinet sat lopsided only five feet away. I tried to imagine the two bodies shoulder-to-shoulder, facedown, between the cabinet and my chair.

"Do you know if Mildred was down here, too, or if she was found elsewhere?"

"Down here. Look, who are you investigating for, anyway?"

"Did you know Mildred?"

He shrugged. "I met her a couple of times. She was a regular. Her and Jesse were friends."

I gave him a look of doubt, curious as to what it would elicit.

"All right, maybe they had a little thing going, but what's the big deal?"

Bingo.

"Did you tell the police that?"

"No." He was indignant. "Why should I? Jesse was my friend. I figured—what do you call it?—his wife and kids, they don't need that kind of news." He shook his head vigorously. "It wouldn't a done any good. I mean, why should I say anything? Hell, it couldn't a meant beans. If it did, Jesse would have told me."

"It could have meant that Mildred had a jealous lover who came in here and killed them. Did you ever think of that?"

"Look, lady, I don't know what your angle is, but some crackhead came in here, wanted bread, didn't get enough, and blew them away for the hell of it. Just look around you. This isn't what you would call a prime location, you know what I mean? I mean, why the hell do you think my store looks like this? 'Cause I like bulletproofing? No. I'll tell you why. Because this is all I got, and at this corner, I can't *give* the sucker away. Every month, I'm able to save a little, you know what I mean? So who knows, maybe one of these days I'll be able to ditch this joint and move to Florida, you know?"

"Jesse lived on Fifth Avenue."

"Yeah. So what of it?"

"It's hard to imagine this store financing an apartment over there."

He scratched his head and examined his fingernails, "Look, I don't know what his money situation was. I mean, I know his wife came from big dough, but money wasn't something Jesse and me discussed, you know what I mean? Like a guy's entitled to some privacy." He hoisted his feet from the desk, ignored the papers that fell to the floor, and squashed the cigarette between the worn heel of his shoe and the floor. "Look, I got a lot of work to do. You done?"

"Ray, you and Jesse were friends. Do you think that he and Mildred were lovers?"

"Well, like I said, he never came out and said it, but he was a gentleman, you know what I mean?" He nodded. "A real gentleman. So all I can tell you, lady, is that they were friendly, real friendly. Actually, one time I asked him about her—well, not really asked, but I made a comment about her, if you know what I mean, and he told me my mind was in the gutter. So who knows? But I'll tell you one thing, she sure spent a lot of bread here. And this wasn't the closest liquor store to where she lived. We had to deliver a couple of cases there once for the holidays. She had a store half a block from where she lived, but she liked coming to Jesse. You go figure."

"Just one more question. Had you ever seen Noah Alexander?" I handed Ray his picture from the paper.

"Not before he killed Jesse."

"Thanks for your time, Ray." I held out my hand.

"My pleasure, Ms. Sloane." He kissed my hand. "Maybe next time, we could do lunch, you know what I mean? There's a fine little pizza establishment just around the corner." He whistled and in an instant Tiny opened the door. My escort.

Joey was sliding a half pint of Wild Rose into a bag and through the opening to the same man who had been there when I first arrived. A line four deep was waiting patiently. Joey buzzed me through and I nodded good-bye.

The snow had already melted and traffic had been reduced to a crawl. Getting over to the West Side was going to take time. I hopped on the Ninety-sixth Street crosstown bus and went to the club. A swim was just what I needed to ease the stiffness from my workout with Zuri the day before.

S I X

I was watching *An Affair to Remember* with Cary Grant and Deborah Kerr when Carmen called and asked whether I could keep Charlie for a few more days. She was having such a good time in Kansas City—which surprised me, but I've never been there—and if I would take care of him, she could stay longer. I assured her that it was fine for him to stay. "Lemme talk to Charlie," Carmen requested in what sounded like a perfectly sane voice.

As I had frozen Cary Grant just as he was about to put two and two together regarding Deborah Kerr's no-show at the Empire State Building, I was eager to finish the film and the last few tissues in the box.

"He's out shooting pool." Charlie, who was quite comfortably curled in my lap, looked up as if to say, Can we get back to the movie already or what?

"Oh, Sydney, you're just being silly." Carmen was beginning to bug me. Apparently, asking to talk long distance to a cat is not silly. As I see it, this is a personality quirk that many pet owners share—the need to talk to Bowser or Puffer over the phone. I don't know how many times vacationing friends have called to talk to their pets. I feel more than slightly stupid holding the earpiece of the phone up to their cat or dog while a voice through the receiver yells very slowly, "HI, SPOT! HI, BOY. CAN YOU HEAR ME? YOU HAVING FUN WITH AUNT SYDNEY?" And they always yell. Why do they do that? Just like people who shout at blind people and foreigners. But pet owners make it worse; they have to know whether Bowser recognized their voice. Now, how should I know? There I am, looking like a fool, holding the telephone receiver out to this poor animal. Just to get on with my life, I told Carmen that Charlie heard her and did a little jig to the sound of her voice.

When the movie was over, I tried to read, but it was impossible. I just kept nodding off until finally at midnight I dragged myself off the sofa and climbed into bed. The radiator sounded like a gaggle of plumbers, pliers in hand, all banging on the pipes, but as far as I could tell there wasn't any heat forthcoming. I pulled a sweatshirt on over a pair of flannel pajamas and let Charlie climb under the comforter.

I should have stayed on the sofa, where I had been quite happy in the arms of Morpheus. In my own bed, I suffered through a fitful night's sleep. I kept waking and falling back to sleep, exhausting myself further with dreams about David and my mother.

* * *

At 7:30, Charlie started mewing. I reached over, rubbed his head, and told him to be still, that everything was all right.

"Perhaps your kittycat knows better than you, Sloane."

I bolted upright and saw the figure of a man standing at the threshold of my bedroom. "Who are you?" I slowly reached for the nightstand.

"Uh-uh-uh," he cautioned me with a singsong lilt. I could hear him cock the trigger of a gun. "You know, the security in this building sucks. You should talk to someone about it."

"That's a great idea. I'll do that, thank you. Now, if you'll excuse me . . ."

"Funny, you're funny. Forgive me if I don't laugh, I'm a little tired. Now why don't you get dressed? We have a breakfast date with a very important man, okay?"

As my eyes adjusted to the light in the room, I saw that he was of average build, dark complexion, and he either had a nervous tic in his right eye or he found me inspiring in my sweatshirt and flannels. His overcoat was large enough to be concealing other weapons and he stood like a man used to waiting for long periods of time. He was calm, deliberate, and not altogether unhandsome.

"Do you often barge into women's rooms uninvited?" I asked as I slid off the bed covers.

"Just get dressed." He motioned to the bathroom with his gun and leaned against the door frame.

There are three coffee shops in the immediate neighborhood, ranging from great to salmonella city. It figured that my date was waiting for me at the botulism capital of the Upper West Side. Fortunately for the population, it was almost empty when we arrived. There was a cashier applying orange lipstick in the reflection of a compact mirror, a bag lady with a lisp at the end of the counter telling her coffee cup to wake up and smell the Danish, and a bald, gaunt hunchback at a tiny booth, looking sadly vulnerable as he snored softly, his mouth gaping open, revealing a minimum of teeth.

My escort, whose name I still hadn't caught, motioned with his head that I was to join a man sitting at the booth farthest from the door, closest to the bathrooms. Oh goody. Ringside seats. Not only does it stink by those tables but more often than not someone will get stuck in the bathroom—a situation that could make the bravest panic.

My host was reading the *Times*. As I neared the table, he said, "Please have a seat, Ms. Sloane." His English was too perfect. He didn't look up from his paper. I considered suggesting we change tables, but it was too early to be cocky.

He wore a thin gold wedding band on his left hand and a ruby and diamond ring on his right pinkie. There was some sort of raised writing, almost like hieroglyphics, on the pinkie ring. His hands were beautiful, almost graceful. He wore a Rolex watch, a thick gold bracelet, and several gold chains around his neck. He also wore reading glasses. All in all, he looked more like a creative director at an ad agency than Mr. Big, if, in fact, he was Mr. Big.

"You could have called and asked me to join you," I said as I slid onto the maroon vinyl seat across from him. A cigarette burned unattended in the ashtray. The smell was nauseating, even for me, at that hour. I reached over and stubbed it out. He didn't seem to mind.

"It wouldn't have been nearly as impressive, would it?" His teeth were straight, white, and probably capped. He folded the paper, removed his glasses, and looked me straight in the eyes. His were dark brown, protected by thick black lashes. I kept my sunglasses on.

"Oh, I see, that's supposed to be impressive. Well, sir, you are batting zero. May I have a cup of coffee?"

"By all means. I had hoped you would join me for breakfast." He pushed the plastic-coated menu toward me. His posture was perfect. I pushed my back against the booth and my shoulders down.

"Just out of curiosity, who are you and what do you want from me?" I kept my hands in my lap.

He waved to the waiter and motioned for my coffee. "My name is Caleb Simeon and I want to do business with you. I want to hire you." He paused as the waiter placed my coffee in front of me. "Would you like to order?"

"I'm not hungry, thank you."

"Not even a glass of juice?"

"No, but please, don't let that stop you." I added half a teaspoon of sugar and two prepackaged creamers to my coffee while he ordered three eggs over easy, grits, a double order of bacon crisp, a toasted bagel with a schmear of cream cheese on the side, and a side of stewed prunes. Chances were likely that in less than an hour he'd regret it.

"If you simply wanted to hire me, you would have called CSI."

"I've offended you." He looked honestly confused, but I wasn't buying any of it.

"Why don't you just tell me what this is about?"

"This has to do with Noah Alexander. I understand that you are looking for him."

I sipped the coffee, which smelled like old socks and tasted remarkably like cardboard.

"I, too, am looking for him."

"Just how did you learn I was looking for him?"

"Shelley told me." Caleb's smile was slow and cold. He held my gaze as the waiter slid the green-rimmed plates in front of him. "Thank you. Nothing else for now."

Caleb's cohort, who was smoking a hand-rolled cigarette at the end of the counter, kept his eyes glued on us.

Caleb cut his runny eggs with a knife and fork and mushed it together with the buttered grits. "When Shelley told me you had spoken with her yesterday, I thought perhaps we could be of some use to one another. You see, Ms. Sloane, I, too, want very much to find Noah. Very much indeed."

"And why is that?"

"Among other things, he is making life increasingly more difficult for Shelley. That distresses me. It would be easier for her if she wasn't living in constant fear of the unknown. She should know once and for all where he is. Could you pass the pepper, please? Thank you."

"You want to find Noah because he's making life difficult for Shelley?" I took another sip of coffee and gave up.

"He also owes me a sum of money I am simply not able to walk away from." He said this with a wave of his hand, forcing the slimy eggs off his fork and back onto the plate.

"That's funny; Shelley didn't mention you."

He sniffed and gingerly patted the corners of his mouth with a flimsy paper napkin. "Be that as it may, when Shelley told me you had been to see her, I made it a point to find out who you were." He leaned slightly over his plate and smiled. "You are well known and respected among most of your peers." He sounded like a fortune cookie. When I didn't say anything, he continued. "I'd like to hire your services."

"You want to hire me to find Noah?"

"Precisely." He buttered a piece of bagel, holding the knife as if it was a spatula, flipping his wrist back and forth as he worked first the butter and then the cream cheese over the surface of the bread.

"Because he owes you money and he's causing Shelley grief."

"That's correct. I'm also prepared to pay twice your usual fee."

"Well, that's very generous of you. What did you say your relationship was with Shelley?"

"I didn't. But we're friends. Close friends."

"Obviously. Did Shelley tell you why I was looking for Noah?"

"She mentioned an unlikely story about a long-lost brother. Is Noah Alexander your brother, Ms. Sloane? He often said he was an only child."

The bag lady at the counter had her head in a Red Apple shopping bag and was shouting, "Wake up, you thtupid thit; I'm talking to you!" Her voice was muffled by the contents of the bag.

I simply smiled at him.

"I thought as much. I'm curious, though. What is your interest in Noah?"

"Strictly professional, Mr. Simeon."

He pulled several napkins from the dented metal dispenser, wiped his hands, reached into his breast pocket, and pulled out a folded piece of paper. This he placed on the table and slid it across to me. It was trapped between the scratched Formica and his index finger. "This should be a sufficient deposit. I will give you a check double that amount when I see Noah." He released the paper and returned to his meal, dabbing a piece of bagel into the egg yolk.

I unfolded the check and glanced at it, hoping to get some information about Mr. Simeon. It was a cashier's check made out for more money than our last two jobs combined. "Mr. Simeon, there is something you should know about me. First of all, I can't be bought. Secondly, I don't scare easily and I don't like your tactics. Contrary to what you might think, sending a goon to break into my apartment and escort me here is not impressive. As a matter of fact, it's rather passé. As for my services, I'm not available. Now, this might come as a surprise to you, but I have better things to do than watch you eat your breakfast." I shoved the check into his eggs and pulled on my gloves.

His laughter took me by surprise. "Now I am certain you and Noah are not related. You've got balls. However, before you leave, Ms. Sloane, let me tell you two things. One, I do not easily take no for an answer." He paused and took a sip of coffee. "Two, you're just a woman and you could get hurt playing with big boys. Please understand I'm telling you this for your own good."

Caleb Simeon didn't strike me as the sort of man who would be looking out for anyone but himself. And, though I have no interest in educating the endless Neanderthals I come in contact with, threats bug me.

"It's been my experience that when a man like you says 'big boys,' Mr. Simeon, that's all they are, boys. But take a good look, because I'm a woman. And believe me, no boy is a match for this woman. In the future if you need to talk to me, Mr. Simeon, I suggest you use the phone." I slid out of the booth. "Thanks for the coffee."

His goon on the counter stool started to stand as he saw me leaving. I saw Caleb in the mirror, motioning for his sidekick to join him and leave me alone. I pushed through the smudged glass door with my back.

It was going to be another bitterly cold day. With a wind-chill factor of ten below, the day was prime for staying indoors. I turned the corner and started west. Shoulder-ing my way against the wind, I thought about the zeros on Simeon's check. It had added up to a lot of money. It wouldn't surprise me if David had stolen money from Simeon, but it would have to have been quite a sum if Simeon was willing to spend a small fortune to get it back. But before anything else, I needed coffee. I can't seem to get going in the morning without two cups of coffee and a quick glance at the *Times*.

The first thing I did when I got home was to check the locks and find out how Bruiser got into my apartment. The lock on the service door that led into the kitchen had been jimmied. He was good at his work. Though it was a relatively easy lock to pick, the job was clean. I'd have to call Lonnie the local locksmith and have him install something a little more challenging.

Charlie rubbed up against my leg and purred that he was ready for breakfast. The smell of tuna in gravy first thing in the morning is enough to keep me from ever having a cat, but it seemed to make Charlie quite ecstatic. I started a pot of coffee and left him noisily scarfing down huge mouthfuls of tuna moo while I went and showered. By the time I was finished, there was some coffee made, none of this aging gray liquid the coffee shop tries to pawn off as the real thing. Wearing the thick blue terry-cloth robe Caryn had given me for Christmas two years earlier, I went into my office to jot down a few notes. I lighted a fake log in the fireplace and Charlie stretched out in front of it and began licking himself free from anything remotely resembling breakfast. I couldn't blame him.

There was something bothering me about Caleb Simeon, something more than his arrogance and his in-effectual attempts at intimidation. I didn't know who Simeon was, or whether he was after David Sloane or

Noah Alexander. I continued with my notes, jotting down everything I'd done since starting my search for David. It's a tedious process I sometimes hate, but I was enjoying it that morning.

When I was finished with my notes, I decided that the warmest course to take was to make a series of phone calls from home. I did a half hour of yoga and then changed into jeans and a black sweater before I called Gil.

He picked up on the first ring and barked his name into the receiver. Not in the mood for his ill temper, I cut right to the point. "It's Sydney, Gil. Anything on the prints?"

I could hear his uneven breathing. Finally, he said, "Nothing yet, Sydney. Look, why don't you give it a break for a day or two and let me get back to you on this, okay? I'm getting swamped here, you know what I mean?"

"No, I don't know what you mean." I jabbed at the fire with a poker. Orange sparks shot up crazily and disappeared. "Do you want to tell me what's on your mind?"

He sniffed once. I waited. Finally, he said, "They can't find 'em."

"Who can't find what?"

"David's prints are missing."

"That's impossible."

"That's what I said. Look, Marcus has a clerk working on it. I figure it's probably buried in some old graveyard file room, but in the meantime I can't cross-reference the prints."

"Let me get this straight, Gil. They can't find David's prints or his files?"

"They can't find his files. It's as if he never existed."

"Is this possible? What usually happens to old files like that?"

"Files can get lost, Sydney. The police department isn't perfect, but the thing is, it should be on computer and it's not. I can't get anything on David."

"When Noah was arrested, his prints didn't match with any prior arrests?"

"Not a thing, which only makes it a stronger case that this *isn't* David. You know, I was thinking that maybe after David went to Israel, one of Nathan's friends did him a favor and eighty-sixed his records."

It was true that Dad had friends loyal enough to do that for him, but it had to have been done without his knowledge. He was a stickler for the law and I know he would have told me if a friend had taken that upon himself.

I didn't say anything. Gil was grasping at straws and we both knew it. It didn't make sense that David's records were suddenly missing. There was nothing I could do to trace the police files, so I left it in Gilbert's hands. When we finally hung up, he was repeating that it was all coincidence and sticking to his belief that David had no connection to Alexander.

I checked my notes. I wasn't sure what good it would do, but I wanted to meet Jesse Washburn's wife. I called and discovered that Dorothy Washburn was very accessible and would be delighted to meet me. We arranged to meet at her apartment the next afternoon.

I called Brian Cermack again. After being on hold, forced to listen to static-filled Muzak, I was finally put through. His nasal whining voice was like nails on a chalkboard. "I can't help you, miss. The few times we met, he insisted he was in Brooklyn at the time of the murders. Now, as I explained to him, I have limited resources for validating his story, but as far as I could check, he was lying through his teeth. Two reliable witnesses definitely saw him on the Upper East Side at the time of the murder. Besides, the blood on his shoes matched Keller's. DNA tests proved it was her blood. About a month after I met him, he fired me. I was told that his case was being handled by a private attorney. No, sorry, I don't know who that would be; no one ever told me. Listen, I'm on a real tight schedule here. Good luck, okay?''

Cermack was still listed as Alexander's attorney in the files. I called the office and left a message for Kerry to check into this.

Whereas some women know the number of their hair salon or masseuse by heart, I have Lonnie the locksmith's number indelibly etched in my mind. An ex-con gone straight, his first free time was the next day. I arranged for a neighbor to let him in. As Lonnie had spent time in the cooler for burglary, I suppose I could have been nervous about his being alone there. However, Lon is more trustworthy than most priests I've met.

Then I decided to pay Shelley another visit. I didn't believe for one minute that Caleb Simeon was her friend, but he knew who she was. There was no answer when I called. Instead of waiting, I threw on some old hiking boots, jacket, scarf, gloves, and the beret I had finally found at home and braved my way through the wind and cold to the subway.

SEVEN

The train was empty as I rode down to Shelley's neighborhood. It was 10:30 when I arrived at her building. I had picked up a little stuffed piggy for Andrew on my walk from the subway. Despite the thick socks and heavy boots, my feet felt frozen as I shuffled in the foyer and rang her bell.

A young Hispanic man, pushing a stroller with a screaming child, was leaving Shelley's building. I buzzed her twice, held the door open for the stroller, and didn't bother waiting for her to respond. By the time I reached the last flight of stairs, I still hadn't heard her buzz the outer door. Chances were that she wasn't home and this was a wasted trip, but I figured as long as I had come this far, I might as well go all the way. I knocked softly at first and then a little harder. When there was no response, I tried the doorknob. To my dismay, it turned easily in my hand. I opened the door slightly.

I took out my gun and called her name. At the sound of my voice, Andrew started crying in his bedroom, blocking out any noise beyond that point. I gently pushed the squeaking door open and called out to Shelley again.

My heart was pounding so hard against my chest, I could almost see my jacket moving with the beat. I slowly entered the apartment.

I peeked in at Andrew and saw that he was holding on to the bars of his crib and screaming. When he saw me, he stopped for a second, realized I wasn't Mommy, filled his little lungs with air, and started screaming again. I placed the little stuffed piggy in his crib and shut the door. I then carefully inched my way into the apartment.

Nothing in the kitchen had been disturbed. There was a bottle in a small pan of water on the stove. Both the water and the bottle were cold. A salad, still in the clear plastic container from the local Korean grocery store, had wilted on the kitchen table and an untouched light coffee beside it was scummed over.

I could smell what lay ahead of me.

I swallowed hard and held my breath as I moved into the living room, where I found Shelley lying in what must have been the total sum of her body's blood.

I felt weak as I crept closer. Her throat had been slit from ear to ear. I jumped back, as if my body were being jerked by an invisible force. My eyes stung, and though every fiber in my body was screaming, I was silent. All the air seemed to evaporate from my lungs. After seven years on the force and ten years as a private investigator, I'm still not able to look at death, anyone's death, without feeling a sense of loss. But this woman wasn't a stranger. She was someone I knew, however briefly. She was the mother of my brother's son.

I leaned closer. Her eyes were open and I got the eerie feeling that she could see me standing over her, helplessly clutching a gun that couldn't do her a bit of good. I slipped the Walther into my jacket pocket. Rage was like a sharp pain that started in my chest and shot through me like an electrical current.

The smell of death and garlic was almost over-whelming. My hands shook as I knelt down beside her. Apparently, her killer knew just what he was doing. Why did I assume it was a he? Could a woman do this to another human being? Sure. Why not? I like to think the world would be a less bloody place if women were in charge, but who knows? People kill for all sorts of rea-sons. Power. Jealousy. Love. Money. Fear. Knowing what little I did about Shelley, I ruled money out right away. Fear? Not likely. What would there be to fear from Shelley? Besides, this carnage wasn't the result of fear. The cut was clean and flapped open like a crazy smile. Her blood had pooled around her and a thin stream had inched toward the kitchen before it dried. Her long dark hair was glued to the rug, encrusted with her blood. She was lying on her back, her left arm tucked awkwardly under her body. Her left leg was stretched out, and the other slightly bent. She was wearing the same jeans and sweater I had seen her in.

It was then I noticed her right hand.

My stomach pitched violently and I let out a cry when I saw her tongue lying in the palm of her out-stretched hand.

I bolted up and leaned against the wall, trying to stave off nausea. My rage did a quick nosedive into grief and I staggered away from the unforgivable viciousness of her death. I opened the window that looked out onto the airshaft, took deep breaths of the cold air, and loosened my scarf. I was overcome with heat and numbness at the same time. The pavement below was strewn with broken bottles and garbage. I leaned out the window and retched. The cold air struck me like a slap in the face and the silence of the weekday morning was broken only by the sound of a television blaring commercials from an apartment above. All I wanted was to be out of there, to take Andrew and get the hell away from the stench of death, but I was riveted in place.

I needed my rage. At that moment, there was no room for pain or grief. Grief would only dull my senses, and though the pain was there and real, it's sometimes confusing for me as to what really hurts. No, I needed to get angry enough to see past the blood and the waste so that I could focus.

Nothing, aside from Shelley's body, looked askew or out of place. I walked the perimeter of the room and noticed that there were five cigarettes in the ashtray next to the sofa. All were Shelley's brand, four were smoked only halfway and folded in half. One was smoked almost to the filter. The tip of that filter was pinched.

During our visit the day before, Shelley had had three or four cigarettes, none of which she smoked more than halfway. I took a plastic bag from her kitchen, in which I placed two of the cigarette butts.

Andrew, who had been still, heard my movements and started crying in the front room. I went back to the kitchen, warmed his overdue bottle, and called the police.

When the first officers arrived, Andrew and I were sitting on the steps in the cold hallway playing a sluggish game of peekaboo with his new piggy. As soon as the commotion began, neighbors started popping their heads out from behind their brown painted doors. Andrew responded favorably to the woman in a faded housedress directly across the hallway. Her name was Malita and it turned out that she baby-sat for Andrew whenever Shelley was in a bind. I asked if she would watch him until I could find his grandparents.

"What happened?" she whined as she reached out her thick, scarred arms for Andrew.

"I'm not sure." I shrugged. "There are police in there now. They'll probably be by to ask you a few questions." I handed her his bottle and asked, "Did you see Shelley today?"

"Nah. Last night around eight. She went to get some milk for Andy and asked me if I wanted anything from the deli. She's like that. Why? What's goin' on over there?" She shifted Andrew in her arms, half-resting him on her generous belly, and craned her neck to see into Shelley's apartment. "I hope to God nothin' happened to her; it would kill her mother, you know what I mean? They're a close group of people. I know."

"Does she have any close friends?"

"Friends? I dunno. I suppose so. Why?"

"Did you see her when she got back from the store?"

"Sure, she gave me my lottery tickets and the bologna she got for me."

"Was she alone?"

"What the hell happened over there?" She started to push past me. I gently held her shoulders and blocked her way. She was a good seven inches shorter than me and didn't really have her heart into crossing the hallway.

"Whatever it is isn't nice. I promise you the police will tell you soon enough. I'm a friend of Shelley's, and I need to know if you saw anyone going in or out of her place last night."

"Well, I didn't see nobody, but I heard her door open around nine-thirty. She's got a squeaky door ya

---

can't miss, you know what I mean?'' She shifted Andrew in her arms. He looked as cozy as Charlie next to my fireplace, fighting to keep his eyelids open. ''I know it was nine-thirty 'cause I was just getting ready to watch 'Coach.' I was in the kitchen getting my coffee and Stella D'ora breakfast cakes.''

''Did you hear the door again?''

She shook her head. ''Nah. But I don't hear nothing when I watch TV.''

I had come to see Shelley to ask about Caleb Simeon. When I asked Malita, she didn't remember ever seeing anyone who fit his description. I ran my hand over Andrew's smooth cheek and said, ''I'll tell the police where Andrew is. Thanks for your help.'' Just as I was returning to apartment 4B, Officer Edwards stopped me in the hallway.

''You say you discovered the body, miss?'' He was tall and slender, with sandy brown hair that fell gently onto his forehead.

Malita cried out, ''Body? Oh my God. Shelley's *dead?*''

''I'm afraid so, ma'am.'' He motioned for me to go into Shelley's while he calmed Malita.

And so began a long afternoon.

Officer Edwards's partner was an unpleasant pasty white doughboy who was convinced that I had something to do with Shelley's gruesome end. By three o'clock, I had been taken to Manhattan North and questioned by a lanky, smelly detective sergeant named Collier. They had nothing to hold me on, so I left after promising to stay in town.

By the time I reached my office, I was hungry, cold, and depressed. The last person I expected to see in my office was Gilbert Jackson, but there he was, laughing and having an altogether fine time flirting with Kerry.

"Hey, boss, this old geeze is trying to finagle information out of me. How do you like that?" She made a face of mock surprise.

"Who are you calling a geeze? Say, what the hell is a geeze? Listen, Sydney, we have a few things to talk about here."

Gil followed me into my office and shut the door.

I shivered as I slipped out of my jacket. I kept the scarf around my neck and opened the office door Gil had just closed. "Kerry, do you have the number for that deli around the corner?" She did, and I asked her to order a club sandwich on rye toast.

"I need to talk to you." Gil perched himself on the radiator and motioned me toward him. "I've been waiting here a long time. We both know I don't have a lot of time."

"Gil, there are two things I have to tell you. First, don't try to push me around in my own office, okay? I'm hungry, I've been held captive for the better part of the afternoon, enduring the stench of one of your fellow officers, and I have a headache the size of Nebraska, so I'm not in the mood for anyone, *anyone*, trying to shove me around. Secondly, your zipper's undone."

"What the—" Gilbert threw his hands over his securely closed zipper and turned his back on me. "Ha-ha. Very funny." When he turned back to me, there were dark red splotches of color on his cheeks. "What the hell's the matter with you?"

I shrugged. Apart from everything else, I was hungry. If I didn't get some food in my system, I'd only get more ornery. Already, I could feel my body buzzing. I took a deep breath. It's moments like this when I've been known to blow the proverbial gasket.

"I heard you were at Manhattan North," Gil said.

"I went to see Shelley Gomes. When I got there, she was dead. They slit her throat. I've never seen anything like it."

"Who's 'they'?"

I shrugged. "It had to be a they, wouldn't it? I mean, could one person do that?" I knew, of course, that one person could have easily done that to Shelley, but I couldn't get Simeon and his gorilla friend out of my mind.

He squinted at me and tapped his finger against the side of his nose.

"*They* is just a pronoun, Gil, nothing to take to heart." I leafed through some papers on my desk, but all I could see was Shelley's face caked with blood and her dead eyes staring at nothing. I squeezed my eyelids shut and was surprised that in doing so I was able to block out Gilbert's voice.

"I'm serious, Sydney." When I opened my eyes, I saw that he was now sitting on the canvas chair across from me, playing with a plastic cigarette.

"I'm sorry, what did you say?" I rubbed my forehead and tried to shake off my sudden exhaustion. It seemed as though a week had passed since I'd awakened to a stranger in my bedroom.

"I said, I don't like the idea that when you poke your nose into something, all of a sudden people start dropping like flies. This isn't the first time, kiddo." He took a drag off the pretend cigarette.

"Are you saying that I'm somehow responsible for Shelley's death?" I hunched forward on my desk.

Gil rubbed his mouth and jaw and started turning a pale shade of red. "You know that's not what I'm saying. Don't go putting words in my mouth. What I am saying is that I think it would be a good idea if you steered clear of this from now on."

"I have an obligation to my client and I'm not doing anything illegal. I'll have to ask you to leave now. I have better things to do than listen to your drivel."

"Drivel!"

"That's right, drivel." I slammed the desk with my fist. "You had the gall this morning to suggest that somehow all of David's files were missing and that it was just a coincidence. A young mother is brutally murdered and you—"

"And I tell you to let the police take care of it— you're goddamned right!" He slapped the arms of the chair and raised his voice to match mine. After a moment of rigid silence, he shook his head. "Look, I don't blame you for that broad's death, but I would rather not see a replay of it with my best friend's daughter. And as far as—"

"She was a woman, Gil, not a broad."

"Woman." He chewed on his lower lip and stared at his lap, anything to keep from looking at me. When he finally spoke, he sounded worn-out and fed up. "Who's your client?"

"I don't have to tell you that." Normally, I'd tell Gil anything, but I was cranky and sad and he was pissing me off. I get my stubbornness from my father, who preferred to call it persistence.

"Yeah, well I'd be willing to bet Waldo you don't have a client, which means that you're just prying, kiddo."

"Bet Waldo?" I looked at him, amazed. I'd never seen Gil willing to bet away his eighteen-year-old sheepdog before. "You would be willing to lose Waldo over something as stupid as this?"

"No. Because you know as well as I do, kiddo,

---

that you don't even have a client." I knew I was cranky because my day started with an intruder, segued into murder, and faded into harassment, but I wasn't used to this sort of escalation of words between Gil and me. The friction between us was getting sharper and uglier, and it didn't look like rationale was about to pop up and save us.

"You're right—I don't have one client, Jackson, I have two."

Kerry slipped into the room, took the wallet from my purse, and left.

Gilbert took a deep breath and crossed his legs. "Really? Who?"

As far as I was concerned, Shelley and Andrew were both my clients. However, I knew the kind of response that would get me, so I poked my nose in the air and said, "None of your business."

"Sydney, no other officer would take this guff."

He was right, but by now I wasn't going to give in. "What was it you wanted from me?"

"Sometimes I don't know why the hell I put up with you, you stubborn, ill-tempered pain in the butt." He pulled out a lighter and lit the end of his plastic cigarette.

I stared at his crossed eyes as he watched the end of the fake cigarette ignite and start to melt. He jumped out of his chair, shook the flame out, threw the cigarette into the garbage, and started wagging his finger at me.

"You might think things are funny now, but lemme tell you something—" The more he talked, the redder his face grew. By the time Gil stormed out of my office, he had sworn not to lift a finger to help my investigation and ordered me to leave the finding of Noah Alexander to the police. As he was leaving, he stopped in the doorway and added, "You think it's David? Well, you know what I think? I think you're just feeling guilty about everything that passed between you two and this is your way of playing it out. Instead of looking for your dead brother, maybe you oughta be talking to a shrink." With that, he slammed the door so hard the print of Modigliani's *The Cellist* teetered and fell to the floor.

I listened as he slammed through the outer door.

Several seconds later, Kerry was standing in the doorway, holding a brown paper bag and my wallet. "Want to talk about it?" She handed me my lunch and put the wallet back in my bag.

"He'll get over it." I unwrapped my club sandwich and felt nauseous. "I was the same way when I first quit smoking."

"Right. But it's not him I'm concerned about."

"Me?" I shrugged. "Oh, I'll be fine. My main concern right now is that I get some information on who could have wanted Shelley Gomes dead."

"You think this is connected to the murders at the liquor store?"

"I don't know, but it is connected to David." I offered Kerry half my sandwich.

"Thanks." She took the canvas seat Gilbert had vacated and pulled it up to the desk. "Your brother must have some good contacts."

"Why? What did you find?"

"A death certificate on Noah Alexander. Crib death in the late forties. How did you know?"

"A hunch." I tried a bite of the sandwich and discovered I could keep it down.

"Which means that everything else was forged."

"No big surprise. I wonder what the hell he's up to."

By the time we had finished lunch, paid bills, and reminded an old client that he was still in arrears (Kerry uses a husky voice and calls as Ruth, the grandmotherly accountant for CSI who "knows it's just an oversight,

Dolly''), it was almost five o'clock. Kerry was off to rehearse with Bo.

The thought of going home to an empty apartment didn't bode well. A quick mental check of who was home and who was not reminded me that Zuri was on a date, Carla and Benjamin were in California with their kids on a sorely needed holiday, and Larry and John, who own a brownstone in the Village and dote better than anyone else I know, would be too solicitous. They would try to absolve me of my guilt and ease the pain. At this point, I knew nothing could allay the pain and I didn't want absolution. Cathy and Bev were a possibility, but then Cathy would want all the minute details. I ached for Caryn, and actually started to dial Max's number at his island getaway, but then the sirens went off in my head and I remembered Eddie. A freelance photojournalist for several major news magazines, Eddie Phillips is known best for his portraits of human suffering and his practical jokes. We go back to the early seventies when I was at the Police Academy and he was just back from Nam. He spends 50 percent of his time out of the city, so I crossed my fingers as I dialed the number.

"Be home, be home, be home," I chanted as it rang once, twice. Eddie was just the person I needed. He was a friend, an associate, and if anyone could schmooze their way past a police barricade, it would be Eddie. My mind was racing. I knew there was no way I could get near Shelley's apartment without having to answer to Detective Collier, a stomach-turning notion; however . . .

Eureka. He was in town and agreed to meet me at six o'clock at the Tin Horn Bar & Grill, which is three blocks from his apartment near Times Square.

That gave me an hour.

I pulled a pack of Life Savers from my pocket and

with it the cigarette filters I'd lifted from Shelley's. I popped a cherry-flavored candy in my mouth and held the plastic bag up to the light. Shelley's ugly death had frightened me and made me sick, but it also enraged me. I was convinced that the killer was connected to David. Find David, you find the killer. But what if they're one and the same? They can't be. Even if David was capable of murder, he wouldn't mutilate. Especially a lover. Or would he? How the hell should I know? I *never* knew the guy, and we were raised in the same home, hid the same liver and wax beans in our pockets once a month, skipped Sunday school together, tormented Nora's dates.

Who was I kidding? I was convinced that Caleb Simeon was connected with Shelley's death. A low-grade panic started in the pit of my stomach. Now, more than ever, I had to find David. Especially before Simeon did.

It felt like a red-hot poker was burning between my eyes.

I tossed the bag onto the desk and called my friend Jimmy, who taught forensics at a local criminal college. He didn't think it could be done, but he said he would try to check the DNA from the saliva on the cigarette filters. On my way to the Tin Horn, I stopped by Jimmy's and gave him the filters. He had gained weight since he'd taken on his new job as professor. "Sydney, Sydney, Sydney, you're as gorgeous as ever, green eyes." He wrapped his thick arms around me and gave a squeeze. I felt almost petite with his arms around me, which, at five eight, is not an easy feat for me.

"And you're putting on the pounds, James. What does your lovely bride have to say about this?"

"More of me to love, baby, more of me to love." He howled with laughter. "Okay, okay." He wiped his eyes with a cloth handkerchief. "Let's see what you've got here."

He held out his hand and I gave him the plastic bag with the cigarette butts.

"Mm-hm." He held it up to the light and squinted. "Mm-hm."

"What?" I squinted up at the bag he dangled between us.

"Nothing, but it sounds good, huh?" Jimmy's laughter was almost infectious. "One of the first things I teach my kids—get yourself a convincing grunt. Makes people think you know what you're doing. Unfortunately, too many of them have great grunts and not much else." He gently placed his hand on my shoulder and sighed. "I'll call you as soon as I have anything. But Sydney, I've never heard of this being done. I need time."

It felt like I was running out of time.

E I G H T

By the time I arrived at the Tin Horn, Eddie was waiting at the end of the bar, well into a pint of dark ale. He's the sort of man you couldn't miss if you wanted to. At six three and 210 pounds, he is imposing. When you add to that his thick black beard and unruly fringe of shoulder-length salt-and-pepper hair, he manages to attract attention wherever he goes. The light was reflecting off the top of his head when I walked through the door.

"Mmm-mm-mm." He shook his head and stayed hunched over his beer. " 'Tis pity she's a dyke." He nodded to the empty stool to his left and eyeballed the bartender, a Paul Lynde look-alike.

"Are you ever going to come up with a new line?"

"I don't think so." He petted his beard slowly, giving it a gentle tug every time he reached the end.

"Good thing, I don't think I'd recognize you without it." I slid onto the bar stool and kept my jacket on. We were close to the front door, and ever since finding Shelley, I'd been unable to warm myself. "Thanks for meeting me, Edwardo."

"Anything for you, Little Darlin', you know that."

"What can I getcha?" Paul Lynde was standing in front of me.

"A Remy up, please. You ready for another?" I glanced at Eddie's mug and ordered a refill for him. "So." I sighed.

"So." He raised his right eyebrow. "Rumor has it you had a busy afternoon at Midtown."

"In a city this size, you'd think there'd be more secrets."

He shrugged. "My information today was nothing more than a result of happenstance. It's true." He held up his right hand—a very large white palm with almost burgandy red lines—and tried to work his face into innocence, a difficult, if not impossible, thing. "I just dropped by Frankie's office to say hello when Toby came in with the news that you and Detective Collier were spending a cozy afternoon together, holed up in an interrogation room."

Toby, a staff reporter for the International News, handles newsbreaking articles concerning celebrities. Ed once told him to title his column "Divorce, Death, Dining, and Discos." Toby has always struck me as the sort of gnat who likes to sit under the staircases at baseball games and look up little girls' skirts.

"That must have pleased him," I said as I watched

the bartender set my drink on a cocktail napkin in front of me.

Eddie polished off his beer and traded the empty pint for one full of amber ale.

"Probably. I take it that's what this is about," Eddie continued.

"Yes. How much do you know?"

"Let's see, a young woman was murdered in her apartment and you came along out of the clear blue sky, found her in her living room, whereupon you called the men in blue and gave her baby to the neighbor."

"And?"

Eddie shrugged and put a big dent into his second beer. He wiped his mouth with the back of his hand and said, "That's all I know, Ms. Sloane. Can it be that you're looking for a knight in shining armor to clear your good name?"

I laughed. "No, I think I'll leave my name alone, thanks. However, I do need your help."

I told him the whole story, starting with David and ending with Shelley's death. By the time I had finished, we were through another round of drinks.

When I was done, Eddie stared at the dregs in his glass without saying anything. Finally, he sighed.

"What?" I drained my glass. I didn't know which I welcomed more, the way the cognac warmed me as it was going down or the way it was starting to numb the back of my head and my arms.

He tugged on his beard and asked, "You got dinner plans?"

"Nope." I glanced at my watch. It was after 6:30. I had to eat before I had anything more to drink.

"We're going to a table, Clint," he informed the bartender. "Just add it to our check."

I left Paul Lynde's astral twin a tip and followed

Eddie to the back of the restaurant, which was deceptively large. It was a long, narrow cavelike space with booths lining both sides of the room. Everything was dark mahogany and the seats were covered in black leather. Only two booths were occupied, one by a single man reading *The Racing Form* and the other by an elderly couple who held hands as they read the menu. Eddie led us to the last booth on the left, right next to the kitchen door.

He took the seat facing the restaurant. Reluctantly, I slid into the seat across from him. I hate having my back to the room, any room. This has nothing to do with my profession. I've always been funny about that. When I was twelve, Minnie told me that I had probably been shot in the back in a previous life. Thanks, Min.

"The food here is great. Sticks to your ribs, know what I mean?" Eddie winked at the waitress as she placed a menu in front of me. He folded his big hands on the tabletop and said, "Claire, I want you to meet an old friend of mine, Sydney. Sydney, Claire."

Claire was hanging on to her apron the way cowboys link their thumbs on to their belts. She was young, full-bosomed, and when she smiled, her eyes sank into her cheeks. She wore false eyelashes and orange lipstick.

She looked at me and said, "You're known by the company you keep, you know." She laughed flirtatiously and shook Eddie's shoulder. "Only kidding, hotshot." She turned to me. "Can I get you something to drink?" she asked.

"Coffee, please."

"Coffee?" She raised her dark eyebrows. "You sure she's one of *your* friends?" Claire teased Eddie. She turned and sashayed off in the direction of the bar, saying, "I know, I know, a pint of Courage."

"What a pisser." He watched her backside. "Been

here for three years now. You don't find waitresses like her anymore."

"What's good?" I scanned the menu and realized how hungry I really was.

"Everything. I'm partial to the shepherd's pie or the liver and onions, but I usually have whatever Claire says."

The menu listed a host of comforting high-cholesterol foods from chicken pie to warmed apple cobbler with melted cheese. When Claire returned with Eddie's ale and my coffee, she suggested prime rib, mashed potatoes, creamed spinach, and blue cheese on the salad to start.

By the time we finished ordering, the restaurant was filling up with pre-theater diners.

"I need someone to get into Shelley's building and talk to her neighbors. There's a chance that I know who did this to her, but I don't know why."

"Who?"

I shook my head.

"Why do you do that? You get me suckered in, I swallow the bait hook, line, and sinker, I'm ready to lay myself on the line for you, and what do I get in return? Bubkis. You won't even tell me who snuffed this gal."

Claire placed our salads in front of us and carried the four other salads she had lined up her arm to another table.

"It's not as if I'm withholding information to hurt you, and you know it." I jabbed a forkful of iceberg lettuce and what looked like bottled blue cheese. "I have a responsibility—"

"Yeah, yeah, yeah." Eddie stuffed a biscuit in his mouth. "I don't need to hear the old pledge again, Sloane. I know it by heart. The altruistic 'I have the responsibility to make sure the world is a safer place' bullshit.'' He slathered butter on another warmed biscuit and continued. ''Well, I got news for you, this world is not a safe place, not for anyone, so trying to protect people is, as I see it, nothing more than an exercise in futility. However, I do understand that this theory wouldn't suit a woman who makes her living either probing into the lives of or protecting virtual strangers.'' He shoveled half his salad into his cavernous mouth and continued. ''I'm gonna help you. But I want you to know it's not because we're old friends or because I happen to be between assignments right now. I'm gonna help you because I owe you one.'' His smile was slow and boyish. ''Like they say, Sloane, an elephant never forgets.'' He rested his elbows on the table and poked his fork in the air for punctuation. His clear brown eyes were filled with affection.

I tried not to blush as I remembered. A year earlier, Toby had called me in the late afternoon and told me that Eddie was on a serious binge and needed help. I dropped everything and met them just as Eddie was being ousted from a Blarney Stone in lower Manhattan. The weasel, Toby, left me in the backseat of a taxi with my dead-weight friend, who was singing ''Hello, Collie'' to the tune of ''Hello, Dolly!'' at the top of his lungs to our patient lady cabdriver. I brought him home with me and found out that Sheila, his live-in lover of four years, had been killed that weekend in a boating accident. We spent that night together. He needed to vent his pain and at that point I hadn't been with anyone since the night before Caryn left for Ireland a year earlier. One thing led to another and before we knew it, Ed and I were both crying and making love. Neither of us mentioned it again.

''I never said I have a responsibility to make the world a safer place, Ed, but I do have a responsibility to my client.'' So there.

''I stand corrected.''

"Okay."

"So how 'bout an instant replay?" He waggled his eyebrows.

"Please, Ed, I'm eating. That's gross."

"Gross? It was gross? I didn't think it was gross, I thought it was nice." He ceremoniously placed his knife and fork down.

"It was nice. As a matter of fact, it was a lot of fun, but I wouldn't do it again."

"Really?" He sounded surprised.

"Really. I mean, it happened, and I don't regret it, but let's face it, guy, you're not the girl of my dreams." I laughed at his mock bewilderment.

"I'm not?" He lifted the napkin off his lap and peeked. "Damn, that's the story of my life." He dropped the napkin and snapped his fingers. "Shoot."

The rest of dinner was filled with small talk and Eddie flirting with Claire. Over coffee and dessert, I gave Eddie the name of Shelley's next-door neighbor. I also asked for any information he could dig up on the Washburn/Keller murder.

By the time I got home, it was after 9:30 and the windchill factor was somewhere around fifteen below. Charlie glanced up from the sofa and shot me the look of an abandoned lover forced to spend an evening alone.

Charlie, however, is a forgiving soul, and after a delicious dinner of savory stew, he snuggled beside me on the sofa. I lit a fire, put on a 1957 recording of Ella Fitzgerald and Louis Armstrong, and read the newspaper.

There was no mention of Shelley in the paper, but it was a morning edition. The eleven o'clock news carried the story. They showed footage of the outside of her building and then showed a mug shot of Noah. "The police are asking anyone with information to call." Then they flashed the number on the bottom of the screen. "All calls will be confidential.'' The anchorman read the number again and tightened the muscles around his eyes, affecting a more serious look as he said, ''The police have stepped up their search for Noah Alexander. They hope to have him back in custody within the next twenty-four hours. Again, anyone with information should call . . .''

I like remote controls. You can do anything you like to a television from across the room. You can turn it on, off, change stations, turn it up or down, convert it from television to VCR. Why, this little gadget has given me a newfound sense of freedom. I ran through the channels twice before I gave up. It was almost 11:30 and I was exhausted. In bed I went through a mental checklist for the next day. My first stop in the morning would be to see Mildred Keller's old apartment building. I had scheduled a meeting with Jesse Washburn's widow, Dorothy, for later in the afternoon. Chances were that the health club would be empty between eleven and twelve, which meant I could probably grab a middle lane in the pool. My only decision now was whether I would go to Keller's before or after my swim.

Before I could make this decision and set the alarm, I was fast asleep.

By 9:45 the next morning, I was on the Upper East Side, standing in front of a neat three-story brownstone tucked between two others just like it. Eighty-eighth is a quiet street where, with just a little imagination, you can transport yourself back to the turn of the century.

The sky was thick with gray clouds, just the sort of day that brings to mind Edith Wharton's overcast view of New York.

An overhead light was shining from the front second-floor apartment, which I took as an invite. There were eight buzzers in the foyer: a basement apartment, two on the first floor, two on the second, and three on the third floor (one of which had been Mildred Keller's home for seven years). That gave me two choices, 2A or 2B. I pressed 2A and waited. There was no intercom, just a buzzer system that was fine once upon a time but insufficient security for any building nowadays, even one just a stone's throw from Gracie Mansion. I heard a door open from the floor above and I smiled sweetly up at the dark figure.

Most people will buzz in a woman, and I was no exception. When I entered the darkened hallway, I heard a strong voice from the second-floor landing.

"Are you from the city?" She held on to the newel post as she craned her head forward to get a better look at me. She was about five two, thick in the middle, and wearing several sweaters.

"No ma'am, my name is Sydney Sloane. I'm a private investigator. I was wondering if I could ask you a few questions." I was halfway up the steps and digging into my jacket pocket for my ID.

"Where the hell's the inspector?" She looked past me, as if they were right behind me.

"Gee, I don't know." I stopped on the second-to-the-last step, followed her gaze, and shrugged.

"I've been waiting for those stupid bastards for three days now. Three days! You know what that's like?" She screamed into my face. "That's like waiting for the Messiah, that's what it's like. I'm freezing to death in here. You think they care about an old lady? They don't know from old ladies! These are the kind of people who care only about themselves. These are the schlemiels headlines are written about, you know what I mean?"

I didn't, exactly, but I made a sympathetic noise.

"So who are you?"

I handed her my ID and said, "I was wondering if I

could ask you a few questions about an old neighbor of yours."

"Does it feel warmer out here, or what?"

"Well, I just came in from outside, so I wouldn't really know."

Just then, she straightened her back and really seemed to look at me for the first time. She sighed and handed me back my license without having looked at it. "You think I'm a nutcase, right? Here I am yelling at you like a senile old fart and you just stand there nodding. Good breeding, right? You must have nice parents. Come on." She started paddling toward her apartment. "We'll freeze no matter where we are, so we might as well sit down, right?"

Her apartment had once been the living and dining rooms of a private house. Now it was a two-room apartment. The renovation work had been done in a time when it was still believed that people needed more than twelve square feet in which to live. The ceilings were close to sixteen feet high, the original woodwork was intact, and glass French doors divided the apartment. I assumed the kitchen and bathroom were off the second room.

"I've lived here forty-odd years and I'm telling you, I never once had trouble like I have with this new schlemiel landlord. Cheap bastard."

It was a cozy space filled to overflowing with pictures, books, plants, and the comforting scent of turpentine. I glanced back past the French doors and saw that though an ornate bed dominated the left side of the room, the rest of the space was an artist's studio.

"You're an artist." What a detective.

"Artist, schmartist . . . I paint." She breathed into her cupped hands and pointed to a chair. "Sit down. You want some tea?"

"No, thank you. You have a great apartment." I sat.

"Yeah, I like it, too. So does that piece-of-shit land-lord, except he thinks it should be three apartments, so what does he do?"

"He shut off the heat?" Call it a wild guess.

"You got it." She shook her head as she plopped down on the sofa across from me. "So, enough with my troubles. What can I do for you?" As she spoke, I could see her breath. Two small space heaters were working away—one in the back studio and the other to her right, next to the telephone.

"I'm an investigator. My name is Sydney Sloane. You are?"

"Sonia. Sonia Rothman."

"Sonia, I'm investigating the murder of a woman who used to be your neighbor. Her name was Mildred Keller. She died about six months ago."

She nodded. "What do you want to know?"

"Do you remember her?"

"Sure I remember her. I'm cold, not senile."

"Did you know her well?"

"We lived in the same building for about seven or eight years, I guess, but she wasn't what you'd call a social butterfly. She was nice enough, but quiet. She minded her own business, which was fine with me be-cause, unlike Mrs. Pain in the Ass across the hall, I like to mind my own business, too." She tucked her hands under her armpits and kept her gaze on me.

"Did you have any contact with her?"

"Not really. Only passing in the hallway, that sort of thing. There were maybe three or four times when we had a conversation that lasted longer than hello, good-bye. Like I told the police, she was the sort of neighbor most people wouldn't recognize in the checkout line at the grocery store. But me"—she tapped her forehead—"I have this thing about faces. I never forget a face." She sniffed. "Her face was a lie, you know what I mean?"

"No."

"What she did with the outside had nothing to do with the inside. I wouldn't have trusted her as far as I could drool, but then, I don't trust most people."

"Did she live alone?"

"From what I know, yeah, but that doesn't mean anything. Hell, she could have been living with the Seven Dwarfs and I wouldn't have known."

"Did she ever have any visitors?"

Sonia shrugged with her face as well as her shoulders. "Who knows. Everyone has visitors sometimes. Even that pain in the ass across the hall has visitors, and believe me, no one would want to spend time with her."

I was about to ask another question when the phone rang. It was the city inspector calling to make sure she was there.

"I've been here for three days, and you know why? Because I'm stuck to my seat, it's so damned cold in here." She winked at me as she spoke. "Mm-hm. I'll tell you something—I've had it with waiting for you and the city to help me out here. If you're not here in fifteen minutes, I'm going to call Channel Two and have Mr. Juarez do an exposé on how you bastards are killing babies and old people."

She dropped the receiver back in the cradle and nodded once. "There. Let's hope that'll do it."

"About Ms. Keller—" I began.

"You know what I think, dear? I think you should talk to Julio. He lives on the third floor, the apartment right next to hers. I have a feeling he'll be able to help you more than I can."

"Do you know if he's home?"

"He should be. He works nights. Apartment Three

C. But be careful," she warned with a twinkle in her eye, "he's a real ladies' man."

I handed her my card. "If you think of anything that might be helpful, give me a call."

"All right." She glanced at my card and tucked it into her sweater pocket.

Just as she was walking me to the door, her buzzer rang. I hurried up the stairs as she started lacing into the unsuspecting civil servant.

As I reached the third-floor landing, the door to apartment 3C opened. Julio was seeing someone out. His friend was in his late twenties, slender, and strikingly handsome. After we bumped into each other, offered our apologies, and he fled down the stairs, I stopped Julio before he could shut the door.

"Julio?"

"Yes." His voice was deep and soothing.

"My name is Sydney, Sydney Sloane. Sonia suggested I talk to you."

"If it's about the landlord, I'm with her, across the board." He started to close the door. I blocked it with my foot.

"It's about your old neighbor, Mildred Keller. I'm an investigator and I need to ask you a few questions."

He took a deep breath and leaned against the door frame. His silk forest green and blue striped robe fell open on top, exposing a hairless, sculpted chest. "I told the police everything I know."

"I'm not the police."

"You're not? What are you, private?"

I nodded.

He brightened up. "That's a moose of a different color. Come on in. It's a little messy, but what the hell."

He opened the door to a very small cavelike room. Everything, including the floor, platformlike bleachers—

which had been built to create a sense of space—and the walls, were covered with gray industrial carpeting. His bed was a mattress on the floor and apparently slid into the base of one of the platforms. It was covered with crumpled gray and white sheets. The room smelled of stale smoke and brandy.

"I won't keep you long." I perched on the platform nearest to the door and watched as he found a cigarette, lit it, and returned to bed.

"That's good. It's still the middle of the night for me."

"I understand. Sonia has reason to believe you might have known Mildred Keller better than most of her neighbors."

"Well, we were the only two on this floor for almost seven years. Which doesn't mean we were pals—the lady was definitely a loner—but we talked every now and then. I was probably in her apartment three times tops. I tried to get it when she died, but, honey, let me tell you, this landlord was on it like a fly to shit. It took them less than a month to convert her place into two studios. And we are talking teeny." He blew smoke rings into the air and poked his finger through the center of the last one.

"She lived alone?"

He nodded and flicked the ashes into a nearly empty brandy snifter.

"What was she like?"

"She was like a librarian, you know? Slender, pale, buttoned up and battened down. She was in her late forties, early fifties, but she she was kind of pretty."

I was tempted to ask why he would be surprised if women in their late forties were pretty, but instead I asked, "What was her apartment like?"

"It was a large one-bedroom, faced the back, classy. Not at all what you would expect from her, you know what I mean? I mean, from the way she looked, I kind of expected that she'd have books all over the place and taste, but the lady was elegant. I mean, we're talking refined. Her apartment was great, very chic, and from what *I* could tell, probably an art collector's dream house. She had a shitload of artwork on the walls, the real stuff, too, I think. You could tell that her furniture was quality stuff. Like I said, it was a real class act.''

''Do you know what she did for a living?''

''She worked at the UN, but I don't know what she did there.''

''Did she ever have any visitors?''

''Sometimes. Not often, though.'' He took a deep drag off the cigarette and squinted at me through the smoke. ''Tell me something. Who really wants to know?''

''I'm working for a client who has reason to believe the man being held in connection with her death is innocent.''

He slid his legs under the tangle of sheets and yawned. ''You know, you're the first female private investigator I've met.''

I smiled and asked, ''Did you know Jesse Washburn?''

''Was that the guy who was killed with her? No, I never saw him. After Mildred was killed, the cops showed me a picture of him, but he didn't look familiar.'' He yawned again, this time talking through it. ''He might have come here, but I never saw him.'' He shook his head as if to rid himself of the yawns. ''Sorry.'' He repeated his last sentence clearly and added, ''Mildred and I had real different schedules. And believe me, it's hard enough to keep up with myself. There's no way I could handle someone else's life.''

Now I was stifling a yawn. At this rate, I'd have the

guy toss me a pillow so I could join him in a nap. "I guess she was a pretty subdued woman."

Julio snorted a laugh and dropped the cigarette into the glass. It made a tiny hissing sound and the bulb of the glass filled with gray smoke. "Everyone has a tiger inside them, lady, it's just a matter of setting it free."

"Is that so?"

"Trust me, I know what I'm talking about."

"Did Mildred ever set her tiger free?"

"It sure sounded like it from here. I mean, I don't have X-ray eyes, but if I did, you can bet your ass there were a few times I could have saved money in video rentals and watched her walls." His laugh was low and dirty. He crossed his arms and smiled mischievously. "The librarian was definitely a tiger."

"Is that right?"

"Oh yeah. I mean, I'd see her in the halls all buttoned up and serious, looking at her feet instead of facing you head-on—but there was no doubt about it; she had a lot of passion in her." He rubbed his chest with his right hand. His left nipple was small and hard.

"Did you ever meet any of her friends?"

"Only one. A guy."

"Can you describe him?"

"Yeah, he was hot-looking. Not my type, but hot. He looked like inside he was controlling either fire or ice, you know? But you want to know what he *looks* like, right?" He mirrored my nod. "Okay, let's see, late forties, early fifties, dark complexion, salt-and-pepper hair, unbelievable eyes—they looked almost black. Definitely not what I would have expected Mildred to hook up with."

"Did he have any identifying marks or scars?"

"I don't know. I don't think so."

"What about his clothes or jewelry? Can you remember anything about that?"

He gave it some thought and finally said, "Nope, nothing that stands out, except maybe that he wore a lot of jewelry. Heavy stuff, very gold, very bulky."

"Did you ever talk to him?"

"No."

"Did you ever hear him talk to Mildred?"

"No."

"Would you recognize him if you saw him again?"

"Maybe. Probably." He paused and then added, "Yeah, I'd recognize him. You don't forget eyes like that. They were like little licorice candies."

I wondered where I could find a picture of Caleb Simeon. Julio told me where he worked and gave me his numbers, in case I needed to ask him any further questions. I gave him one of my cards and let myself out of the apartment.

I passed Sonia, who was standing in her doorway, her hands tucked under her armpits, yelling at the city representative. "See, see how cold it is. Would you want your grandmother to have to live with this cold?" She huffed into the air and pointed to the little clouds of breath.

Within forty-five minutes, I was in lane three of an empty pool. Apparently, not many club members like to swim when it's below five degrees outside. Minnie says I take after my great-uncle Amos, who was a member of the Milwaukee chapter of the Polar Bear Club until he froze to death at the age of seventy-seven, but she's wrong. The thought of baring my flesh to take a dip in the icy waters of Lake Michigan is about as inviting as taking a little stroll on broken glass or eating fire.

The place was so deserted, I decided at the last minute to use the Eagle and rowing machines before I left. After an hour and a half, I felt rejuvenated as I braved the cold and walked the fifteen blocks to my office.

N I N E

The woman who answered the door at the Washburn apartment pushed her chins into her throat and stepped back from the threshold as she gave me the once-over. She kept a firm hold of the door-knob. "Yes?"

"Hello. I'm Sydney Sloane. I have a two o'clock appointment with Mrs. Washburn." I held out my card.

"You're a woman." She sniffed twice and crossed her liver-speckled arms under her low-hanging bosom. This was obviously a sensible woman. She wore flat sturdy shoes, a permanent-press wash-and-dry dress with a floral pattern that showed few spots while bringing out the color in her blushless cheeks, and she knew, without assistance, that I was a woman.

"Yes, I know." I smiled.

"Wait here." She opened the door, stepped to the side, and snatched the card out of my hand. With the precision of a marine drill sergeant, she clipped off through an archway into a hallway. Her footsteps trailed off.

I unzipped my jacket as I checked my reflection in the Victorian mirror that covered a good portion of the left wall in the foyer. The entranceway was six feet by twelve feet but looked larger thanks to the mirror. Black and white ceramic tiles lined the floor and a pine tavern table had been placed prudently under the mirror, a catchall for keys, papers, gloves, tickets, whatever. The wall to the right was covered with antique lithographs of boats and stormy scenes of the high seas. A dozen tulips, the shade of a new harvest moon, leaned gracefully from a vase at the end of the table. The walls were eggshell white and though there was a living room straight ahead, I turned to the right and peered through the diamond-shaped window cut into the swinging door that led to the right half of the apartment. I saw a darkened dining room with a long, formal Hepplewhite mahogany table surrounded by eight matching wide-bottomed chairs.

"Just what do you think you're doing?" The drill sergeant was practically in my ear.

I opened my mouth to respond but was quickly cut off. "Mrs. Washburn will see you now," she said with all the disgust she could muster up. This lady definitely needed an attitude adjustment. "Follow me," she grunted. I did and was led at a jogger's pace through a deceptively long hallway to the last room.

"In there." She nodded toward the room, turned on her heels, and was gone.

I knocked softly on the half-closed door and pushed it opened.

"Come in." Dorothy Washburn was poised with her left hand on the Steinway baby grand and her right hand on her small sunken chest. She looked as if she had taken deportment lessons from Loretta Young. She wore a floor-length lounging outfit made of gold lamé and rhinestones, circa 1965. Her lips seemed to spread across almost the total width of her jaw and were highlighted with fire-engine red lipstick. She was painfully slender, but her posture was schoolgirl-perfect. Her thin, long neck seemed to stretch unnaturally out from her collarbone and precariously held her head in place. "Please shut the door," she said in a thin voice. I did.

"Thank you for taking the time to see me, Mrs. Washburn." I slowly advanced into the little room. There was space enough for the piano, a small table, a love seat, and a chair. Wherever you looked, there were splashes of vibrant colors. A vase of anemones sat on the piano, atop a Guatemalan shawl of rainbow colors. There were several throw rugs, one more colorful than the other, all haphazardly tossed on the floor, overlapping one another with a carefreeness that seemed out of place when I looked at Mrs. Washburn.

"Please call me Dorothy." She motioned to the white love seat and waited until I was seated before speaking. "Clara was surprised that you're a woman." Her smile revealed large yellowed teeth. "Chauvinistic, I suppose. I told her Sydney and she assumed you were a man. I imagine you get that a lot." Her words slurred together when she spoke, not distorting the sounds but running them all together as though a sentence was a word and a paragraph a sentence.

"I do." Sunlight poured into the corner room from the two shadeless windows. "This is a lovely room."

"My youngest daughter, Leslie, decorated it just a month ago. It had been Jesse's office." She inhaled at length and slowly released a barely audible sigh. "Actually, I like what she did so much that I've hired her to do the living room. She's just getting started in interior decorating." Dorothy Washburn glided to the chair and settled onto it in one flowing movement. "Is it unusual that a woman would choose your line of work, Miss Sloane?"

"Not really. There are more of us than you would imagine."

"You just woke up one morning and decided that you wanted to be a private detective?"

"Not quite." I wasn't here to discuss my history. It couldn't do her any good to know that after my initial stab at theater I'd joined the police force and wound up in business with Max after my father was murdered in a courtroom by a psychopath who had a thing for little boys, his own son in particular. Often people need to shift the focus from themselves to me. I suppose it makes the question-and-answer period seem more equitable.

As I wasn't volunteering any background information, Dorothy picked up the ball.

"Well, what can I do for you?" She crossed one leg over the other and carefully draped the lamé over her bony kneecaps.

"Mrs. Washburn, as you know, Noah Alexander has accidentally been released from prison. I'm trying to locate him."

"I don't see how I could be of help to you. I've never even seen the man."

"I realize that. I should tell you up front that I have reason to believe Noah Alexander was not responsible for your husband's death. May we still continue this interview?"

Mrs. Washburn stared at the throw rugs and seemed

to give my question some serious thought. Finally, she said, "I think the only thing worse than seeing my husband's killer go free would be that an innocent man was accused of his death."

I nodded. "Is there any possibility that Mr. Washburn might have known Alexander? Do you remember your husband ever mentioning Noah Alexander or someone who might have fit his description?"

The rhinestones on the front of her outfit reflected the sunlight. "Not that I can recall, Miss Sloane, but that's not to say it never happened. Jesse was having a lot of trouble at the store. The neighborhood was never great to begin with, but he was adamant about that damned place. I told him a thousand times it wasn't worth the aggravation, but men are funny. Jesse was raised in that neighborhood and loved it. The steady decay of the area would have broken another man's heart, but Jesse wasn't like that—he honestly believed he could make a difference."

"With a liquor store?" I asked with more irony than I meant to show.

She waved her hand listlessly in front of her. "That was more a romantic notion than anything else. His father had owned a liquor store in the same area and his grandfather before him. Family traditions, Miss Sloane, run deep, like blood. He was fulfilling a lifelong dream with his store."

"All of Mr. Washburn's income was from the liquor store?"

"Hardly." She looked at me as if I were an ignorant child with whom to be tolerant. "Our income came from several sources."

She continued. "My family was old established money. Hangers. Wire hangers." She smiled modestly and readjusted the fabric of her dress over her knees.

"After the army, Jesse wanted to work with his father, but he worried about me, about being able to take care of me. So instead, he worked with my father for several years." She sighed. "He just hated it. The truth is, in the beginning I couldn't have cared less about the money. I would have been content to put my money into trust for our children and live on what he made." She shook her head sadly and touched the back of her neck, "But Jesse was a proud man, he had to be the breadwinner. About twenty years ago, Jesse's father died and left him some real estate."

"Including the building on Lexington?" I asked, referring to the corner building where the liquor store was housed.

"Yes, that and other properties. Jesse could have quit working with my father then, but he didn't. I think he had a sense of obligation to Father. Anyway, Dad loved Jesse like a son. He was aware of Jesse's loyalty, and when he died about ten years later, he saw to it that Jesse had a separate inheritance, separate from mine and my brother's. About three years after Dad was gone, my brother happily agreed to buy Jesse's share of the business. Jesse was good with money, he invested carefully." She inhaled deeply. "It was a natural progression that he'd go back to his roots, open the store, try to make a difference in the community."

"Was the store making money?"

"That's not why he was in business. To be honest with you, I don't know how much money it brought in. All I know is, he was happy. He'd come home from work glowing. I never saw that in all the years he worked for Dad. As happy as I was to see that Jesse had finally found something he loved, it made me sick that he'd denied himself for what he thought I wanted." She brought her hand to her throat and slowly shrugged her right shoulder. "The business now belongs to someone else. I understand its transformation during the last six months is a testament to our changing times."

"Do you know the current owner?"

She barely hid her distaste. "Ray something or other. He and Jesse met in the army. I met him once, but I don't know him, no."

"Did you think it was strange that Jesse left the store to Ray?"

"Absolutely not. But he didn't just leave him the store, he left him the entire building. You didn't know Jesse . . . he was a giving man. Besides, no one in our family would have known what to do with it."

I noticed a framed picture on the piano. I walked over to it and commented, "What an attractive family you have, Mrs. Washburn."

In the center of the picture, Mr. and Mrs. Washburn sat on a deacon's bench, holding hands. Jesse Washburn was strikingly handsome. He had a full head of gray hair and, though slender, looked quite muscular. The couple was surrounded by two men and two women. The men were both dark and appeared to be in their mid- to late thirties. The one who stood to Jesse's left was slightly balding and thickening around the middle and had a lovely, almost self-conscious smile. The other looked impassively at the photographer, his hand placed formally on his mother's shoulder. The woman who was obviously the youngest in the group looked to be in her late twenties and was standing to Dorothy Washburn's right, her hands on her hips and her head cocked to her right as if she was somehow just slightly removed from the scene. She was pretty, slender, and casually dressed in pants and a sweater. The other woman was older and colder, more like the humorless man standing behind Dorothy. Her dark brown hair half-covered the right side of her face as if it was the only thing left for her to hide behind. I brought the picture to where Dorothy sat and perched myself back on the love seat. "Are these your children?"

"Yes. That was our last family photo. It was taken about four months before Jesse died. That's Leslie, my baby, the resident decorator." She pointed to the pants and sweater. "That's Paul, our eldest. He's an accountant, married, and living in Connecticut. Ever since Jesse died, he's wanted me to leave the city and live with them, but I was born here. I'd go crazy in Connecticut." I could envision the round face of the balding man entreating his mother to please move into the safety of the suburbs.

"This is Lloyd. He doesn't look very happy there, does he? I think he and Paul had just had a little tiff before this was taken. He's thirty-eight. Quite handsome, don't you think?"

"Yes, very."

"That's what I think. But he can't seem to find a woman to settle down with. He's too picky, if you ask me. Then again, his work seems to absorb all his time."

"What does he do?"

"He's a computer programmer. He had thought he'd stay in the navy, but he left that, and I'm just as glad. Now he lives in Washington, which I think can only help his chances of finding a nice girl, don't you agree?"

Yes indeed.

"And this is Marcia." She pointed to the Veronica Lake look-alike. "She's just a year younger than Paul. She's a psychotherapist and her husband's a podiatrist." Dorothy held the frame in her lap and stared at the photograph. "It is a handsome family, isn't it, Miss Sloane?"

"Yes, very."

"Do you come from a close family?" She sounded far away, as though she was addressing someone from the past rather than me.

"Somewhat . . ." I cleared my throat. "Mrs. Washburn . . ."

"Mom! You're not going to believe what I've found for you. Only the most fantastic violin case from the eighteenth—oh!" She stopped short when she saw me. "Sorry. I thought you were alone." Leslie Washburn was wearing faded jeans, pointed cowboy boots, a beige fatigue sweater, a midlength blue Air Force coat from the forties, and brown leather gloves. A brightly colored scarf was tied around her waist and another around her neck. She was, quite simply, the most beautiful woman I had ever seen.

"Tsk, Leslie, must you be so loud?" Dorothy rose from her chair, returned the picture to its proper place, and opened her arms to her daughter. "This"—she pointed to me—"is Sydney Sloane. We were having a nice discussion before you so rudely interrupted us, weren't we?"

Leslie removed her gloves as she brushed her lips against her mother's cheek. She then came to me with an outstretched hand. "Nice to meet you. Sorry about the interruption, but I'm wired today. I hit a bonanza while I was antique hunting." She clasped my hand warmly between both of hers.

Mother taught me not to stare, but she also told me not to snoop, and where would I be if I followed that dandy little piece of advice? Besides, I wasn't staring. I had to look at her; she was holding my hand. Like her father, thick dark lashes and brows framed her light blue, almost gray eyes. When she smiled, her lips parted ever so slightly, revealing a small but sexy overbite. A blue headband covered her ears and kept her dark hair pulled back off her face. As she stood there holding my hand in hers, I could feel all the blood rushing to my face. I gently pried my hand away before it got all sweaty.

"Shall I leave you two alone?" she asked her mother.

"I don't know. Miss Sloane? Is there any other way I can be of help to you?"

"I do have a few more questions."

"Leslie, be a good girl and make me a cup of coffee, would you please?" Dorothy put her hand to her chest as if she had been stricken. "Where *are* my manners? I apologize, Miss Sloane. Would you care for a beverage?"

"No, thank you. I'm fine."

Leslie rolled her eyes and went to the door. "Mom, I think I saw your manners in the den. You want me to get 'em for you?" She winked and closed the door behind her.

Dorothy positioned herself by the piano. "Of all our children, Leslie is most definitely her father's daughter."

"Were you ever married before, Mrs. Washburn?"

She looked puzzled. "No. Jesse and I were married for just over forty years."

"Do you know if your husband ever had an affair?" There is no delicate way to ask some questions.

Color rose to Dorothy Washburn's cheeks. "I'm surprised at you. Your appearance of decorum is deceptive."

"It's not. However, sometimes I have to ask questions that sting. You see, Mrs. Washburn, I can't ignore a line of questioning because it's ugly or upsetting."

"I don't understand how this could possibly help you locate this Alexander person."

"As I said before, I have good reason to believe that Noah Alexander was not responsible for your husband's death. Therefore, I have to explore every other possibility." I left it at that. The possibility that an ex-husband or lover of Dorothy's eighty-sixed Jesse and Mildred was implausible, but I had to ask. I asked again whether Jesse had ever had an affair.

She pressed her fingertips to her forehead and squeezed her eyelids shut. "Jesse was a very virile man." She turned away from me and walked to the window. "Leslie is a blessing, but we hadn't planned for her, if you know what I mean. Giving birth to her put an enormous strain on me, both physically as well as emotionally. After she was born, our intimate life was somewhat . . . altered." She placed her hand against the windowsill.

She turned her doelike eyes on me. "I loved him very much."

"I can see that."

"He knew he was free to look for sexual release elsewhere." The words were difficult, but she seemed somehow relieved having said them. She paused. "We had a very full, wonderful marriage filled with so much love and affection. But that's not what you asked, is it?" Her voice turned cold. "We hadn't made love in many years." She paused. "Were they lovers?" Her eyes were wide and almost panicked.

"I don't know." Given another set of circumstances, I might have alluded to Ray's innuendo that Jesse and Mildred were involved, just to get information, but I liked Mrs. Washburn. Besides, what the hell did I know?

"I like to think not."

Like my mother always said, "Let thy speech be better than silence, or be silent." I said nothing.

Finally, she said, "The thought of his killer being free is like having a knife twisting inside me."

"I can imagine that it is."

"I still wake up every morning and reach for him. Forty years is a long time." She sighed. "It was such a senseless killing."

"Most killings are."

"The police were convinced that this Alexander was guilty." She sat on the piano bench.

"Yes, I know. However, since then, new evidence has surfaced that may change that."

"What evidence?"

There was a knock at the door.

"Come in." Dorothy straightened her back even further, as if it was possible.

"Coffee's on." Leslie carried a small wooden tray with a demitasse of steaming espresso.

Dorothy rose and took the tray from Leslie. "I'll have this in the other room." It was a smooth dismissal, and one I didn't mind. I was just as glad not to answer her last question.

"You've been very kind, Mrs. Washburn. I appreciate your having taken time for me."

Her face was expressionless. "You're welcome." She put the tray on the piano bench and extended her right hand to me. "Leslie will see you to the door, won't you?"

"Sure." Leslie went into the hallway.

"If you find out anything new regarding Jesse's death, you will let me know, won't you?" Mrs. Washburn asked softly as she took my hand.

"Yes. I promise." I released her hand and followed Leslie into the hallway.

"Did you meet Clara the human look-alike?" Leslie asked.

I laughed and told her I had. "She's bright—she knew right off the bat that I was a woman."

"That makes two of us."

Again my cheeks flushed. "People usually expect to see a man when they hear my name," I explained. On the way out, I was able to examine the family photographs and portraits that lined the hallway. "I love the work you did in your mother's sitting room. You have a gift for decorating."

"Which comes as a huge surprise to me because I always thought I'd be a teacher or a nurse, something practical like that." We reached the foyer. "But then I hated school and the sight of blood makes me sick."

"Yeah, me, too." In my mind, all I could see was Shelley.

"Well." An uneasy silence descended upon us as she shifted her weight from one foot to the other and I pulled my gloves from my pockets.

"Well, it was nice meeting you." I stepped toward the door.

"Which direction are you headed?" she asked as I turned the knob of the door.

"West."

"Through the park?"

"Yes." There wasn't much choice, as we were on Fifth Avenue and the park divides east and west.

"I mean, are you walking?"

It was only three and I could see there was still plenty of bright sunlight. "I hadn't thought about it. It was pretty cold before."

"The sun's made it almost warm out there. If you walk, I'd like to join you. I need to burn off some of this energy."

"All right." The idea of walking back to the office wasn't altogether unappealing and a chance to question—and look at—Leslie Washburn was an unexpected bonus.

"Great. Let me get my coat and tell Dot I'm history." She disappeared back into the hallway, which gave me an opportunity to see that from *any* angle, Leslie Washburn was a knockout. Now, I'm no slouch, but the last time I looked like that in a pair of jeans, I was twenty-five. Then again, Leslie probably was twenty-five. Twenty-five. At twenty-five, my tush was in its proper place and the laws of gravity hadn't yet kicked in.

Leslie was right: It was now about thirty degrees above zero, a warming trend if ever there was one. As we started across the park, she asked why I was visiting her mother. I told her.

"You're a private investigator?" Her voice rose with excitement. "Mom never mentioned you." She pushed her hands farther into her pockets. "So what's up?"

"I have reason to believe the man accused of killing your father is innocent."

"Alexander? Go on. How come? The police were convinced it was him. Hell, *look* at the guy—he looks like a killer! Don't tell me he's the one who hired you?"

"He didn't hire me."

She nodded once. "So why call Dot? That doesn't make any sense. What could she know about the shithead who killed Dad? Unless you know something that the police don't know. Do you?" She had a bounce in her step like a little girl hopping, skipping, and jumping circles around you, all the while asking a bizillion 'why' questions.

"Did you know Mildred Keller?" We made our way over a frozen dirt path that led us past a deserted playing field.

"No. I hardly ever went to Dad's store. But wait— don't change the subject. I don't understand why you would need to talk to my mom. What could she possibly tell you?"

"As it turns out, nothing, but more often than not people don't realize what they know. They'll say something in passing and, as it turns out, it might just be the thread I was looking for."

"Is that right?" There was something in her smile that made me momentarilly self-conscious.

_____

"Were you very close with your dad?"

The smile faded. "Yes, we were very close. He was my best friend when I was growing up. My hero. Dad was a very special man. Gentle. Genuine, you know what I mean?"

I nodded knowingly, remembering my own hero, Nathan.

Her smile returned slowly. "But then I hit adolescence and parents were just not cool, you know what I mean?"

"Mm-hm. Between thirteen and sixteen, I don't think there was anything more painful for me than having to be seen in public with my folks."

"Oh God, yes." She shrieked with delight. "Restaurants were the worst!" Her laughter was infectious, bubbling up slowly from someplace deep within and then spilling out, touching me like a tickle. Before I knew it, we were sharing stories of the agonies of adolescence as we crossed through the park.

"I saw the family portrait. Your dad looks like he was a nice guy."

"They don't make men like him anymore. Maybe they never did. I mean, he was charming, funny, loving, in touch with his feelings—everything you could ever want in a man. When I was growing up, I thought all men would be like him. God, was I disappointed." She took a deep breath, pulled off her headband, and combed her fingers through her long hair.

The bogus gaslights suddenly lit the pathways and the park drive. "I like your mom. This must be hard on her."

"Unless you've been through it, you can't understand."

We walked in silence for the next twenty paces. I understood too well the gamut of emotions that come with the violent death of someone you love. Nathan's murder threw me into six months of incapacitating depression. Then one day, Max came to see me. It was eleven in the morning, and Caryn had already left for her studio. Max let himself into the apartment (Caryn had given him a set of keys), came into my darkened bedroom, and ordered me out of bed. I suggested he not hit himself with the door on his way out and pulled the sheets over my head. He told me then that I had options: Either he would yank me out of bed and personally dress me or I could bathe and dress myself while he made a fresh pot of coffee. When I finally joined him in the garden, he told me we were going for a little drive. An hour later, we were at a shooting range in Nyack, where Max handed me my Walther and said, ''We all loved Nate, but we can't die because he's gone. You've got to let go, Sydney.'' By the time I was finished, the magazine was empty, the target was in tatters, but the noise was still deafening. I felt Max's hand on my shoulder and realized it wasn't gunshot I was hearing but my own screams.

''Tell me something.'' Leslie stopped to scrape mud off her boot. ''How did you ever get involved in this line of work?''

''It's a long story.''

''I have time, and seeing as though it's colder than I thought, I need something to keep my mind off my frostbitten feet.''

''A friend talked me into it.''

After we left the shooting range, Max and I had gone to the boat basin in Alpine for a walk. It was his idea that we pool resources, energy, contacts, brains, money, and brawn and go into business together. I'd quit the force eight months earlier and knew I didn't have it in me to spend another day without a game plan.

I pointed to the skyscrapers south of the park and said, "Beautiful, isn't it?"

She followed my gaze. "Yes, it is." She blew into her hands and rubbed the palms together. "Okay, it's obvious you don't like to offer information, so I'll ask questions. Isn't it a dangerous line of work?" She kept her head down as we forged ahead, trying to stay in what was left of the waning sunlight.

"No more so than most other jobs."

She made a face of disbelief.

"Seriously. With most jobs, there's some element of risk involved. Take window washers, okay? They know there are risks involved in their line of work, but if they come prepared and know how to protect themselves, it's as easy a job for them as it would be for you to decorate a restaurant."

"Now, there's a rotten analogy. Almost like comparing apples and cantaloupes." As we passed the lake by the boat house on the Seventy-second Street transverse, two teenage boys were practicing jumping up and down curbs with their skateboards. Both were wearing torn jeans and high-top sneakers without laces. Neither of the boys were wearing gloves, which only made me flex my fingers, which were buried deep in my pockets.

"All I'm saying is, any risk we take is dangerous to us on some level. That's why we call them risks."

"Yes, but you risk getting killed, whereas I risk only having to recover a sofa."

"You're still putting yourself on the line, and probably taking more of a risk than I do on any given day. Believe me, private investigators don't live TV lives. Most of our work is done on computers."

"No!" This thought seemed to delight her.

"Yes." I found myself being just as playful in return.

"Say, listen, want to stop for a coffee over there?"

She nodded toward the end of the park, which we were nearing. "I have to admit it's colder than I thought."

The idea was tempting, but I couldn't. "I need to get back to the office."

Her eyes, now gray against the cold white sky, looked like little saucers. "Well, listen, if you're not busy tonight, maybe you'd like to have dinner with me? I mean, we both have to eat and, who knows, I might be able to shed light on your investigation. Like you said, you never know what you can learn. What do you say?" She arched her brows and looked like a lonely little waif, a look I was certain she'd used successfully on Jesse in the past.

Leslie was—however remotely—involved in my search for David, which would have normally been reason enough for me to say no. However, I threw better judgment to the wind and said, "That sounds nice. Anyplace in particular?"

"Let's see. I could go for either Italian or Thai food. How about you?"

"Italian sounds good. I know a great dive called Bruno's."

We had reached Central Park West and had to raise our voices above the traffic.

"Sounds fine. Should I pick you up or meet you there?" She rubbed her hands together, trying to create heat by friction.

"Why don't you pick me up and we'll have a drink before we go." Bruno's is one of those places you take people to rather than let them meet you there. The front of the place looks like an old bakery, so if you don't know it, chances are likely you'd pass it up, not realizing there's a restaurant hidden in the back.

"Okay." She hailed a taxi as I quickly scribbled my

---

home address on the back of one of my cards. "Eight o'clock?" she asked.

"That's good." The cold was more penetrating as the sun began to sink over New Jersey. Snow felt imminent.

"I'll see you at eight." She jumped into the backseat of the cab she had flagged down.

I stood there for several minutes, staring blankly at the Dakota and thinking about Leslie, when I realized how cold I was. I checked my watch and decided rather than footing it the fifteen blocks back to the office, I'd be better off taking a taxi and having time for a shower before dinner.

Kerry was on the phone when I walked in. "Hang on a second, Max. She just walked in." She held out the receiver to me.

"I'll take it in there." I continued past her into my office.

"Max!" I had the receiver in my hand before I took off my coat. "What's the matter, pal? Did she dump you already?"

"Quite the contrary, my love. She wants to marry me. But you know me—not the marrying kind of guy."

"I don't know. I always thought you'd be a good husband." I took off my jacket and put it on the back of my chair.

"My ex-wife would disagree. I'm calling to get an update on David."

I told him about Caleb Simeon's early-morning visit and Shelley's gruesome death. "I just met Mrs. Washburn."

"Washburn?"

"Noah Alexander allegedly murdered two people,

Jesse Washburn, the owner of a liquor store, and a client, Mildred Keller."

"So, where are you now?"

"Well"—I settled into my chair—"as much as I hated David, I'm convinced he couldn't kill anyone. Now, Alexander is accused of cold-blooded murder. David is Alexander. Therefore, Alexander has to be innocent of murder." I put my feet up on the desk. "I just have to prove it, that's all."

"Anything else?"

"Yeah. From the description Keller's neighbor gave me, it sounds like this Caleb Simeon might have been a visitor of hers."

"Proof?"

"Hunch."

"That's all the proof I need. More?"

"Kerry was able to trace a death certificate for baby Alexander."

"Good for her."

"That explains how David took on another man's identity—a very professional job, I might add, because the cops bought it lock, stock, and barrel. Now, David would have to have a damned good reason for dumping his own identity, but I haven't been able to figure that out. I haven't had time to just sit down and think things through. I need to write it down and look at it." I glanced at my watch. It was almost five.

"Listen, you want me to come back? Maybe I can help."

"Oh no you don't. I've been your excuse too many times in the past."

"What? Me?" Max feigned innocence. I could almost see his handsome face, tanned and bug-eyed, staring at the receiver in disbelief.

"Now, now, my dear, you can't always come racing

home to Auntie Sydney just when the going gets tough. I'm sure Gerta's a very nice—"

"Glenna," he corrected me.

"That's right, Glenna."

"All right, tell me, what are you going to do next?"

"Well, I have a dinner date."

"You have a what?"

"A dinner date."

"With Minnie?"

"No."

"With whom?"

"No one you know."

"Wait, wait, wait, wait. No one I know? You haven't had a date in over a year, and now, all of a sudden, poof, a dinner date . . . and you won't share the details?"

"It's just dinner, for God's sake," I teased him.

"Just dinner?"

"Stop repeating everything I say."

"You haven't had a date for over a year. Am I correct?"

"Yes." I smiled despite myself. "Okay, you want details? She's an interior decorator, very young—"

"What's young? Fourteen, eighteen?"

"You are a pig. You know that, don't you? She's in her late twenties," I said, guessing, "but she seems a lot older. She's bright, nice, that's it."

"Uh-huh, and where did you meet her?"

"She's Jesse Washburn's daughter." I tried to toss this off.

"The stiff?"

"Yes."

"You're dating the stiff's daughter?"

"Who said *dating?* We're just having dinner together, that's all."

"Wait a minute, *I* date clients and suspects—that's

135

me, not you. You're the one who always has to be properly introduced. You're the one who's always been too shy for casual dating. What the hell's going on there?"

"This isn't dating." I switched on the desk lamp.

"Is she gay?" he asked.

"We didn't talk about it." I could feel my defenses rushing to the forefront. I took a deep breath. "But yes, I have a feeling she is."

"A hunch?"

"Yes."

"Okay, so she's gay, you're gay, and you're going out for dinner, right?"

"Right." I stopped. "Wait a minute, are you saying because we're both gay and going out to dinner that it's a date?"

"You're saying it's not?"

"I won't even dignify that with a response. You've *got* to hear how stupid you sound without my pointing it out." Damn it. Now I was pacing. I hate pacing. It makes me nervous.

"Did it occur to you that just maybe this has been planned to get you off the track? Or maybe Washburn wants to keep her eye on you for other reasons?"

"Of course I thought about it, and it doesn't make sense. But now you're starting to piss me off. I don't like you questioning my professional judgment, Max. And you of all people should know how much double standards irk me. What's this bullshit—I can do this but you can't?"

"Come on, you know I'm on your side."

I counted to ten.

"Syd? I'm holding up my white shorts." He paused. "I was being a bully. I'm sorry."

"It's okay." I stopped pacing and carried the phone to the window.

"She cute?"

"Incredibly."

"Be careful."

"I will."

"And Sydney, I don't want to come home and find you married, is that understood?" He laughed softly.

"Oh God, Max, you're so queer."

"You should talk."

"I have to go. Are we okay?" I asked.

"We're fine. If you need me, you call, all right?"

"Yes, dear," I said in my best June Cleaver impersonation. "In the meantime, just enjoy the rest of your vacation. Stop calling in and stop worrying about me. By the time you get back, all of this will be history. Okay?"

"Okay. I-love-ya-good-bye." He gave me his standard exit line.

"Good-bye." I heard his end click off. I hung up and stared out at the street. Max was right in suggesting that Leslie could have been planted, but there was also a possibility that he was simply jealous. Though we'd been friends since I was a rookie and partners for the last ten years, he had only known me as a couple with Caryn, with whom I had lived for sixteen years. In the beginning, it had been difficult for Max to accept that I was gay and not the least bit interested in sleeping with him. However, once he got to know the two of us, he and Caryn became inseparable and his loyalty to her unfaltering. When Caryn made her decision to move, Max assumed I would turn to men. I hadn't. I never told him about the night with Eddie. But then, there was a lot I never told Max.

I hadn't heard Kerry when she came into the office. She sneezed. "Shit."

"That doesn't sound good." I went back to the desk and tossed her a box of tissues.

"Yeah, well I thought I'd go home, have a bowl of soup, send out a few resumes, and then take a candlelight hot bath while sipping expensive cognac." She stretched back into the sofa and smiled. "How about you?"

"I want to take a shower and then I'm going out for dinner."

"Oh? Who with?" She pulled herself upright, folded her hands on her lap, and smiled like my best friend in high school, Mona Schneider, who wore braces for two years and never once showed her teeth during that time.

"None of your business." I smiled back at her.

She crossed her hands over her heart and looked wounded. "To the quick. Why not just open my veins? Hmmm? What am I, an employee? A peon who is not fit to share the good along with the bad and the ugly? Fine. Fine. If you think that I care that you're fooling around with one of your clients, you are sorely mistaken." By now, she had worked her way over to the doorway and was leaning against the frame, à la Garbo in *Camille*.

"Did you listen to my entire conversation with Max?"

"Just some." She walked to my desk and perched herself on the edge. "You know my theory, Syd; Max is in love with you. I know you think I like to make things up, but I know what I know, and I know he's got it bad for you. I think you're insane to pass on a guy like him simply because there are about three men in the whole of New York City who are not either crazy, married, or gay. I mean, let's face it, women throw themselves at Max and what do you do?"

"You're just jealous."

"You're right. I know you don't notice, but that's one sexy man." She blew her nose.

"I notice. I just don't care."

"So, who's the lucky gal?"

"Her name is Leslie."

"Uh-huh. She's a pubescent decorator." She blew her nose again. "Are you serious about her?"

"It's just dinner." I swiveled to the left and switched on my computer, a Macintosh Plus that's perfect for mechanical morons like me. "That's all. Dinner. Period."

"Did I suggest more?" She sneezed again, grabbed a handful of tissues, and blew her nose for about a minute and a half. She took a seat on the chair opposite me and said, "Listen, can I come in at one tomorrow? I have a reading of a new play at the workshop that goes from ten-thirty until twelve-thirty." She was pulling on her over-the-knee boots and barely looked up.

"Whenever is good. But the way you sound, you may not want to come in at all." By now, I had opened a new document and Kerry knew I was no longer with her. I vaguely heard her telling me to have fun, and when she said good-bye, I told her to break a leg.

I had enough time to input the notes I had written earlier and add to the list. After about twenty minutes, I had a chronological list of people from Noah Alexander to Sonia Rothman. Beside each name, I listed their relationship first to David, then to either Jesse Washburn or Mildred Keller. After that, I noted when they were interviewed, what impressions I got from them, and the possibility of how and where they might fit into the scheme of things.

By the time I finished, the streets were dark and crowded with nine-to-fivers conducting the business of life after work. I decided to walk West End Avenue rather than Broadway because it's less congested and prettier. These very streets are testimony to the best-laid plans of mice and men. West End Avenue—sandwiched between Riverside Drive with its mansions and Broadway (originally the Boulevard, and slated to be a residental street)—

was, at its inception, designated as a commercial avenue housing businesses ready to cater to the homes on Broadway and the mansions on Riverside Drive. Now it's one of the quietest streets in the city, as it is one of only two avenues (Park being the other) that prohibit bus traffic.

When I got home, I poured myself a light gin and tonic, drew a hot bath, blasted Vivaldi's *Four Seasons,* and unplugged the phone.

There is nothing more relaxing than a hot bath on a cold winter's day.

By 7:45, I was ready for Leslie Washburn.

T E N

I was at the opera with my mother and David. Suddenly, there was silence. The singers were continuing their grand gestures, their mouths were opening and closing, and the musicians were furiously playing their instruments, but there wasn't a sound. A small Asian man dressed as a woman in Kabuki came to the side of the stage and started signing the opera. When I turned to David to ask about this, I discovered that he had turned into a German shepherd puppy. My mother kept telling me to sit still and enjoy the show. At the back of the theater, there started a funeral procession winding through the aisles. Behind the child-sized casket, there was an old woman carrying cymbals, which she clapped loudly together every three steps. As she neared our aisle, the sound became shattering.

I reached for the phone.

"Sydney, it's Gil."

"What time is it?" I could barely get my eyes to open, let alone focus on the alarm clock.

"Seven o'clock. We got to talk."

"Seven in the morning?" I pulled a pillow over my head.

"No, seven in the evening. What's wrong with you? What, are you asleep?"

"Brilliant deduction, Sherlock."

"Well, get up. I'm on my way over."

"Right now?"

"Right now." He clicked off.

Through the venetian blinds, I could tell that it was a clear morning. I tried moving out from under the covers and quickly realized that the heat had been turned off. West End Avenue apartment buildings may look impressive, but that doesn't mean beans when it comes to heat and hot water.

Bed felt like that big, warm, safe place it had when I was little and hated school. Inevitably, I'd put off getting out of bed for so long that every morning it was a race just to get out the front door. I can still remember my first-grade teacher, Mrs. Lillian Daniels, standing at the front of the room, her scowl in place, tapping her orthopedic-shod foot while waiting for me to climb into the garbage can as punishment because I kept blowing the *P-Q-R-S* sequence in the alphabet.

That was one of my historical facts I had shared with Leslie the night before over dinner. Whatever notion I had to interrogate her had fallen by the wayside and we wound up having a very nice evening. And though it had nothing to do with the case, I did learn one very important lesson that night. I realized that after a year and a half of being single, I was lonely. Not for friendship—I have a wide and varied circle of friends—but I've missed companionship, romance, flirting.

This thought was enough to catapult me out of bed. I raced from the bedroom to the bathroom, where it was equally cold. Adding insult to injury, there was no hot water. Charlie burrowed into the warmth under the bed covers, and though the thought of cat hairs all over the flannel sheets didn't delight me, the little guy had to keep warm.

By the time Gil arrived, I had a pot of coffee brewed and, because I was starved, breakfast for both of us.

"What's that?" Gil asked as he straddled one of the kitchen chairs and heaped three teaspoons of sugar into his mug of coffee.

"It's a little thing called breakfast. Have you heard of it? Innovative idea." I took the cover off the pan and checked the omelet. Perfect.

"Ha-ha." He sipped his coffee. "I'm not hungry."

"Mmm." I divided the omelet in half, put two slices of oatmeal toast on each plate, and joined him at the table.

"So, what brings you to my humble abode at this stupid hour?" I buttered a piece of toast.

"Murder."

"Now whose?"

"Same one. That little girl died a nasty death." He surveyed his plate. "What is this?" He poked at it with his fork and made it sound as if I'd given him a plate of worms.

"It's an omelet with cream cheese and scallions. You'll love it." I poured myself a second cup of coffee.

"Well, as long as you went to the trouble . . ." He first salted and peppered and then tasted it. He grunted

---

143

his approval. Cooking for some people can be such a pleasure.

"So." Gil sighed as he cut into his eggs.

"So." I smiled.

"So we both acted like assholes the other day, right? Right. In the meantime, has your friend Mr. Phillips been able to give you any information?" In two bites, half of his breakfast was gone.

"Eddie?" I got up and went to the refrigerator. "Why would Eddie have information for me?" I pulled out a jar of strawberry jam and took it back to the table.

"Why? Because you asked him to get in there and get information about this Alexander schmuck, who I'm tellin' you isn't David." He raised his hands before I could get in a word. "I know, I know, hold off for a second, would you, tiger? Lemme just tell you a few things, okay?" He gulped some coffee and wiped his mouth with the back of his hand. "We found prints at Gomes's apartment, very clear, very incriminating."

"Noah Alexander's."

"That's right. Look, he had motive, access, and it might explain why there was no forced entry or apparently any struggle. I'm telling you, this man's killed before, Sydney, and given a chance, he'll probably kill again. He's brutal."

"I agree with you. But look, I've been thinking about this. Who says that the person who killed Shelley is the same one who killed Washburn and Keller? Maybe there are two killers. Maybe the murders are completely unrelated. I mean, everyone's so quick to assume that Noah Alexander is responsible for all three killings, but what motive would he have to kill Shelley? They were lovers."

"Right, and lovers never kill lovers." His sarcasm was loud and clear.

"Okay, okay, but you have to look at the bigger

picture. The more I learn about this case, the more I'm convinced that the man you think is Noah Alexander is being framed, just like he was the last time."

"I see, so now you think Washburn was a frame." His plate was clean.

"I do."

"Mm-hm. And you still think David is Alexander, right?"

"That's right."

"But there's no evidence to support that."

"Sure there is. There has to be. You just haven't bothered to look for it because you refuse to believe that I might be right. Check Shelley's apartment for photographs. I saw one there the other day that was David as sure as you're Gilbert Jackson."

I finished breakfast and poured us each another coffee just as the radiator started clanking loudly. I took that as a positive omen.

" 'Bout time," I muttered to the metal antique in the corner.

"Mind if I smoke?" He pulled out a pack of cigarettes that were wrapped up in a sheet of white paper. "These yahoos have me wrapping up my cigarettes and writing down when, where, how, why—it's a load of shit." He pulled a pencil out of his shirt pocket, made his notations, and then rewrapped the cigarettes with the paper and two rubber bands. He then lighted the cigarette.

I slid an ashtray in front of him.

"Tell me one thing—do you have any proof that it's David and he's being framed?"

"No." Not conclusive. "But you don't have proof that they're not one and the same. The prints—"

"I told you, David's prints are missing."

"And you still think it's a coincidence? Why?" I took a deep breath. "Gil, Noah Alexander died of crib

---

145

death in the late forties. With his birth certificate in hand, someone created new ID. I think that someone is David. You don't. It's as simple as that."

"How do you know that?" He leaned back and took a long drag off his cigarette. If nothing else, he was going to relish his smoke.

"Funny thing, it's what I do for a living."

"Sydney, that little girl was murdered by an animal. Do you know what he did to her? First he cut out her tongue and then he slit her throat."

"I know, Gil, I was there, remember?" I got up abruptly, took the dishes, and put them in the sink. Bastards. All I could imagine was her fear, her panic, her pain. I grabbed the side of the sink and held my breath.

"Do your people have a lead?" I needed to change the direction of the conversation.

"Not much." He paused. "Nothing."

"I don't get it. Who was watching her place?"

The silence that followed was my answer. I turned to Gil and stared at him in disbelief. "No one? You've got to be joking."

"I'm afraid not." He looked as pained as if Shelley had been one of his own kids. I turned back to the sink and rinsed off the dishes with cold water.

"Well," he sighed, "my instincts are just as good as yours, kid, if not better, and I don't get a feeling about this like you do. Now put yourself in my shoes for one minute here. What am I supposed to do? Go to my boss and suggest that Noah Alexander is actually a thirteen-year-old corpse who's now being *framed* for three murders? Even if I thought there was a chance that you were right—and I don't—I'd have to be out of my mind to put myself out on a limb like that. You know me . . . I'd bend over backward for you, but the truth is, I don't think you called this one right." He rubbed his jaw. "I came here to tell you about the prints at Gomes's apartment and to ask you nicely to lay off the case. Whoever he is, this guy's crazy, Sydney, and I'm afraid you'll get hurt."

"I understand." I kept my back to him and stared at the dishes in the sink. Fortunately, the phone rang before either of us could continue. It was Eddie. "Hiya, stranger, how are you?"

"I've got information for you," he said.

"Good. Listen, I have a guest right now. Can I call you back in about ten, fifteen minutes?" He agreed, and I turned back to Gil.

By now, the radiator was clanking up a storm and I could hardly hear myself think.

"So, wadda ya say?" Gil was savoring the last few drags of his cigarette.

"I say I can understand your position better than I did before and I think you're sweet for worrying about me, but you know as well as I do that I can take care of myself. I won't lie to you and say, sure, sure, I won't pursue this, because *this* is my job, Gil. I do this for a living."

We stared at each other for a long time until finally Gil nodded, put out his cigarette, and stood. As he started toward the front door, I slipped my arm through his. "David's not a killer. You know that," he said softly.

"I do. Which means neither is Noah Alexander." I smiled. "We're just at one of those little impasses." We were standing at the front door. Carmen gets the *News* delivered, and I get the *Times*. I retrieved both papers off the floor and said, "Listen, Gil, have you ever heard of a guy named Caleb Simeon? Tall, dark, thickset, early fifties, brown eyes, salt-and-pepper hair. Likes jewelry."

Gil pressed the elevator button and pushed the corners of his mouth down. "Nope. Never heard of him. Of course, that description only fits about twenty-five million people. Who is he?"

I shrugged. "I don't know. That's what I'm trying to find out."

"Is it connected to Alexander?" He took a half-step toward me.

"No." The wrong answer popped out of my mouth before I could stop it.

"You need help?" The elevator door opened.

"I'll let you know."

He held open the elevator door with his hand. "You wouldn't hold back from me, right? I mean, I came here to share with you and I would expect the same from you, kiddo."

"And you would be right to expect that." I shooed him into the elevator, "I'm already running late and I haven't even taken a shower. We'll talk, okay?"

"Okay," he said begrudgingly as the wooden-inlaid elevator door closed between us.

Okay, so I lied. But it wasn't really a lie. There are just some times you shouldn't offer information, and I knew that until I had something I could substantiate, Gil wasn't in a position to use anything I could offer him. So in essence, it would have been a waste of time for both of us.

I grabbed my coffee and went into the office to call Eddie. The apartment was finally heating up and I removed one of two sweatshirts I had been wearing. I dialed his number. He picked up on the first ring.

"Phillips."

"Sloane."

"And who were you entertaining so early this morning?" he cooed into the phone.

"Gil Jackson," I cooed back.

"He's a little old for you, don't you think?"

"I always go for maturity, Eddie, you know that."

"That I do. It's a shame I'm so much younger than you." He chuckled. "So, I went to Gomes's building yesterday and met some of her neighbors. By the way, you have a time of death yet?"

"No."

"I do. Between ten and midnight two days ago."

That meant that by the time I'd found her, Shelley had been dead for close to twelve hours.

"No one's seen Alexander since he was arrested, and most of the tenants know him by sight. Now, the people who live there like to mind their own business because in a building like that strangers come and go all the time, if you get my drift. Oddly enough, the only stranger anyone remembers seeing was a cable repairman. This was around nine o'clock the night she was killed. The cable worker was described as being a big guy, wearing overalls, carrying a small metal box—everything that says repairman, except for one thing."

"What's that?"

"Cable didn't have anyone scheduled to go there that day."

"Who gave this to you?" I wiped off the lens of the binoculars with my sweatpants and looked out the window.

"A Spanish guy on the first floor. Hernandez, Robert."

"Did he give you anything else?" Across the street a traffic cop was writing out a ticket to an irate Hasadic gentleman whose car, complete with wife and child, was double-parked. He waved his hands in the air and stomped his foot as she continued to scribble out the fine. She was wrong, and if he fought it, he'd win. He looked like he'd fight it.

"The repairman was Caucasian, but dark, big, and

he was smoking a cigarette. He had short hair and dark eyes. Sound like any of your playmates?''

I grunted. ''Anything else?''

''Apparently she was a nice, quiet woman who was devoted to her kid. Her parents have him now. The funeral's tomorrow.'' He told me which funeral parlor she was at and suggested we go together. ''Oh yeah, one other thing, for some reason Collier has it out for you. What'd you do to him?''

Detective Collier was the officer who had drilled me after Shelley's murder. ''Search me. Maybe he doesn't like private investigators.''

''Maybe. In any case, I'd steer clear of him.''

''Did Hernandez actually see a cable truck outside?''

''No. He was just taking newspapers to the basement when he ran into him.''

''How big is big?''

''About my size, only fuller.''

That could have been either Simeon or his goon.

''The guy smoking the cigarette, do you know if it was hand-rolled or store-bought?''

''Gee, I don't know. I didn't ask.''

''Maybe you could find out today. So, none of her neighbors heard anything?''

''Nope.''

''Damn.''

''Also, I read up on the Washburn/Keller murder like you asked.''

''And?''

He sighed. ''And there's not much to tell you. Seems pretty cut-and-dry. The two were killed, executed really, at about four-thirty on August twenty-four of last year. It was a Friday and an eyewitness placed Alexander at the scene of the crime. Though the murder weapon wasn't recovered, blood matching one of the victims was found on his shoes. They booked him that same day.''

"Slam, bam, thank you, ma'am.''

"That about sums it up.''

Since the radiator had warmed the place up a little, Charlie had come out from under the covers and was wailing that he wanted his breakfast and he wanted it "neow.''

"I owe you for this, Mr. Ed.''

"Nah, even-steven. Besides, I got a couple of great shots there, some good character profiles and one really nice rooftop shot that plays with light and angles. Beautiful. Anyway, no one knows I'm helping you.''

"Gil did. He asked if you had found anything new and interesting at her building.''

"Those guys are so nosy down there.''

He suggested again that we go to Shelley's funeral together.

"I don't think so, Eddie. I don't know when I'm going to get there or where I'll be coming from.'' It was a limp excuse, especially since, during the last ten years, he and I have been to more funerals together than either of us would care to remember. It usually helps to attend these things with a friend, but I knew that going to Shelley's wake was something I had to do alone. As soon as I hung up with him, I fed Charlie and called Jimmy to find out about the DNA. I knew he had said he'd call me, but I was feeling antsy. He wasn't in yet, which wasn't so odd considering it was barely 8:30. I went back to my desk.

As hard as I tried to ignore it, Leslie Washburn was very much on my mind. I could see her in my mind's eye from the night before, sitting across the table from me, slightly flushed from the wine, and comfortably leading the conversation from one topic to another. She had worn an emerald green turtleneck that made her eyes look almost hazel in the candlelight. It was when I caught myself staring in space that I said out loud, "You don't have time for this right now, so cut it out." Charlie looked up from licking between his toes, meowed loudly, blinked once majestically, and returned to his toes. "Sorry, Charlie, you can't lick your feet and be arrogant at the same time. Doesn't work."

I folded yesterday's newspaper and tossed it onto a pile next to the fireplace. Then I took the day's *Times* with me into the bathroom, where I turned on the hot-water tap and held my hand under the limited flow of water. It was cold. It would stay cold for another few minutes. I stared at my reflection in the mirror as I squeezed the toothpaste onto my brush. "She's nice, I'll give her that," I said out loud. "She's *very* nice. Nice and beautiful. And young. Don't forget young. But not too young. I mean, she looks a lot younger than she really is, which isn't really all that young, is it? So you're ten years older than she is, no big deal. It's not as if she's twenty . . . three. The woman's almost thirty, for God's sake. Thirty's not *that* young. Or *too* young." I shoved the toothbrush into my mouth to prohibit any further conversation but took it out just as quickly. "I mean, hell, you were ten years younger than Caryn, right? And did that bother you? No. But it did bother her. So how do you like the shoe being on the other foot? You know what the problem is?" I pointed the red brush at myself in the mirror. "The problem is, you like her. And that scares you, doesn't it?" I smiled impishly. "Screw you. I'm not scared, I'm just . . ." I waved the toothbrush gently over the sink like a magic wand while I searched for the right word. "I'm just talking to myself. That's all. I'm just standing here in my bathroom, talking to myself—no, not only talking to myself but trying to pick a fight with me. What am I, *nuts?*" I felt under the shower nozzle. The water was nearing tepid. I made a face at myself in the mirror, finished brushing my teeth without further conflict, and started reading the newspaper.

After a few minutes more, the bathroom mirrors were steaming up.

Once I was out of the shower, my answering machine was blinking away. I listened to the three messages as I dressed. Jimmy called and said to chill out. If he was lucky, there might be something in a week, but even then the possibility of getting any result wasn't likely.

The second message was from Minnie. "Sydney dear, your sister called to tell me that she's worried about you. Apparently, your phone call had more of an impact on her than you realized. She wants me to convince you that you need to go into therapy. What do you think?" Click.

Maybe. After all, I was talking to myself.

The third message was from Carmen across the hall. She was back from Kansas earlier than expected and she wanted to see her little boy.

I did twenty minutes of yoga and decided to go to the office before calling anyone. I slipped the semiautomatic into my purse and stopped by Carmen's apartment as I headed for the office.

"Oh, Charlie Kitty, come to mommy kittums." Carmen's face was hidden behind a sea-green mud pack when she greeted him. Her lips barely moved. Charlie looked up at me and I could swear he shrugged.

"Looking good, Carmen. Is that the latest fashion in Kansas?" I held out a bag filled with food and water bowls and the toys that I could round up without moving large pieces of furniture or appliances.

"Ha-ha," she said without cracking the mud pack. "I thought I heard you leave before, so I put this shit on." She glanced in the bag. "Did you two have a good time?"

"Divine." The elevator door opened. "Gotta run. See you later."

"Wait!" She caught the elevator door. "Don't you want to say good-bye to Charlie?"

"Nope." I wiggled my fingers as I pressed the CLOSE button.

It was 9:30 when I left my building. The cold had died down and the streets were glistening, which meant there was no ice and I could walk at a fast clip. I chose to go a few blocks out of my way and walk through Riverside Park rather than on the avenue. After three blocks, I was aware that I was being followed.

I slowed my pace and walked over to the stone wall that faces New Jersey. A tug was pushing a garbage trawler up the Hudson and a dozen gulls followed noisily behind. I fished my sunglasses out of my purse. Out of the corner of my eye, I could see that my tail had stopped to tie a shoelace. Clever. I cleaned the glasses with my scarf and slid them on. I turned my right side away from my distant companion and slipped the Walther into my jacket pocket. One of the things I like best about the Walther is that it's small enough to slip into a pocket or an evening bag while at the same time carrying enough power to make me feel protected.

There were a handful of joggers—one of whom was a nun in full habit and sneakers—and about half a dozen people walking their dogs. Four bicyclists passed and two homeless people slept soundly on their respective benches, surrounded by the total sum of their possessions. My tail started south. His nonchalance was commendable. He was about five ten, slightly built, and his face was pockmarked. He passed me. I let him get about twenty feet farther south and I started east, walked up a steep hill and then along a short stone wall that divided the street and the park.

He caught up with me again on West End Avenue and Eighty-third Street, a block away from my office. At the corner, I bought a newspaper. Mr. Shadow studied the display in the window of a woman's shoe store. As I passed him, I handed him the newspaper and said, "I'm going to be in my office for a few hours. You might need this to keep yourself occupied."

Without glancing back, I went to work.

E L E V E N

I locked the office door behind me and saw that there were seven messages on the answering maching on Kerry's desk. Five of them were for Max, all women, all breathy, none of which I bothered to write down. The other two messages were from Minnie and Nora, both of which baffled me. Minnie had already called at home and Nora never called, especially at the office.

I glanced out onto Broadway and saw the Shadow leaning against a lamppost across the street, reading the sports section of the newspaper. I turned the radiator down and settled in at my desk. My first call was to Minnie.

She sounded out of breath when she answered. "Yeah, hello."

"Minnie? Are you all right?"

"The voice sounds familiar, but I just can't place it."

"Very funny. I've been busy, you know?"

"You were supposed to keep me updated. Anything I learn now, I either hear on the news or read in the papers." She took a deep breath and lowered the pitch of her voice. "I spoke with Nora last night."

"So you said."

"Don't sound so excited."

"I'll try not to. She left a message here for me."

"She's quite upset."

"I wonder why."

"Who knows? I read about that poor Gomes woman. Were you the unidentified woman who found her body?"

"Yes." I took a deep breath and told her everything I had learned so far.

"So Gilbert still doesn't believe it's David, eh?" she asked when I had finished.

"Nope. And right now I have a shadow following me."

"Oh, I used to love that song." Minnie started humming "Me and My Shadow." "They don't write songs like that anymore."

"Mmm." I switched on the computer.

"I wonder what's up with Gilbert."

"What do you mean?"

"Usually he weighs your opinions carefully. Now he's just out and out rejecting your ideas. Did you offer him any proof?"

"I don't have much. But I did tell him to look at the pictures at Shelley's. He knew David, so he'd have to see my take on it. Couple that with the fact that Alexander's

ID was bogus and David's prints are missing, it just doesn't go down real well." The familiar clicking from the Macintosh Plus sounded like an old friend coming to life. "That his prints are missing really bothers me."

"My dear, you know better than that. Bureaucracies thrive on misplacing whatever is most necessary. I always thought my father would make a marvelous bureaucrat. Do you know why?"

"No. Why?"

"Because every time we would try to piece together a jigsaw puzzle, your grandfather would deliberately hide a piece in his pocket. He thought it was amusing watching us kids crawl around on the floor looking under the chairs and sofas for a little piece of cardboard."

"So that's where Dad picked up that little stunt."

Minnie's throaty laugh filled the receiver.

After my call with Minnie, I was looking up Nora's number in the computer when my thoughts were drowned out by a cacophony of sirens. I went to the window and saw my friend the pockmarked tail sitting on the pavement, leaning against the building, his hands both turned palms-up and his head at an odd angle, as if he had fallen asleep while watching TV. His left leg was sticking straight out in front of him and his right knee was bent. The newspaper I had given him was lying on the sidewalk, starting to blow away, and a small semicircle of people had started to gather around him. The phone rang.

"CSI, can I help you?" At first there was silence. "Hello," I said.

"You got a choice, Sloane."

The voice was low and menacing. I strained to hear him through the background noises.

"Lead us to Alexander and nobody else'll get hurt,

or keep thumbing your nose and watch how many people will bite the dirt around you."

"Dust. People bite the dust, not the dirt. I don't know what you're talking about." At the moment I said it, I felt a weight in my chest. I knew all too well what he was talking about.

"Yeah, well take a peek out your window."

I carried the phone to the window. Paramedics had my shadow spread out on the concrete and were working on him. I checked the pay phone on the corner. It was empty.

"You didn't need to go to all this trouble just to get my attention."

"Like you said, you don't scare easy." It wasn't Caleb I was talking to, but the voice was familiar. It had to be his gorilla playmate.

"I'm still not scared," I said.

"No?"

"No, but you do have my attention."

"Good."

"I don't know where Alexander is."

"You got till Monday to find him."

That gave me less than three days.

"How can I contact you?" I asked.

The line went dead. I hung up the receiver and saw that a crowd four deep had gathered and people were straining to see the dead man. A cover had been placed over his body. I scanned the onlookers, trying to pick out a familiar face or one that might be more interested in me than the stiff. The gorilla could have been calling from anywhere while one of his friends did the dirty work. Whoever would eighty-six a tail in broad daylight was cocky enough to hang around and watch the circus.

One thing was certain: The dead man wasn't one of Caleb Simeon's friends. But who the hell was he? From the warning call, I guessed he must have been a cop, but was he one of Gil's associates sent out to make me feel safe and sound, or was I being tailed because I was a suspect?

I went back to the computer, angry at myself. Angry that I hadn't seen what must have been a second tail and mad as hell that two innocent people had lost their lives in a matter of forty-eight hours. When I reached for the keyboard, I realized my hands were shaking.

I brought up the list I had created the night before and stared at the black and white screen. Chances were likely if Gil ran a check on Simeon, he'd come up with a blank, but I had to do something. Caleb Simeon had proved that he wanted Noah—or David; I still wasn't sure which—badly enough to kill for him. Repeatedly. Brutally. There was no way, given my resources, that I would be able to get an ID on him, but at least Gil had a chance. He was out of the office when I called, so I left a message.

I tried to study what was on the computer screen. Lists like this create more questions than answers, but they also help me to focus on details.

Why did David feel the need to create a new identity for himself instead of simply using stolen ID? Who was he hiding from? And why would he go to the trouble to establish this new identity only then to turn into a killer?

Presuming David could kill another person, what would have given him cause to kill Washburn and Keller, two apparently innocuous people? Money? *Had* he become a junkie since I'd last seen him? It wasn't an altogether-inconceivable thought. But cold-blooded murder? No. It just didn't feel right. I rubbed my forehead and tried to see it from another angle.

What about Mildred Keller? Who was responsible for her living beyond the means that a salaried United Nations worker would make? Did she come from

---

money? Were she and Washburn lovers? Was he the one who paid for her original artworks and antique furniture? Or was it David? No, scratch that idea. David never spent his own money on women. Who was the man Julio had seen at her apartment? Was it Simeon or one of the other 4 billion men who fit that description? But if it was, what would be the connection between them? And how the hell did David fit into all this? Simeon and David were connected, but how? Did Simeon know David as David or as Noah Alexander?

As I was typing out my list of question marks, the phone rang. I answered on the second ring and flipped on a voice-activated tape recorder at the same time. If it was Caleb or his little friend, I wanted to have something to remember him by.

"Sydney? It's Leslie."

I flicked off the recorder. "Good morning."

"Am I disturbing you?"

"No, not at all."

"Good. Listen, I was wondering if you could be free for lunch today." She sounded subdued.

"Are you all right?" I asked.

"Yeah, I'm fine. It's just that, well, I have a client in your neighborhood, just a few blocks away from you, actually, and I thought maybe we could have lunch together."

She sounded uncomfortable. I agreed to meet her at 12:30 at Ernie's on Seventy-sixth and Broadway.

On the way there, I bought a bag of oranges for Marcia, one of our neighborhood bag ladies. She walked me halfway to my lunch date and we talked about how screwed up the system was and now she felt safer on the streets than in a shelter.

* * *

Leslie was seated at a window table with a cappuccino when I arrived. She was staring into her oversized coffee cup as though she were scrying like Nostradamus, peering into the cloudy liquid and waiting for a vision.

"You look just like you sounded on the phone." I hung my jacket over the back of my chair and pulled at my sweater, which was covering my gun. I'd left my purse at the office and I was only slightly uncomfortable with the gun tucked into my waistband.

She sighed. "Why is it that things are never easy?"

"Never say never. Some things are really quite easy." I glanced around the restaurant. The chic eatery was scattered with the Ladies Who Lunch set. Any of Caleb's cohorts would have stuck out like a sore thumb.

"Yeah? Tell me one thing that's easy." She finally picked up her chin and looked at me.

"Rita Jean Philliatro, the school you-know-what when I was in seventh grade. She was easy." She laughed despite herself. "And from what I can see, your smile upon occasion."

"You're cheating."

"I didn't know there were rules."

She sighed and ran her slender fingers through her hair. "My family doesn't like that we had dinner together last night."

"I beg your pardon?"

"Actually, my brother doesn't like it. Lloyd was in town last night to have dinner with Mom and she told him about your investigation and that you and I had gone out for dinner. Basically, he read me the riot act and insisted that I never see you again." She sighed.

"Really? I don't understand. Why?" He probably thought I was out to corrupt his little sister, but from our dinner last night, I knew her family was aware she was gay and didn't make an issue out of it.

———

She shrugged and bit her lip. Just then, a waitress in black stretch pants a size and a half too small came waddling over to our table. It seemed possible that if she made a sudden move, she might explode.

"You ladies ready to order?" Her lips were painted deep purple and she wore black-rimmed glasses that magnified her eyes, which were partially hidden behind limp mousy-colored bangs. She looked out at the street.

"I'll have a cappuccino and we'll order later," I said.

"A decaf cap or a regular?" She sniffed.

"Regular." I waited for the waitress to move away from the table. "Why don't you tell me exactly what happened," I said gently as I rested my elbows on the table.

Leslie's eyes were glacier blue, especially in contrast to her black turtleneck, but she looked tired and lonely. Whatever Lloyd had said to her, it had doused some of the fire in her eyes. She wet her lips and started. "Well, I got home at around—what, twelve o'clock last night?—and I was surprised to see that Mom was still up. She called out to me and asked me to join her in the den, which I did. What I didn't expect was to see Lloyd there."

"Lloyd's the ex-sailor?"

"Yeah. We used to be really close, but we're not what you'd call bosom buddies anymore. Dad's death seems to have had more of an impact on him than the rest of us. It put a distance between us that hadn't been there before."

The waitress slid my cappuccino onto the white tablecloth and looked from me to Leslie and back again. "Wanna order now or later?"

"Later," said Leslie, and the waitress toddled to the next table. Leslie moved the bud vase with its three purple tulips to her right. On the fourth finger of her right hand, she wore a ring, a thin band of gold with an emerald. She

164

continued. "Anyway, Lloyd was pissed at me. He said that I didn't have the right to drag the family into this, which didn't make *any* sense to me, so I asked him what the hell he was talking about. Then he tells me I'm killing Dot." She took a deep breath and balled her graceful hands into little fists. "I mean, give me a break. Who the hell was standing there in the middle of the night having a conniption fit? Me? You bet your ass not." She was beginning to raise her voice. Apparently when Leslie gets excited, she reverts to a New York dialect. The color was returning to her cheeks and as she pushed her shoulders back, I could see a flame in her eyes. "So I asked him what the hell he was talking about, because as far as I was concerned, you weren't the enemy. If anything, it's just the opposite. I mean, you want to find the son of a bitch who killed Dad, right?"

"Right."

"That's what I told him. But he wouldn't let up. He wanted to know everything we talked about at dinner."

"What was your mother doing throughout this?"

Leslie shrugged. "Mom's pretty chauvinistic, I suppose. I mean, she has a lot of women friends, but she refuses to go to a female doctor or lawyer. I suppose Lloyd's kind of taken Dad's place in a way, so she just lets him say what he wants and then afterward she'll tell me not to take it so seriously."

I shook my head as I poured a packet of sugar into my cappuccino and watched it slowly sink through the steamed milk.

"Anyway, there's something I want to clear up with you." Leslie ran her hands along the tabletop.

"What's that?" I looked up.

"Have you told me everything?"

"With regard to your dad's case?"

She nodded.

"Yes."

"Do you have any reason to make my father look like an asshole?" She held on to the side of the table until her knuckles were white. She was sitting as straight as an arrow and looked as if she could take me in one round. At that very instant, I was painfully attracted to Leslie Washburn.

"The last thing I want is to make any member of your family, especially your father, look like an asshole. As far as your mother is concerned, I not only liked her but I can't imagine that she has a dishonest bone in her body. I don't know your other siblings and I doubt that I ever will. So that leaves only you." I took a deep breath. "I like you. I like you a lot. I think you're funny, bright, unbelievably attractive, and very sensitive. I had a great time with you last night and I hope that was just the beginning of a new friendship. However"—I paused until she looked me straight in the eyes—"right now I'm in the middle of an investigation and the last thing I want to do is involve you. You see, not only could you get in my way but you could also get hurt." I flashed on to Shelley's lifeless body. "I wouldn't want that."

"What do you mean?" She had loosened her grip on the table and was frowning at me.

"I mean, Lloyd may have had a point, Leslie. Regardless of where he's coming from, the fact is, you could be in danger right now."

"Oh Christ, you make it sound like cops and robbers." A nervous laugh escaped her.

"It is." I didn't return her smile. I still hadn't told her about David. Now I knew I wouldn't.

We gave our order to the waitress, who was pushing pasta. We both opted for salads. Leslie chose the niçoise and I ordered the spinach salad—without mushrooms. I hate mushrooms. I don't see how people can willingly eat fungi.

After lunch, Leslie looked more relaxed and was obviously in better humor. "Now what?" she asked as she downed the last of her second coffee.

"Now I go back to work. How about you?"

She shrugged. "Maybe I could help you."

"No. You can't."

"You never know, I could be great at detecting."

"I'm sure you could, but no is no. Get it?" I signaled for the check.

"What if I said I wasn't ready to leave just yet?" She leaned forward and spoke very softly. She was wearing Paris, one of those rare scents that gets better as the day wears on.

I just stared at her.

"Who had the green eyes in your family, your mother or your father?" she asked.

"Neither. My father's mother did. Both of my folks had brown eyes. Listen, I really don't think it's a good idea to see you again until this thing has blown over."

"That's silly." She arched her right eyebrow.

"You could be in danger."

"I could be in danger crossing the street. Does that mean I should never take a chance and just stay put on the same old corner?" She shook her head. "No, of course not. You're not like that and you wouldn't expect me to be, either." She smiled at the hostess, who retrieved the check and my credit card. "Thank you for lunch." She reached across the table and squeezed my hand. "Now, I have an idea. It won't take long and I won't take no for an answer. Okay?" She stood up. "I'm going to the ladies' room, I'll be right back. Oh, and just in case you're thinking of leaving me here . . ." She took my leather jacket and left me waiting for the receipt.

She might be a good detective, after all, I thought as I watched her sashay to the ladies' room with my jacket in tow. I wondered whether she had taken my jacket to go through the pockets or simply to get her way.

When she returned, I had paid the bill and slid the receipt into my back pocket. She handed me my jacket and grabbed her coat off the back of her chair. "Shall we?"

I examined my jacket as I followed her to the door.

Once out on the street, I slipped on my jacket and tucked my hands into my pockets. She linked her arm through mine and started uptown. I didn't budge.

"What's wrong?" Her eyes grew wide with innocence.

"Just where are we going?"

"Well, I have to look at a lamp over at an antique store on Amsterdam. Your opinion would be helpful."

I shook my head.

She took a deep breath. "You want the truth?" Her voice curled up in exasperation.

"That would be nice." With my free hand, I slid my sunglasses onto the bridge of my nose.

"Okay." She heaved a huge sigh. "First, I thought we could go to your apartment. Then, given my powers of persuasion, I had hoped I might be able to seduce you and we could enjoy a cozy, passionate, basically hedonistic afternoon together."

Passionate. Just the way she said it was exciting. When I found my voice, all I could say was, "I can't." Now, an afternoon of passion was probably just what the doctor would have ordered, but apart from the fact that I'm old-fashioned and like to know someone for more than twenty-four hours before I reveal several small but curious scars, I had a brother to find and I was running out of time.

Her shoulders went limp. "Oh, Sydney, say you can."

"I can't."

Without another word, we started uptown again. This time, my hands were swaying at my side and hers were tucked in her pockets. We walked a few blocks in silence while I engaged a private dialogue in my head. I should have said yes. But I had to say no. Figures, I finally meet someone who has all the qualities I've been looking for and she's off limits. Then, of course, there was the big question: Could she have wanted to get intimate for reasons other than the fact that I'm irresistible?

Nah.

When we reached Seventy-ninth Street, I told her I had to make a phone call. I went to a trio of phones at the corner and chose the one on the left. There was no sound in the earpiece. I moved to the middle stall and found that someone had jammed the coin slot. Feeling a little like Goldilocks, I waited patiently for the third phone. It wasn't long before I was talking to Kerry.

"Hey, boss, what's the scoop?"

"Anything interesting?" I watched Leslie as she window-shopped at Woolworth.

"Hell yes. I got a date *and* a job as a result of the reading I did this morning." She rattled off the details. After she had finished, I told her I wanted background information on Lloyd Washburn. What the hell? People usually squirm when they have something to hide.

I hung up with Kerry and joined Leslie, who had moved onto window-shopping at the equivalent of a K Mart shoe store.

"So should I be embarrassed?" she asked.

"That you're window-shopping at Fayva? No."

When she smiled, a little dimple cut into her right cheek. "No," she said almost coyly.

———

"What about?"

"You know." She half-shrugged and nodded south.

"You mean your suggestion for how to spend a winter afternoon? Absolutely not." I reached out and squeezed her shoulder. "You have to know that if this were any other time, I would have said yes, but I can't. I just have too much to do. And Leslie, it really could be dangerous. I don't want anything to happen to you."

"So I didn't make an ass of myself?" It was hard not to stare at her mouth when she spoke. What can I tell you? I like overbites.

"Not as far as I'm concerned."

"Then you're just being a coward?" she said flirtatiously as she squinted from the sunlight.

"That's it." I linked my arm through hers and walked with her to the corner of Eighty-sixth and Broadway. She was persistent, but finally, after seven blocks, she realized I wasn't going to give in.

At least not now.

As we stood at the bus stop, the skies clouded over and I wondered whether this wasn't some sort of warning. She refused to leave until I agreed to try to have dinner with her the next night. I left as she hopped onto the crosstown bus.

Back at the office, Kerry was already trying to get a line on Lloyd and Detective Collier was cooling his heels in Max's office.

"I told him to wait in there." Kerry pointed to Max's door. "I didn't like his attitude and I didn't want him out here listening to my business. I figured this way, he can't get into too much trouble. Besides"—she smiled—"I've learned that snooping through Max's office can be both educational as well as entertaining."

"Officer Collier," I said as I opened the door between our two offices, "what brings you all the way up-town?"

Collier was sitting at Max's desk with his heels hiked up onto the blotter. His bony index finger was excavating the inside of his left ear and he was leafing through the *Post*. He raised his eyebrows and nothing else when I greeted him.

"Where the hell have you been?" He wiped his ear finger on his already-soiled suit jacket.

Max's office would have to suffer the cooties a little while longer. Without responding to Slob Collier, I simply closed the door and went to my desk. I had better things to do than watch Martin Collier gross out.

After a count of three, he was standing in front of my desk, his long, sad face the color of crimson. He threw his overcoat on the chair. "Don't do that again," he snarled as he leaned onto my desk. This did not bode well. I pulled a ruler out of the top drawer and promised him that if he didn't remove his dirty little hands from my desk, I'd give him cause to remember his Catholic schooling.

After a brief but tense few seconds, I suggested that he take a seat. "Collier, just for the record, you didn't have an appointment to see me and I don't like being harassed. Now, as long as you're in my office, I'll have to ask you to behave like a gentleman, difficult though it may be."

"Cut the bullshit, Sloane. Where were you this morning?" He crossed his stiltlike legs and tucked his fingers under the waistband of his pants.

"Majorca. And you?" I mirrored his movements.

"We're not gonna get anywhere if you keep acting like a smartass."

"Why don't you tell me just what it is you want. The sooner you get to the point, the less time we have to spend together."

171

"A good man died this morning and I'm willing to bet my detective's badge that you had something to do with it." His eyes seemed colorless. "Did you hear what I just said?"

"Yes, I did," I assured him. "Who was the good man and why should I have had something to do with his death?"

"He was killed right outside. I know you knew he was there. He told me that when he checked in at around ten o'clock this morning." As he spoke, he kept his head tilted birdlike to the left. Words seemed to escape from the right side of his mouth.

"What was he doing downstairs?" So it wasn't one of Gil's men, after all. Which meant I was one of this idiot's suspects.

"I'm here to ask questions, not answer them."

"I knew I was being followed this morning, but I didn't know why. I also knew that a man was killed across the street between eleven and eleven-thirty this morning. I had nothing to do with his death. Why was he following me, Detective Collier?"

"I wasn't born yesterday, believe me. I know you had more to do with Shelley Gomes's murder than just finding her, and I'm going to prove it. I've had it up to here"—he sliced at his nose—"with you and your type."

"Really, and what type is that?"

"Listen to me, you little bull dyke, nothing and nobody is getting in the way of this investigation. Do I make myself clear?"

"I'm not a bull dyke. Why, just looky here—I'm wearing nail polish," I said à la Sophie Tucker, and waggled my red painted nails in his direction.

"You're a sicko." He looked at me with contempt and popped his knuckles one by one, pulling each finger by the tip. "Now, what were you doing there Wednesday?"

"We've been through this already. I told you eighty-eight times, I'm looking for Noah Alexander."

"But you said you saw Shelley the day before."

"That's right."

"So why did you go there Wednesday?"

I looked blank.

"Why did you go there Wednesday?"

"I've already told you. Look, Collier, no matter what I say, you're going to twist it around to fit your scenario that I went there to kill her."

The smile was arrogant. "Why did you go there Wednesday?"

I had told Collier repeatedly during our afternoon at the precinct that I had gone there to see whether she had any pictures of Noah Alexander. "I wanted to ask her out on a date."

"What about Alexander? What are you, in cahoots with him?"

"Cahoots?" I laughed.

His forehead turned red. Within a matter of seconds, his whole face was flushed. "I don't like you, Sloane. I don't like your attitude and I don't like outsiders coming in and making things more difficult for me and my men. Do you understand what I'm telling you?"

"And let's not forget your love of homosexuals. Tell me, do I detect a threat, Martin?" I said sweetly.

"I never make threats." His smile was sour as he puffed out his small chicken chest. "Now, I want you to answer some questions, Sloane. We can do it here or we can take a drive down to my precinct."

I glanced at my watch. "I have ten minutes."

"How well do you know Noah Alexander?" He started his line of inquiry. The next twenty minutes—I let him ramble on—was almost entertaining. Collier would ask questions, wipe beads of sweat off his thin upper lip, and I would answer calmly, which made him sweat more. Yes, I was investigating the Washburn/Keller murder. No, I had never met Noah Alexander. No, he couldn't know who my client was. No, apart from handing the officer—whose name was Stewart Cohen—the newspaper, I had no further dealings with him.

Collier was convinced Noah Alexander was responsible for Officer Cohen's death, as well as Shelley's. He knew I was an accomplice but couldn't figure how I actually fit into the picture. Apparently through association, I was just as guilty. I never mentioned Gil: Why saddle an old friend with an introduction to the sort of cop I've always hated? There are people who need to make themselves feel bigger by trying to make others feel smaller—you can find them in any line of work from elevator operators to presidents. Martin Collier was just this sort of man.

If I told him about Simeon, I would have been up to my earlobes in Collier for the next few days. The thought of that sent shudders through my body. I stood and thanked him for dropping by.

"You haven't seen the last of me, Sloane." His arms moved like two long snakes as he put on his overcoat.

"Be still my beating heart." I perched on the edge of my desk.

"I don't like little girls trying to be little boys who then interfere with men's work." He jammed his fists into his coat pockets; the left hand pushed through the already-torn lining of his thin overcoat.

I was still laughing when Collier slammed the outer door.

———

T W E L V E

"**W**here the hell have you been?" Nora demanded as soon as she heard my voice.

"I'm fine, thank you, and you?"

"This isn't funny, Sydney. It's bad enough that *you're* involved in that filthy line of work, but I will not have it spilling over into *my* life, do you understand?" I could almost see Nora's fish lips puffing in and out as she gasped into the mouthpiece. Not a pretty picture.

"No, I don't. Why don't you tell me what you mean."

She released a long, loud sigh. "Okay." She took another deep breath. "First, you called me the other day asking me stupid questions about David. I mean, you

---

can't just leave well enough alone, can you, Sydney? You always have to go around stirring up still waters. Then, two days ago, I received a call and the person asked for Nora Sloane. Well, no one's called me Sloane in years, so I just perked right up, thinking that it was someone from grammar school or high school. So I said, 'This is she.' '' Nora's voice went up two octaves and then returned to its normal pitch. "And you know what they did? They hung up on me. Imagine that!" She lighted a cigarette. "Well, I was indignant, I tell you, but at the same time there was something else bothering me about the call. There was something almost . . . familiar about the voice on the phone, but I couldn't place it. Then it hit me." She stopped.

"What hit you?" I finally asked.

"It hit me whose voice it was."

"And whose voice was it?"

"It was David." She paused. "I'd know his voice anywhere, but I couldn't believe it. Granted, you had suggested it, but most of the time I take what you say with a grain of salt."

"Thank you."

"You know what I mean."

I didn't, but I wanted her to continue. "Then what happened?"

"Then, yesterday morning, I got another call. This time, it was a stranger telling me, *telling* me, to go to the telephone booth at the corner of Pratt and Lombard at ten after two. No 'Are you free?' or 'Is this convenient?'—just ordering me to be there at two o'clock. I had half a mind not to go because he was so rude. But then I started wondering if it had to do with David."

"Your curiosity was peaked, eh?" I could easily relate to that feeling.

"Well, yes, I suppose it was. Of course, I called

Byron first and told him what had happened. He said he would meet me there in case it turned out to be dangerous—after all, we didn't know what I was going to find there. There could have been anything from a bomb to a dead body.'' I could hear her excitement.

"Or a phone call," I offered.

"Or a phone call." She cleared her throat and regained control over her voice. "Which is precisely what happened. It was a call." She stopped.

"From?" I indulged her in the old game of dragging the good part of the story out of her.

"Who do you think?"

I hated this game. "Minnie?" I suggested.

"Can you be serious for a minute or does everything that happens to me have to be a joke for you?"

"I'm sorry. David?"

"Yes. David." Her voice was barely a whisper.

"What did he say?" I could feel my heart racing.

"Well, he sounds just fine."

"For a dead man."

"You know, Sydney, you make it sound as if you're disappointed he's alive." She sighed. "I told him you're trying to find him."

"Why did he call you?"

"To say hello. To tell me that he loves and misses me." So there.

"And where has he been for the past thirteen years?"

"Quite honestly, Sydney, I didn't ask him. I was just grateful to hear that he was alive, which is probably why he called me and not you."

She had me there. Nora takes after our mother in this respect. The best way to describe them is to imagine you are sitting down to dinner and there, in the center of the table, is a dead moose. Now, I would ask, "What's with the dead moose?'' Mom and Nora would ask you to pass the peas. I would ask about the moose again and again until finally either Mom or Nora would slam down their forks and ask why it is I have to spoil a perfectly fine meal.

Which isn't to say I'm right and they're wrong. It simply means that we operate from different starting points. However, Nora's holier-than-thou attitude has terminated more than one of our conversations in the past. I took a deep breath and tried again.

"What did you talk about?"

"He said he was in the States but couldn't tell me where. It was a quick call; we didn't get a chance to say much."

"But you told him I was looking for him?"

"Oh, he already knew *that*." Na na na na na na.

"And what did he say?"

"Nothing. Just that he knew you were looking for him."

"And did he happen to mention that he's wanted for three, maybe four murders?"

There was a "pass the peas" silence. Finally, Nora took a deep breath and through clenched teeth said, "No."

"Did you make plans to see him?" I asked.

"No." She paused. I could barely hear her breathing on the other end of the line. "He said he had to make it quick and that he was sorry that it all had to be so strange. He said he went to see Mom and Dad and made his peace with them." She gave this solemn moment a pause.

Unlike my sister, and obviously my brother, too. I'm not one for graveside chats. Graves give me the willies.

"Did he say anything else? Where he's staying? Where he's been? Where he's going? What he's up to?" I threw my hands up.

"All he said was that sooner or later I'd understand. Sydney, I don't understand."

"Neither do I."

"Well, all we can do is trust him," she said.

Right. "Wait a minute. Why were you so mad at me when you called? You can't be mad that David's alive."

"Oh my God, I can't believe I forgot to tell you this." Her initial anger returned. "Last night, I was sitting here with Byron watching a PBS special about the rain forests and the phone rang. Byron answered and the caller asked for Nora Sloane." She took a long drag off her cigarette.

"Who was it?"

"Would you wait a minute? I'm getting to that. Anyway, I got a little excited because David had called before and asked for Nora Sloane."

"But it wasn't David."

"No. I got on the line and they didn't say anything at first. I said hello a few times and it sounded like they had dropped the phone. Well, just as I was about to hang up, a man came on the line and asked if he could talk to *David*."

"What did you say?"

"Well, I was about to say, 'He's not here,' but then I realized that something wasn't kosher, so I asked, 'Who *is* this?' and he said it was an old friend."

"What did you say?"

"I said, 'If you're such an old friend, then you'd know David died thirteen years ago.'" Nora sounded quite pleased with herself. "Then I asked him how he got my number."

"And what did he say?"

"He said that you suggested he call."

"What did he sound like?"

"What do you mean what did he sound like? He sounded like a man."

"Did he have a high-pitched voice or was he nasal? Did he wheeze or lisp? Did he have an accent?"

"Oh God, how do you expect me to remember that?" She whimpered. "Let's see, he had a normal voice." She gave it some more thought. "It was lower than Byron's and fuller—you know what I mean?"

I did. Byron's voice is as thin as a chiffon scarf. I have never been able to envision my brother-in-law speaking forcefully enough to have any impact on a jury.

"Now that I think of it, he did have a slight accent, like a hint of one, but I don't know where from. It was really slight." She paused and added, "He could have been English, maybe, or European. You know how their English is always so much clearer than most Americans'? Wow, I'm surprised I remembered so much."

"What did you say when he told you I'd suggested he call?"

"I told him that if this was your idea of a joke, it wasn't very funny." I could just see Nora pushing her small shoulders back and thrusting her large bosom forward in righteous indignation. "But I knew you wouldn't do a thing like that."

"Thank you. So then what happened?"

"Well, I asked him again who he was. He wouldn't tell me, so I told him, 'That makes you sound like a coward to me.' He started to laugh at that, so I hung up on him."

"Pretty spunky, Nora. I'm proud of you."

"The hell with you, Sydney. I don't like getting involved in this sort of craziness—it just scares the hell out of me. If you had heard that creep laughing on the other end of the phone, you might think twice about what you do for a living."

"I'm sorry you got scared. I don't think you'll be bothered again."

"Who was it?"

"I don't know."

"Then how can you tell me I won't be bothered again?"

She had a point. "Well, let me put it this way, I have an idea as to who it is and I think he was trying to get a message either to me or to David." I was certain the caller was Caleb Simeon, which proved to me that he was actually after David, not Noah Alexander.

"I don't like this one bit. You know, Mother was against this from the very beginning, and I agreed with her. This is no work for a woman. But you've always had to do things your way, haven't you?"

"We come from stubborn stock, Nora. We all have to do things our own way, that's one of the things I've always liked about our family."

"You're being glib, Sydney. This is a serious situation we have here. I don't want any of your crazy friends showing up here intent on scaring my family."

"I'm not being glib and they're not my friends. Is Vicki home?" My only niece and I have been best friends since she was old enough to walk.

"No, she's still away at school. Nonetheless, I don't want trouble."

"I don't blame you and I can promise you that you won't have any from me. Right now, I think the best thing to do is try to forget about all this."

Nora spent the next ten minutes discoursing on the many unhealthy choices I've made with my life, until I finally was able to say, "Look, I have to go, I'm late for an appointment."

"The next time I call you, would you have the courtesy to get back to me sooner?"

"I'll try. Talk to you soon."

I stared at a patch of sunlight that was reflecting off

one of the new high rises across the street and coming to a stop on my office floor. David. Caleb. Mildred. Jesse. Noah. I mused. Somehow these names all fit together. I flicked on my Macintosh.

It bothered but didn't surprise me that Simeon had found Nora. So now I know Caleb wanted David, not Noah, but the thought wasn't comforting. The photograph that I had seen at Shelley's—the one that she said had fallen out of David's book—had been bothering me ever since I had met Simeon. It was the picture torn in half of David sitting on a chair with another man's arm draped over his shoulder. There was something familiar about that arm, the shape, the jewelry, coloring. I'd be willing to bet odds that the owner of that arm was none other than Caleb Simeon.

Kerry sneezed as she entered the office and closed the door behind her. "You'll never guess who's out there." She wiped her nose with a large wad of tissues.

My heart jumped into my throat. "David?"

She shook her head. "Lloyd Washburn."

I took a deep breath. "Show him in."

"You want me to stay?"

"No, thanks. As a matter of fact, now might be a good time to get lunch."

"I'm not hungry."

"Go anyway. The way you look today, chances are, Washburn wouldn't be able to keep his eyes or his mind off you."

"Thanks, chief." Even with a cold, Kerry managed to look great. She was wearing a teal turtleneck sweater, which deepened her brown eyes. Her jeans were snug but not tight and she finished her ensemble with snakeskin cowboy boots. It was a casual, sensual look.

Kerry left the door open and said softly to Lloyd Washburn, "Ms. Sloane will see you now."

———

Lloyd ducked through the doorway as if he was trying to avoid hitting his head on the frame. The humorless man I had seen in the picture at Dorothy Washburn's home was again without humor. I stood and offered him my hand. He glanced at it and seated himself on the canvas chair.

I inspected my hand for contagion, found none, and sat on the edge of my desk. I figured it would be a good idea to have Lloyd looking up at me.

"So"—I smiled a slight but charming smile—"what can I do for you, Mr. Washburn?"

"I want to know just what you think you're doing." His eyes, the color of charcoal, glared straight through me.

"I'm afraid I don't understand."

Apart from the fact that he had ducked through the doorway, I had no doubts that Lloyd's spine had been surgically replaced with a metal rod. The military will do that. He rocked stiffly forward and pushed back into the canvas. "I'm not as naïve as my sister, Miss Sloane, and I don't like the idea of you poking your nose in my family's business." He hissed words ending in *s*.

"Nose poking is my business. Look, I have no intention of hurting your family, Mr. Washburn. My only interest is in proving the innocence of the man accused of murdering your father. Now, I'm not out to slander your family and I have the highest regard for your mother, so you can rest assured that I would do nothing to hurt her. However, I believe in justice and I believe that the man accused of killing your father was framed."

He pulled his gaze away from me and stared at my desktop while he gently stroked his full lips. The Washburns were, if nothing else, a strikingly handsome family. Lloyd had movie-star good looks: a square jaw shaded with dark stubble, a nose that was probably sculpted, and eyelashes so thick, I could barely see his eyes. I watched his fingers as he stroked his mouth. The nails had been recently manicured. His hands were graceful and on the pinkie of his left hand he wore a college ring with a blue stone. A gold watch hung loosely from his right wrist.

"The police told us they had conclusive evidence that he's guilty." Again his eyes met mine, only this time without the rage.

"Circumstantial, not conclusive."

"Then who did it?"

"I don't know."

He sighed. "Look, I know I came across a little strong, but my family, my mother in particular, have all been under a great strain since Dad died. No one, except Leslie—and she's in a world of her own—has the contact with Mom that I do, and I know that this bastard escaping from jail has just scared the hell out of her."

"Is that right? I was actually impressed by how composed your mother seemed."

He let out a soft laugh. "Yes, well she's really quite marvelous at putting on a mask for strangers." An uneasy silence followed. "I understand you have a job to do, Miss Sloane. All I ask is that you keep my immediate family out of it."

I nodded. He could ask. Whether or not I could comply was another matter.

He stood slowly and offered me his hand. "Forgive my rudeness earlier. I was upset."

I placed my hand in his and was surprised. His hand was surprisingly feminine, both cool and soft to the touch. Instinctively, I almost pulled away. He cupped his left hand over mine and drew slightly closer to me.

"You made quite an impression on my little sister. I think she'd like to be friends with you." He smelled like grape juice.

I kept my eyes trained on his without moving a muscle.

"I admire her taste in women. I always have."

It occurred to me the collective libido of the Washburn family could probably populate a small state. I smiled modestly.

"Good luck with your investigation." With that said, he left abruptly, ducking through the doorway on his way out.

T H I R T E E N

After Lloyd's visit, I made a beeline to Tina's. Then, after an hour of jumping rope, sit-ups, and punching the speed bag, Zuri and I decided to try a round in the ring, complete with bulletproof vests for protection.

The first round went smoothly enough until Zuri caught me off guard with a left that sent me flying into the ropes.

"Girl, you're making this too easy for me. I'm liable to fall asleep." She slipped her mouthpiece back in place and bounced lightly on the balls of her feet.

"You look like you're giving dance lessons." I ducked off the ropes and caught her on the arm with a right.

"Why dontcha quit jabbering and start jabbing a little." Tina circled the ring. "You're both looking a little flabby, if you ask me."

Zuri grunted at Tina and turned just enough for me to land a solid hit. She went down fast and landed on her butt. She looked a little like a rag doll, her legs spread-eagle and her gloved hands resting on her thighs. She shook her head and sprung back up onto her feet.

"That's more like it!" Tina hooted from the side-lines.

By the time I showered and changed into a conservative black wool pantsuit and an ivory silk blouse, I had just enough time to make it to the funeral parlor where the wake was being held for Shelley.

The DeSantis funeral home was only four blocks north of where Shelley had lived. I arrived forty-five minutes before the doors would close for the night and was met at the front door by a young man with greasy hair and acne who was wearing a hand-me-down gray suit, white shirt, and black tie. A faded rose was pinned to his lapel. His smile was practiced and discomforting for a boy barely eighteen. I wondered whether funeral directors teach their offspring and employees the mortician's smile, which is actually the same smile that my dip-somaniac fifth-grade teacher wore as he sat at the head of the class after a liquid lunch of a half pint of scotch. It is the handy-dandy all-purpose smile that falsely says, I understand, or I'm listening—which is usually not the case.

"Can I help you?" he whispered as he leaned slightly forward on the balls of his feet.

"Yes, I'm here for the Gomes wake."

He turned and pointed to the door farthest to the left. "Right through there." He smelled like wet dirt and peppermint.

I left my gym bag just outside the door to the viewing room. I figured if anyone was desperate enough to steal a bag filled with smelly workout clothes, they were welcome to it.

The room was large enough to seat seventy-five. Even rows of padded folding chairs divided the space. At the far end of the room was the opened casket, surrounded by several lavish pink floral arrangements. There were about fifteen people divided into three or four groups. No one looked familiar.

I went to the casket, remembering the last time I had seen Shelley, dreading the moment I would see her again.

The DeSantis funeral staff had reason to be proud of their work. Shelley looked both unscarred and at peace as she lay with her soft hands crossed at her chest. A simple pink turtleneck covered her throat and the makeup artist had carefully applied makeup so that she looked fresh and almost natural. I was stunned. I have always hated wakes and the barbaric viewing of dead people, but seeing Shelley like this helped to soften the brutality of her death.

I felt someone's hand on my arm. I turned and was face-to-face with the woman who had to be Shelley's mother. They had the same almond-shaped brown eyes and the same full mouth. Mrs. Gomes was young, no more than fifty—give or take a year—and she wore her added weight in her chest and her hips, giving her a 1950s hourglass figure.

"You knew my Shelley?" She tightened her grip on my arm.

"Briefly, yes."

"Come. Sit." She linked her arm through mine and led me to the first row of folding chairs. "So." She searched my face.

"My name is Sydney, Sydney Sloane, Mrs. Gomes.

I'm so sorry about Shelley. She seemed to be a very special woman."

She pulled back a fraction of an inch. "You're the one who found her."

"Yes."

She studied the tip of my boot. "She told me about you. About how you thought Noah was your brother and you was investigating." She looked up into my eyes.

"Yes, that's true."

Mrs. Gomes raised her right hand and slapped me full force across my face. There was a chorus of gasps behind us. I stared at her, not moving a muscle.

"My daughter is dead and the detective says you probably had something to do with it." Her eyes were filled with hatred and pain.

"The detective is wrong." My body was on fire at the thought of Martin Collier telling a grieving mother that I was somehow responsible for her daughter's ugly death.

"You shouldn'ta come here." She squeezed her hands in her lap.

"You all right, Ruby?" A black man in an ill-fitting blue suit leaned over us, resting his large, calloused hands over the backs of our chairs.

"She was just leaving, Cal. Maybe you could see her to the door."

"You got it." He placed his left hand protectively on her shoulder and tried to slip his right hand under my left armpit. I shook him free.

"Ease off, Cal. I don't need your help." I stood up and glanced at the fifteen sets of eyes on us, then back at Mrs. Gomes. "Soon enough you'll see that Detective Collier is not only inept but that he's also a liar. I liked Shelley and I'm sorry she's gone. I'm very sorry."

I turned and walked chin up past the stunned onlookers. As soon as I was in the hallway, I felt Cal's big hand on my shoulder.

"You okay?"

"Peachy, thanks." I caught our reflection in a hallway mirror. Three small welts discolored my left cheek. I didn't know whom I was angrier at—Simeon for the slaughter or Collier. I grabbed my bag and under Cal's watchful eye left the DeSantis funeral home.

Back out on the street, I was glad for the blast of cold that hit me full force. I walked ten blocks, trying to decide whether to confront Collier now or ignore the fool. I decided he wasn't worth it, hailed a taxi, and headed uptown. Visions of my apartment, a gin and tonic, and dinner danced in my head. I needed to be alone. Needed to turn off the phone, cook a little dinner, and veg out.

Once home, where the radiators were still clanking away, I checked the back door lock. Lonnie had installed a Fichet lock for the kitchen door.

I downed the first half of my gin and tonic as if it was water. Then I broiled a Montery Jack cheeseburger with jalapeño and roasted red peppers, which I washed down with a glass of Perrier-Jouët. By the time I finished the dishes, it was 11:30. It was too late to call Gil, but I dialed his number, anyway. Whether I liked it or not, I needed his help. Just as it started to ring, my doorbell rang. I hung up the phone and went to the door.

Through the peephole, I could see that Caleb Simeon and his sidekick, Godzilla, were standing in the hallway. I got the Walther, slid it into the band of my slacks, and opened the door.

"Well gee, boys, what a nice surprise. And such a civilized entrance. Whatever possessed you?" I addressed my last comment to Godzilla, who proceeded to pick at his left nostril. I looked down and saw Charlie

---

rubbing against Carmen's door. On an average of twice a week, Carmen unwittingly lets Charlie out of the apartment.

"May we come in?" Caleb's smile was tight and thin.

"Both of you? No."

He thought about this and finally said, "You wait here." Mr. Nosepicker, not at all pleased with this twist, glared at me and readjusted his genitals.

I have this theory about men—their genitalia and acts of violence in general. I firmly believe that had men been designed with very short arms, this world would be a safer and, in many instances, cleaner place.

I locked the door behind Caleb and ushered him through the foyer into the living room.

"Have a seat." I gestured to the sofa and went to the armchair.

He stopped at the doorway and surveyed the room. He pushed his lower lip out and nodded slowly. "This is nice, very nice indeed. I don't know why, but I had pictured something a little more . . . cluttered." He tossed his overcoat on the sofa.

"You killed Shelley Gomes," I said flatly.

He paused. "Did I?" He sat in the middle of the sofa and crossed his legs. Dark hair peeked out between the tops of his black socks and the cuffs of his pants.

"Your playmate, Mr. Personality? Well, he confessed on a taped call to my office this afternoon." It felt more like a week ago.

He didn't flinch. Finally, he said, "I'm sorry, but who is Shelley Gomes?"

"Shelley Gomes, your good friend?"

He looked bewildered enough to pass a Collier suspect test.

I shrugged. "Suit yourself. It's simple to match a

voice." He didn't need to know that there was no tape. "Besides, the police have a wonderful little piece of evidence you left behind. Modern technology is amazing, don't you agree? Why, they can test the DNA on dried saliva left on a cigarette butt and get a ninety-nine per-cent–positive ID." I don't often lie, but I'd studied acting and knew I could match him at his own game. "You know you really ought to be more careful when you slaughter people. But enough of this idle chitchat—what is it that brings you here?"

"I am a man of integrity, Miss Sloane."

"Really?"

He smiled indulgently. "As you have agreed to work for me, I wanted to give you a retainer." He slipped his hand into his overcoat. I had my hand on my gun but withdrew it when I saw he pulled out a bulging white envelope with the flap taped shut. He tossed it onto the coffee table, where it landed with a thud. "I have found that in most cases cash is far more appreciated than checks. Is that so with you, as well?"

"Gee, Mr. Simeon, if I say no, will you cut my tongue out, too?"

He folded his hands and sighed. His eyes moved from the envelope to my face and back again. "Pick it up."

"No."

"Why not?"

"I don't believe you have hired my services. If memory serves me correctly, I received a call from Uncle Bozo out there and he told me I should *consider* it very carefully, but I don't remember ever having said, 'Yes siree, I'm the gal for you.' And I know I would have said that if I thought I was. I always do."

"Why are you complicating things?"

"Am I?"

He shook his head. "Women shouldn't talk to a man the way you do."

"I'm sorry you feel that way."

"I believe a woman should know her place. I think more than anything else *this* is where the United States has veered off track. After all, democracy is a marvelous idea, but this equality for one and all is . . . quixotic. Don't you agree?"

"If you feel this way about women, and me in particular, why hire me? Why not hire someone else? Why not hire a man?"

His smile was slow. "You have a vested interest in finding our shared quarry."

"As it turns out, I don't. I thought so when I first started, but things have changed."

"I don't think so."

"Regardless of what you think, the fact is Noah Alexander is not who I thought he was. I received irrefutable information today that my brother is dead and buried. As it turns out, I've been wasting my time chasing ghosts. And as I don't like you, Mr. Simeon, I have no interest in finding your friend Noah."

"I would think *that* would be sufficient reason to continue your search." He gestured to the envelope. "If he's not your brother, then this becomes nothing more than what it should be—a business proposition."

"I play by a different set of rules." I glanced at my watch.

"You know, you're far too attractive a woman to have such a cocky attitude."

"It's an occupational hazard."

"It could be."

"Look, why don't I give you a list of other investigators who might be better suited to you. Or better yet, you've come this far on your own, why don't you just exert a little extra energy and find Noah yourself instead of insisting that I do your legwork?'' I stood, picked up the envelope, and put it back into his overcoat pocket. He wasn't carrying a gun in his coat.

"I'm a stubborn man—forever hopeful, you might say." He rose slowly and held out his hand for his coat. "You know as well as I do that Noah Alexander is David Sloane. He's eluded me for a long time, but I do believe you are my ace in the hole, as they say. I want your brother and I'm willing to do just about anything to get him."

I'd never mentioned David's name to Simeon. I laughed. "You're too much. Believe me, I wanted Alexander to be David just as much as you do, but facts are facts. He's not David and I'm not interested in working for you." We squared off. "What did David do that got you so pissed?"

He took a deep breath before answering. "David doesn't know how to treat his friends."

"David's dead." I stared him down. "I think you should go now."

I walked him to the front door. Sometimes you can sense trouble and you know there's not a thing you can do to alter the chain of events. Then there are other times when sensing it makes all the difference in the world. I pulled the gun from my waistband and opened the door for Simeon. The Walther compact may look little, but it carries one hell of a punch.

"You really don't need that, I assure you," Simeon said with a laugh.

"Better safe than sorry, I always say." I leaned against the door.

He stepped out into the hallway and Bozo started toward me. I pointed the gun straight at Simeon's head and said, "I suggest you ring for the elevator, Bozo, because one move at me and your boss is a dead man."

"Fuck that," Bozo growled.

"Wait, Walter." Simeon stopped him.

"Walter?" I echoed.

Big Walt stopped. His face was now a dull shade of scarlet.

"I am sorry you're not interested in working with us," Simeon said as he pressed his hand over the elevator call button. "The lady is not interested," he told Walter.

The elevator gears didn't engage.

"Even with all that money, I can't entice her." He placed his hand over the call button again. "The elevator is broken?"

"Maybe if you actually pressed the button," I suggested.

I heard movement behind me and turned to see what it was. In that half second, Walter jumped at me and grabbed for my gun. He twisted my hand until the gun fell to the floor. Charlie went racing between our legs. I had forgotten he was prowling around.

Walter swung at me with a right. I ducked and his hand grazed the closet door. He then caught me on the right cheek with a left that sent me flying back. I tried to kick him in the legs to get him off balance. However, he was faster than I could have guessed. He flattened himself against me, sandwiching me between himself and the wall. I don't know which was worse, the smell of cumin on his breath or his groin pushing against me. I lifted my right knee as hard and fast as I could. When he doubled over, I grabbed his head with my hands and pulled it down as I came up again with my knee. I heard the cartilage in his nose crack. His blood sprayed onto the pastel runner. Shit.

Out of the corner of my eye, I saw that Simeon had

closed the door. He was leaning against the closet door, my gun in his hands, apparently enjoying the show. Big Walt heaved himself at me again—saliva and blood spewing from his mouth like a rabid dog—and grabbed my hair. With all his weight behind him, he slammed my head against the wall. A mirror crashed to the floor, shattering glass everywhere. I stumbled and tried to get away from him so I could catch my breath, but the pain in my head was so intense, I could barely see. If I could just get on the floor, I could kick the shit out of him, I thought, but he caught me by the back of my shirt and pulled me back. The next thing I knew, he was pressing the barrel of a gun against my temple.

"Enough." Simeon's voice cut through the haze.

Above the high-pitched wail in my head, the only sounds I could decipher were glass crunching as Caleb stepped back into the apartment and Walter's heavy breathing. Walter wrapped his large left hand around my neck, half-holding my head up, half-choking me. His face was so close to my right ear that I could almost feel his sweat.

"Let go of her," Caleb ordered.

"No." He squeezed my neck tighter and crammed the gun against my ear.

"Put away the gun." Caleb's voice was calm.

It was several seconds before Big Walt put his gun away. He kept his hand firmly around my neck.

"You see, Ms. Sloane, I am a generous man. Here I have spared you your life." He pulled the magazine from my gun and dropped it on the floor. "I don't know how much longer my patience will last, but I suggest you not test it again. Do you understand?"

Uncle Walt grabbed the back of my hair and yanked my head back and forth.

"I thought so," Caleb responded. "Now, what I

want is this. I want David Sloane by six-thirty tomorrow evening or I'll kill your sister, Nora. Do you understand?''

I tried to look up at him but pain shot through my head when I made even the slightest movement.

Bozo rasped, ''Answer the man.''

When I didn't, he pulled back and punched me in the stomach as hard as he could. I returned the favor by retching on him.

''Son of a bitch.'' He threw me down on the broken glass and kicked me in the side.

''That's enough, I said.'' For the first time, Simeon raised his voice.

I was able to move into a sitting position and leaned against the wall. ''I don't know where he is,'' I finally slurred.

''Then you have a busy day ahead of you.''

''What happened to Monday's deadline?''

''It's just been moved up.'' He threw the envelope at me. ''I'm actually a very nice man to work for. Now, we will be here tomorrow at six-thirty. If both you and David are not here, you leave me no choice.'' He dropped my gun into my lap. ''Wipe your face and carry your jacket,'' he ordered his sidekick. Charlie rubbed his face against my leg.

I heard the door close behind them.

An hour later, I had cleaned both myself and the hallway. Apart from a slight headache and stiffness, I was mad.

I redialed Gil's number.

''Yeah?'' He growled into the receiver.

''I need your help.''

''Do you know what time it is?'' He yawned.

In fact, I didn't, but I also didn't care. ''Remember I asked you if you knew a Caleb Simeon?''

''Yeah. What about it?''

"I have to find out who he is, Gil."

"Sydney." He paused. "Why do you act like the police department is your personal secretary? And why is it your calls can never wait until morning?"

"He and one of his playmates just paid me a little visit. Their objective was to rearrange my face. I can promise you his next call won't be to discuss eighteenth-century art."

"Okay, okay, tell me what the hell's going on."

"This guy Simeon is interested in finding David, too. And he knows it's David."

That seemed to wake him up. I gave him an outline of my dealings with Simeon so far and a detailed description of the two of them.

"Why the hell didn't you tell me this sooner?" he spat into the phone.

"I tried. You never returned my call. Besides, you couldn't have done anything with it if I had."

After our call, I was wired. I made myself a cup of Grandma's Tummy Mint tea. I needed to do something to work out the stiffness from having been Walter's personal punching bag, and the kitchen has always been a comforting place for me. The round oak table is one of the few remnants of our childhood. David had engraved his initials in the base of it when he was nine years old. It's still there.

Halfway through the tea, it occurred to me that if Simeon knew where Nora was, he'd know where Minnie lived. I reloaded the Walther and threw on some clothes.

Charlie was curled up on a sofa, but I didn't have litter, so I bundled him up, went across the hall, and knocked on Carmen's door. After a few minutes, her peephole darkened and I heard the latches being opened. Carmen, a night owl as long as I've known her, shook her head and reached out for her straying companion.

"Have you two been pussyfooting around?" She nuzzled Charlie and scratched him behind the ears.

"You locked him out again, Carmen."

Charlie purred loudly.

"I need to use your phone." The possibility of my phone being tapped was remote, but I was edgy and didn't want to take any chances. I brushed past Carmen and made a left into her kitchen. The floor and walls were bright lemon yellow. An overhead light cast a flat, shadowless glow. I plucked the yellow wall phone off its mount and asked Carmen whether I could make the call alone.

"Sure, sure. Do I think this is weird? No, not at all, and you know why? I'll tell you why—because I live in New York and I've actually learned that this is normal." She continued her conversation as she carried Charlie into the living room.

The phone rang once, twice, three times. A yellow and black wall clock loudly ticked away the seconds. After the tenth ring, I slammed the receiver back into the cradle and set out for Minnie's Park Avenue apartment.

I was acting irrationally, I knew that, but in less than twenty minutes I was letting myself into Minnie's. I know the layout of her place as well as I know my own home. Not wanting to wake her, I didn't turn on any lights. All I had to do was see her, know she was safe, and then I'd feel better. After that, I'd crawl into what we call my bed in the second bedroom and get some sleep.

The apartment was dead still. By the time I reached her bedroom, which is at the end of the hallway, my eyes had pretty much adjusted to the dark. The door to her room was opened and I inched just over the threshold.

The bedroom drapes were open and from what light came in from the street, I could see that Minnie's bed hadn't been slept in. I checked my watch. It was after two in the morning. It felt as if the blood turned cold in my veins. If anything had happened to Minnie . . .

Before I could finish the thought, I heard the creaking of the floorboards behind me. I didn't have time to do more than flatten myself into a shadow before someone was standing in the doorway. My adrenaline kicked into high gear.

He took one step into the room. The smell of bourbon surrounded him like a thick perfume.

Still stiff from my encounter with Wally, I decided to play it safe this time around. Just as he was turning, I sprang from the shadows and caught him with a right to the side of his head that sent him reeling. Despite the odor of liquor, he was able to bounce back quickly enough to wind me with a tackle that sent me rolling into the hallway.

I don't like violence. However, between Shelley's murder, the run-in with Walter, and now this yo-yo who had done who knew what to Minnie, I was so angry that I knew I could put him away with my bare hands.

We struggled through the hallway like the projectiles in a pinball game, bouncing from side to side. In the foyer, just outside the kitchen, I had a vision of Minnie frightened and hurt in some dark place. The thought terrified and enraged me. I was able to get in one good kick between his legs, which incapacitated him long enough for me to pin him. When he fell to the ground, I trapped his wrist between the heel of my boot and the floor. I pulled the Walther out and took careful aim at his face.

As we both gasped for breath, there was the sound of keys in the front door. I applied more pressure on his wrist and turned the gun on the entrance. When the door opened, there was Minnie standing in the doorway. A short older man was standing behind her.

"Oh my God," she whispered as she looked from

my face to my feet. Her bug-eyed companion was straining to see over her shoulder.

I followed her gaze. In the light that spilled into the
apartment from the outside hallway, I could see that it
wasn't one of Simeon's goons I had been fighting.

Nope. Lying on the floor, under my boot, was the
end of my search. David, looking more than slightly chagrined, glared up at me and grumbled through clenched
teeth, "Get off me."

F O U R T E E N

Maybe one of you would like to explain just what's going on here." Minnie handed David a Baggie with ice cubes and scowled at me. "You nearly scared the life out of poor Mr. Stone." She glanced at David and reached under the kitchen counter, where she keeps the liquor. When she pulled out the bourbon, she looked surprised. "Did you drink this all by yourself?" she asked him as she held up the half-empty bottle.

"Yes." He straddled a white wicker chair and pressed the ice to his right eye, which was already starting to discolor.

Minnie sighed and poured him another drink. "I want answers and I want them now."

The last time I saw Minnie this mad was when David, Nora, our cousin Benjamin, and I had glued all her closets shut.

David and I looked sheepishly at each other. The mug shot I'd seen of him in the newspaper with longer hair and a thick beard was already dated, but there was still much of the old David sitting there in Minnie's kitchen.

"She started it." He still had the same boyish grin and the thickset jaw hidden under what we once called his baby fat and was now simply several unshaven chins. His left eye still pulled to the outside.

Minnie, however, was in no mood for levity. "You listen to me, David. You don't just pop up from the grave and start making jokes. Now, this may be funny to you, but I'm getting too goddamned old for this nonsense. Now, how did you get in here?" She turned to me. "And why the hell were you beating him up?" She pulled out a Parliament, lighted up, and leaned against the counter.

"I wasn't beating him up."

"Yes you were." David took a sip of his drink.

"I was not. I was defending myself. You're just mad because I won." I longingly enhaled Minnie's second-hand smoke.

"Wait a minute, who jumped who?" David practically screeched.

"I had just had a run-in with your other playmates and I wasn't about to take chances. Do you realize how you jeopardize Minnie just by being here?" I was beginning to sound like Nora on a lecture circuit. It was a sobering thought.

David took ice from his Baggie and put it in his glass. "Minnie, I came here to talk to you. If she stays, I'm leaving." He brought his glass to his lips.

I sputtered.

Minnie shook her head. "You two were like oil and water from the day you were born. Sydney, I want you to go home now. Your brother and I need to talk."

"But . . ."

"David, I want you to agree to see Sydney tomorrow."

"I can't—I'm leaving tomorrow." He got up and took one of Minnie's cigarettes.

"Don't make me repeat myself, son." She offered him a light.

We finally agreed to meet at one the next afternoon at a comedy club on the Upper East Side. Apparently, David knew a manager there, and from what I could tell, he had "borrowed" her keys and made a second set for his personal use.

By the time I got home, crawled between the sheets, and shut off the light, I was so tired that I could barely keep my eyes open. But I couldn't sleep. The thought of seeing David after all these years had me wired.

Shadows moved across the ceiling. When had I stopped hating David? Or had I? The questions haunted me.

If you don't know the subway system in New York, it can be confusing. If you do know it, it can be a great tool for shaking off any unwanted tails. Despite David's bravado, I decided to play it particularly safe that morning and at 10:30 I started playing subway tag. If anyone had followed me from my apartment, chances were likely that I had left them either in Brooklyn or Queens by the time I was back at Grand Central Station just after 12:30.

I hailed a taxi on Vanderbilt and gave the driver my First Avenue destination. David's choice of a comedy club as our meeting place seemed somehow fitting.

Apparently, there were two entrances to the club—

the front door and the basement entrance, which could only be reached through metal doors on the sidewalk and was padlocked shut from the outside. The front door to the club was opened. Stepping into the nightclub from broad daylight had a blinding effect on me. I pressed my back against the entrance wall and tried to let my eyes adjust to the light. There was no sound of movement in the place. Not knowing who else could be waiting, I pulled out my gun as I eased past a small, dirty coatroom, the service bar, and a service area for waiters. Red leather and brass-studded double doors led into a darker, large room cluttered with a small stage, three rows of about fifty black-topped tables, and a bar at the far end. Most of the chairs were upended on the tabletops. The black and red carpeting was tattered and stained. It's funny how places like this change in the daylight. A disco globe reflected bits and pieces of the sunlight from the outer room. The doors behind me flapped shut and my eyes strained against the darkness.

"You should have minded your own business, Sydney. It would have been safer." David was leaning against the bar. As my eyes adjusted to the light—a bare bulb on the stage and two exit signs in pale yellow and red—I could see he held a glass in his left hand. Nora was right—after all these years, his voice hadn't changed.

I ignored the tightness in my chest and took a deep breath. The night before had been so crazy, it didn't have time to settle in that it actually hurt seeing him.

"I was concerned about you."

"Oh yeah. Suddenly my sanctimonious kid sister rides up on her white steed to save me." He drank from the glass. "Why don't you have a seat?"

"How about a drink?" I stepped past an industrial vacuum cleaner that was blocking the aisle.

"A drink? A *drink*? At this ungodly hour?" He

looked around and shook his head. "Why the hell not? You're old enough." He leveled his gun in my direction. "However, you can stop right there. Before we have this little drink together—for good times' sake—why don't you just hand me your gun? Those things can be dangerous."

I paused.

He pushed away from the bar and slowly started toward me. His right eye showed signs of our struggle the night before. "Now, Sydney, you've been in the business long enough to know you can't trust anyone, not even a sibling. In our case, maybe especially a sibling." He held out his hand. "Give it to me."

I handed it to him. He tucked it behind his back, under his belt.

"Now the jacket."

"For God's sake, David, I'm clean." I handed him my jacket and watched as he padded the lining and emptied the pockets. Gloves, tissue, Clorets gum, keys.

He was standing no more than a foot away from me. Family patterns die hard. I could easily have been seven years old fighting the same struggle of being wedged between loyalty to my older brother and hating the power he'd wield over me. I had just spent the better part of a week obsessed with finding him, and our reunion was off to a start that only made me remember how much I didn't like him. Here I was, finally face-to-face with him. The last thing I expected to feel was anger.

This wasn't the reunion I'd expected, but then again, I hadn't allowed myself to imagine anything. No fantasies of what it would be like if we were actually face-to-face again.

I nodded to my jacket, which he had tossed onto the floor. "May I have my jacket back?"

"Nice jacket, Sis. I always said you had class." He

bent down, picked it up, and threw it at me. "Now, what was it you wanted to drink?" As he said this, the tone of his voice and his body language changed in a flash. He was more relaxed, almost jovial. Though David was slimmer than I would have expected, as he headed back to the bar I could see that he carried himself forward, as if at any given moment he would tip over onto his face.

"Champagne? After all, this is a celebration, isn't it?" I slipped my arms through the sleeves of my jacket.

"That all depends on how you look at it. Me? I don't see it as much of a celebration." He scratched under his armpit and suggested I consider something else for my libation. His faded brown hair fell over his forehead. When he brushed it back, I realized that he looked older—a good ten years older than forty-two.

"How about a cognac?" I really wanted an orange juice, but I figured a touch of brandy would have medicinal value.

"Yup. Dad would have been proud of you. But then, he always was, wasn't he?" He patted a bar stool and waited for me to place myself there before he went behind the bar and poured us both a drink. Jack Daniel's neat for himself and a Remy for me.

"Dad was proud of you, too. You were the one who didn't like yourself," I reminded him.

"And you, Sydney, don't forget you didn't like me, either." He smiled as he poured my drink.

"No, I really didn't." We stared at each other. "You know, David, I always felt comfortable not liking you because it was reciprocated."

"Yeah, well that's true enough." His eyes sparkled as he lifted his glass. "Here. To burying the hatchet?"

"I'll drink to that." We clinked glasses and drank to his toast. "It's good to see you."

He nodded. His collar was opened, revealing a few

strands of graying chest hair. He wore a wrinkled work shirt, jeans, and a blue and red striped tie. His beige sports jacket barely covered his shoulder holster.

"So, what happened?" I asked.

He put down his glass, rubbed his eyes, and yawned. "What do you mean what happened? When? In Israel? At Rikers? Pick a segment of history and I'll fill you in."

"Why don't we start with your death." I leaned back into the stool and crossed my legs. He smelled like bourbon and Old Spice, both of which have a noxious effect on me.

"I died of boredom." When he smiled, his eye seemed to pull farther to the left. "Actually, I was made an offer I couldn't refuse." He took another swallow of bourbon and continued.

"Let's see, when I first left the States, I wasn't what you would call a real desirable citizen. As a matter of fact, I had a court date for sentencing, but the idea of spending more time behind bars didn't exactly appeal to me. So I thought, Let me just get the hell out of this country and I'll go straight. When I first got to Israel, I met Basha. Basically, I told her the truth about myself. Then it turned out that her father had connections and they made a deal with the U.S. government—as long as I stayed in Israel, I was a free man. I married Basha and everything went okay for the first six months. Then I realized something very important."

"What was that?"

"I wasn't free. I hated my life, I hated my in-laws, and I sure as hell hated working in their bookstore. I busted my ass ten hours a day, and for what? So I started writing Dad for pocket change. I mean, I couldn't live on what I was making, you know what I mean?" He slid his hand into his jacket pocket and pulled out a pack of cigarettes. He tapped the package against the edge of the bar and slid one of the exposed cigarettes between his lips. "Want one?" He held the unfiltered Indian brand out to me. I shook my head and tried not to inhale the acrid smoke. Indian cigarettes always smell like cow dung to me.

His skin tone had darkened as a result of living in Israel and he could easily be taken as either Italian, Hispanic, or Middle Eastern. He was still a serious nail biter. His hands were almost painful to look at. What little stubs of nails he had remaining on each finger were sunken into the swollen red skin around them.

"But the pocket change from Dad wasn't enough and I discovered two things. One, I have a gift for languages. I can learn just about any language in a matter of weeks—at least enough to get by—and if I study for a few months, I'm able to speak fluently. Well, by then I was bored, so I started the old game. I mean, it was too easy not to. With the number of tourists that come to Jerusalem—and I mean stupid tourists—I was raking it in hand over fist. Wallets, traveler's checks, credit cards—you name it and I could pinch it. The second thing I learned was the more I forged, the better I became at it. I became so good, all I had to do was glance at a signature to duplicate it." Pride washed over his face and for a second he looked almost boyish. "That kept me entertained until my activity was . . . curtailed, you might say." He held the cigarette between his thumb and index finger. I'd never seen him smoke before and he didn't look comfortable with it.

"There were these two men who knew all about me and my moonlighting. They came to visit me one day and made me an offer I couldn't refuse. Remember Roger Farris?"

"Sure." Who could forget one of David's more colorful childhood friends? Rumor was that he had been stabbed to death in a southern penitentiary.

"To make a long story short, he was involved in smuggling and I had the option either to help the government nail him—after which I would be rewarded with the freedom to globe-trot—or not. Not helping them would find me behind bars for theft and forgery, among other things. It wasn't what you would call a real difficult decision to make." He sighed as he dropped the cigarette onto the floor and squashed it under his shoe. He finished off the J.D. in his glass and poured another two fingers.

"Anyway, these guys suggested that if I helped them, they'd help me. I'd be working together with the American and Israeli governments and as my reward I would be given a new identity and enough money to start over elsewhere." He placed another cigarette between his dry lips, lit a match, and inhaled deeply.

"Much to my surprise, I actually liked what I did. I mean, Roger was an asswipe anyway, so I didn't feel any disloyalty when they finally caught him with his pants down. But I mean, I *liked* the undercover work. At first, it scared the shit out of me. I didn't want to die, but then I wasn't really attached to life, so I got into it. Anyway, after they got Rog and I had myself a new identity, I thought, Hey, man, I'm a whole new person; I can do whatever the fuck I want to do. So there I was in Wales and it hits me what I want to do—I want to work with these guys again. So I head back to Israel."

"Did Basha know?" I asked.

"Basha thought I'd died in that explosion, too. There wasn't any other choice. It was too dangerous for her if she knew I was alive."

I gave him a look of disbelief.

"All right, I would have gone nuts if I'd had to stay with her and her family." He grabbed a handful of peanuts from a bowl on the bar and popped a few into his mouth. "Anyway, these guys know me, know I'm good with language, bright, and, if I was nothing else, a great con artist. So they put me through this training program and the next thing I know I'm working my ass off. And I love it." He polished off his fistful of peanuts and wiped his hand on his pants. "We're talking all expense-paid government-approved games of bullshit. It was great. Anyway, about two years ago I came to the States for the first time in over a decade. Someone was stealing secret documents and selling them to the highest bidder. This was all taking place here and having a nasty effect on the Middle East."

I rested my elbows on the bar. "This ties in with Washburn and Keller?"

"Eyup." He drained his glass and dragged the bourbon bottle back to where he was standing.

"Mildred Keller was one nasty broad." He laughed softly and shook his head. "She also had mucho expensive taste. Unfortunately, on her income she couldn't really afford herself. That is until she discovered that she could make a lot of money selling information."

"To?"

He raised his eyebrows, half-closed his eyes, and shrugged. "Any number of bidders. Her last known association was with Iran." He ran his stubby fingers through his thinning hair. "She had a contact at the Pentagon who was supplying her with information regarding chemical warfare. With the documents that she was passing to the Iranians, they would have the capabilities to build a plant that could produce enough mustard gas to wipe out the United States. Not a very nice lady."

"But how does Washburn fit in? I'm a pretty good judge of character and what I know about him doesn't seem very sinister."

"Just incredibly unlucky." He loosened his tie.

"So they weren't lovers?"

"No, not as far as we knew. She was just a steady customer, that's all. She did have a lover, but I never saw him. He might even have been one of those yo-yos she was dealing with."

"Who killed them?"

He took a deep breath. "My guess would be her business associates. Charming bunch of guys. Believe me, they wouldn't hesitate to slaughter their mothers if they thought it would get them a front-row seat in heaven."

David exhaled the smoke, which was smelling more and more like cow dung, over my head. "Then again, it could have been a junkie or maybe even someone who knew them both; there wasn't any sign of a struggle that I could see."

"So you *were* there?"

"Well, yeah, afterward. I had been tailing her all day. When she went into the liquor store, I was waiting for her across the street."

"What did you see?"

"Nothing, really." He slapped his hand down onto the bar, flattening a cockroach, and then wiped his hand with a cocktail napkin. "I mean, no one went in or out of the front door except for her and me. There's a back entrance the killer must have used. There was this one guy who came out from around the street side and hailed a cab on the avenue about five minutes before I went in. He could have done it."

"What did he look like?"

"Tall. That's all I know. He was covered up pretty well."

"Do the police know this?"

"Everyone knows. Look, I told you, I'm protected."

"But they stopped looking for the real murderer."

"Maybe. Maybe not." He shrugged.

"Believe me, they have. As far as this moron at Midtown North is concerned, you and I murdered Washburn, Keller, and Shelley." I stopped short, the air caught in my lungs. "You heard about Shelley, didn't you?"

"Yeah, I did." He started chewing his left thumbnail. "Too bad, she was a nice girl."

"You have a child with Shelley." I was stunned at how flippant he sounded.

"Yeah? So?" He took a drink and wiped his mouth with the back of his hand.

"What do you mean, 'Yeah? So?' " I was so angry, it felt as if my torso had turned into concrete.

He threw his cigarette on the floor. "Look, I don't ever make promises. I like not having to feel responsible to or for anyone. As far as I'm concerned, women are like cars—every few years, you trade them in for a new one. Shelley knew there were no promises." He sniffed and wiped his mouth. "You can glare at me all you like, Sydney, but facts are facts and it doesn't change because you think I'm a jerk."

"Jesus, David, she loved you. She had your child. And she died a horrible death. You're right, I do think you're a jerk."

David shook his head and looked away. We were older and the setting was new, but the dynamics hadn't changed. The friction between us was as vigorous and stiffling as it had been fifteen years ago when we'd last been together.

"Do you know who killed her?" I asked.

"No." He drained his glass again and motioned to my cognac. "Drink up. The party's over."

"What does that mean?" I held the nearly full glass in my right hand.

"It means our little family reunion has come to an end." He chewed on his thumbnail.

"Wait a minute, I still have a few questions."

"Like what?" He glanced at his watch.

"Like if you have such great connections, why did you spend six months in jail? Why weren't you out on bail? Or how about where have you been for the past week? Or why call Nora only to hang up on her and then suddenly show up at Minnie's?"

"If Keller was killed because of business, it was important that my identity be protected. My contacts figured that jail might be the best way to protect me, so it was arranged that the judge would deny me bail. Let me tell you, I was not happy with this arrangement."

"So why set you free now? And why not release you on bail? Why use an attention-getting device like forgery?"

"First, we were waiting for Keller's pals to be rounded up, but it was taking for fucking ever. Just when the accommodations at the Hotel Rikers were really starting to get to me, my guys pull through with these bogus release papers. They figured it was the fastest way to do it. But what happens? My organization doesn't share with New York's Finest and the next thing I know my fucking picture's splattered all over the newspapers. By the time it gets cleared up internally, the damage is done."

"But Gil said there was shit hitting the fan internally."

"Right, because that's what they told everyone. But the higher-ups know the real situation. Me? All I know is, I'm out of jail and the attention is going to blow over—two days after my release, I was supposed to be in Amsterdam."

"But?"

"But Shelley got killed and the media got involved again." He shook his head and grabbed another fistful of peanuts. "Believe me, reporters are murder."

"So where have you been for the past week?"

He looked around the club. "Julie put me up."

"The manager with the keys?"

"That's right." He ate a few nuts and licked his fingers. "Look, it's been grand, but I have a plane to catch. What was your last question?"

"Why call Nora and hang up on her?"

He bristled. "Because I had to protect myself. If there was a tap on her phone, I didn't want to be traced."

"Who would be trying to trace you?"

"Sydney, I'd love to continue this, but, like I said, I'm on the go." He pulled a pack of mints from his pocket and stuck one in his mouth.

"Who's Caleb Simeon?"

He stopped chewing and looked at me. He didn't make any movement to leave.

"It's a hunch, but I think he killed Shelley, or had her killed. Could he have killed Keller?" I asked.

David stared at his empty glass. He said nothing.

"He paid me a visit a few days ago and told me that he was friends with Shelley. He tried to buy my services to find you. He said that Noah Alexander owed him a considerable sum of money. I went to see Shelley to find out if she knew him and that's when I discovered she was dead. The next thing I know, a police officer who was tailing me is killed across from my office. I got a call from his gorilla suggesting I accept his offer and look for Noah. Last night he and a friend visited me at home and tried to be even more persuasive. They threatened Nora, which was what led me to Minnie's. What gives?"

Before he could answer, there was the frightening sound of a gunshot in the outer lobby. I jumped off the bar stool and hit the floor. Just as I was turning around, I saw a man in a white bloodstained shirt come crashing through the swinging doors. Dead.

I didn't bother to watch who followed. I rolled on my side to get behind the bar and held out my hand to David. "Give me my gun." He slapped it in the palm of my hand. He was sweating profusely and his eyes were reddened from drinking. "You know who this is?" I nodded toward the entrance.

"The devil incarnate. Caleb must have followed you here." He inched his back up against the counter and strained to see in the mirror that was hanging over the bar. The top of his head barely brushed the countertop when a single shot rang out and half the mirror shattered into hundreds of pieces.

"He couldn't have followed me," I whispered.

"Then how would he get here?" he whispered back as he wiped glass shards out of his hair.

"Come out, come out wherever you are." I recognized Caleb's voice. There were three sets of footsteps. One was moving toward the stage area, one was dead center, kicking the vacuum cleaner out of the way, and the third set of footsteps had stopped at the doorway. I assumed that was where Caleb was standing, as his voice didn't seem to move. "I know you're there, so why don't you just come out and make things easier for everyone."

The bottles behind the bar were shattered by the deafening spray of an automatic. It came from the stage area and I could hear the marksman laughing. I was terrified. With my belly flattened to the floor, I barely inched out from behind the bar and took aim. I held my breath, squeezed the trigger, and caught him in the center of his forehead with one shot. It was Walter. He looked surprised as he fell backward, spread-eagle onto a plastic potted palm. My ears were ringing as I rolled back behind the bar.

Another round of automatic fire pierced through the upper portion of the bar, sending splinters of wood and glass flying everywhere. It came from dead center. David fell to his side and grabbed his chest. Blood poured out between his fingers and pain was etched on his face. "Fuck," he whispered. He twisted around and called out to Caleb. "Wait a minute." He took a deep breath. "I'll make a deal with you, Caleb." He was carefully examining the splintered bar front as he spoke.

"Oh, a deal? What sort of deal, David?" He pronounced David's name with both contempt and an Israeli accent, making it sound like Dahveed. His voice was still coming from the back of the room. From the sound of his footsteps, the third man, who had been in the center aisle, seemed to be moving closer to the wall opposite the stage. I crawled carefully over the broken glass and mirror to the other end of the bar and followed David's lead. Through the bullet holes in the wood, we might be able to take aim at one of them.

David's voice was getting hoarse. "Well, what is it you want most?"

I wasn't able to see a thing through the small holes in the bar. I was, however, able to catch a glimpse of a shadow moving across the wall closer to me. When Big Walt had caught it in the head, he had tipped the light away from the bar. From the angle of the reflections on the opposite wall, it was shining almost directly on Simeon. If I could distract the third man for just half a second, I'd have a fair chance at hitting him.

The stench of all the liquor, old cigarette butts, sweat, and my own fear was almost gagging. I held my breath and watched the shadow. Shards of broken glass dug into my knees. Right in front of me was the metal caddy that contained the bar bottles, inferior brands they pour if you don't specify a name brand. One quarter-full bottle of White Crown vodka remained intact. I gently slid it out of the rack and emptied the contents onto the floor.

"There's only one thing I want, David, and that's to see you dead once and for all, dead and buried." His voice neared us. "I promised my brother I would avenge him. It is unfortunate your lovely sister will die also, but as you people say, 'Them's the breaks.' "

David's breathing was labored. "Any suggestions?" he whispered. I nodded and gestured that I would take the one on the left if he could handle Caleb. He nodded.

"Do you hear me, David?" Caleb called out.

"Of course I hear you. I'm not deaf. Answer me one question first, okay?"

Caleb sighed impatiently. "What is it?"

"Why did you kill Shelley?"

"Walter just got a little carried away," he said casually. "He was only supposed to frighten her, but the next thing I knew he had cut out her tongue. A sure way to keep her quiet, wouldn't you say?" He laughed softly. "Actually, her death was an act of kindness, David, which is more than I can say about you. Enough now, face me head-on."

David squinted through the hole in the wood and nodded at me. He counted one, two, three with his fingers and I threw the bottle at the shadow on the wall. At the same time, David squeezed the trigger of his gun repeatedly. I rolled out from behind the bar and caught sight of my quarry. He had shot at the bottle and now was firing wildly, shooting up the ceiling and the other half of the already-broken mirror. The bottle had thrown him and he had stumbled backward against a table, losing his footing. I fired three shots and watched him crumple to the floor. Behind me, all I could hear were deafening screams and gunfire.

And then there was silence.

FIFTEEN

From where I was lying, I could see that both Caleb and his associate were sprawled out and motionless. Caleb was on the floor and the third in their trio was lying over a table. As I sat up, I realized I was bleeding from my left arm. I was dizzy from the noise echoing in my head.

"David," I said as I crawled closer to him. He was lying on his back, holding his chest. His face was covered with blood and he was staring at the ceiling. He was still breathing. "David, can you hear me?"

"Why does everyone think I'm deaf?" His voice was weak. "We got 'em?"

"We got them." I gently placed his head on my lap.

I could hear the distant sound of sirens.

"Such a rude interruption." David smiled and licked his dry lips.

"Who was Caleb, David?" I reached for a box of cocktail napkins in the back of the shelf behind the bar and gently cleaned his face.

"A long time ago, I helped jail his brother, Mahmud. They're religious fanatics who like to blow up things. Killing children under five was Mahmud's specialty. It was in the name of God that he blew up a school bus with thirty kids inside. They didn't have a chance." He tried to take a deep breath. "After Mahmud was jailed, Caleb vowed to kill me. Because I usually don't keep the same identity for more than a year, he had trouble finding me. It took the scumbag a long time to catch up with me."

The sirens were wailing louder and louder. David's breath grew fainter and fainter. I tried to reposition him in my lap. When I brought my hand up, it was covered with his warm blood.

"Hey, Sydney, detectives don't cry."

"I love you, David."

"I love you, too, kid." He took his last raspy breath. I gently closed his eyes and pulled his arms over his chest. Every part of my body felt as if it were on fire. In my mind's eye, all I could see was David as a little boy one Christmas morning when he had received a chemistry set. All day, he sat hunched over the set, mixing this and that, threatening to shrink me with a potion if I got too close. At dinner that night, David had announced, "I want to save the world." Dad asked, "From what?" And David had told us, "From ourselves."

I rested my hand on his. For the first time since I could remember, he looked calm. All the tension was gone and a very serene man was what remained sprawled out before me. My brother.

The silence was shattered as sirens screeched to an abrupt halt followed by the sound of police crashing through the front door.

"Oh Jesus." I heard Gil's familiar voice. "Sydney, you in there?" Hurried footsteps followed behind him. "Stay where you are," he ordered the overzealous feet. "Syd. It's me, Gil."

"I'm here." My voice cracked. "Behind the bar."

He squatted beside me and holstered his gun. "Minnie called me and told me where you would be. She was scared. Someone called, told her they were with the police force and that they thought you'd been injured. It was a ruse to find out where you were. As soon as she told them, she knew she'd been taken, so she called me. On my way over here, I heard the call that shots had been fired. You okay?"

"Gilbert, this is Noah Alexander. He didn't kill Washburn or Keller." I could feel the tears burning inside me. I bit my lip and held my breath.

"Oh God." Gilbert took a close look at David and put his hand gently over mine. "You were right."

I nodded, unable to speak.

"Come on, Sydney, let's get you out of here." He tried to pry my hands off David's.

I shook my head. "I'm not ready. Not yet."

Gil stooped down and gently took David's head in his hand. He moved David's head from my lap to the floor, slid his arm around my waist, and pulled me up. Shards of broken glass and mirror had become embedded in my knees and the palms of my hands. I tried to grab on to him to keep my knees from buckling under me, but my hands were useless.

There were about ten police officers in the club now, and five dead men. I saw Caleb's body in the aisle, next to the vacuum cleaner. David had hit him three times, all in the torso. His marksmanship surprised me. Unlike David, whose face was serene in death, Caleb looked as though he might be chasing my brother far into the hereafter.

"Who's that?" Gil pointed to the first man who had been shot and was curled up in a fetal position by the double doors.

I shrugged. "I don't know."

Gil led me to a small round table and tried to ease my jacket off. "The thing that scares me is that one day I'm gonna be scraping *you* off the goddamned floor."

"I told you it was David."

"You tried to. I was just too damned stubborn to listen."

There was a shearing pain down my left arm as he ripped the sleeve off my shirt. I held my breath and slowly released it. "David didn't kill anyone. Nobody. Not Shelley. Not Washburn. Not Keller. Not Cohen."

"Who did?"

I sighed. "That one killed Shelley and Cohen." I pointed to Walter, who was still sprawled out on the plastic potted palm. "It's more than likely that he also killed Washburn and Keller."

"We got a live one over here, boss," said a police officer who was squatting next to the third gunman, the one who had shot at the vodka bottle.

Gil joined the officer, and two medics were right behind him. Gil grabbed the second medic and said, "I don't care what it takes, I want him alive."

Gil looked at me with his hound-dog eyes and shook his head. "I let you down. I let David down." He grunted, shook his head, and then took a chair off a table and straddled it across from me. "I don't know what to say."

"This isn't your fault."

"If I had listened to you—" he began.

"Right. And if I hadn't seen his picture in the first place," I interrupted. "Look, Gil, you and I could rake ourselves over the coals for the rest of our lives, but the truth is, we just do the best we can." I didn't really believe what I was saying, but I had to say it or else I'd start screaming. Pretending that I had a grasp on reality might be all I needed to get me out of there without ripping the place apart.

An older medic who looked like a leprechaun had joined us and was poking at my arm. He succeeded only in enhancing the pain.

"She's going to have a cute little scar there, wouldn't ya say, Gilbert?"

"Adorable. Gimme a pencil, would you?" He pulled his cigarettes out from his coat pocket and started to unwrap them from the rubber bands and tally sheet. "Can you imagine what these schmucks think when they read this?" He held up the white paper and read sample questions: 'Reason for cigarette? What are you feeling?' He shook his head. "I know what they think. They say, 'Jeeze, what's he, nuts? This guy *should* smoke!' "

There was a muffled commotion behind me. Then I heard Collier's voice loud and clear, "Get outta my way, goddamn it."

I didn't even bother to turn.

"You want to tell me what's going on here, Sloane?" He positioned himself between Gilbert and me.

"Detective Collier, meet Lieutenant Jackson." I motioned in Gilbert's direction.

Collier jumped as if he'd been goosed and swung full around to face Gil, who was making his cigarette entry on his tally sheet.

———

225

"Jackson?" He stepped back and shoved his hands in his pockets. "I got word that she was involved in some fireworks up here." He surveyed the place. The third gunman was being lifted onto a stretcher and the other four bodies were being photographed. "Any of these stiffs Alexander?" He pushed out his chin.

Gilbert and I shared a glance.

"You need her, Gil? It's time she went to the hospital," the leprechaun suggested.

"Now wait a minute." Collier gestured that I keep my seat.

Gil took a long drag off his cigarette and stood up. He was a good five inches shorter than Collier, but he towered over the man. "Detective . . . Collier, was it? If you have any questions, I'll be more than happy to answer them as soon as I get everything cleared up here. In the meantime, Ms. Sloane is going to get her arm taken care of. Don't you agree that's the best course of action?"

"Miss Sloane is under investigation in connection with another murder, Lieutenant," Collier hissed. His forehead and upper lip were shiny with sweat.

"Well, I'll personally vouch for her. How's that?" He poked his cigarette in my direction. "Don't leave town, you hear?"

I nodded. I refused to use the stretcher, but because of the glass in my knees, I didn't argue when my Irish medic helped me out to the ambulance. Just as we were about to go, Gil put his hand on my cheek and kissed my face. "I'm glad you're alive." He then turned away. "Now get out of here and take good care of her, Tom."

"You bet." Tom's arms were strong and comforting as he led me past the lifeless body at the entrance and the crowds who had gathered outside. Without my jacket, the cold seemed to blast right through me.

In the back of the ambulance, all I could see was

David looking up at me just before he died. David and I had spent the better part of our lives distrusting one another. It seemed odd that ultimately it was our trust in each other that had kept at least one of us alive.

Still, David was dead because of me. I was responsible for his death, but I couldn't allow myself to think about it just yet. I still had to find out whether Caleb had killed Jesse Washburn and Mildred Keller, and why. Was she selling him information or were they lovers? Or both?

I realized that I didn't really feel anything emotionally. The only sensations I could determine were physical—the searing heat in my arm and my knees. Even then, it was the only pain and numbness that I would allow myself to acknowledge. Someone closed the ambulance door. I lay back on the stretcher and shut my eyes as the ambulance sped through the city streets.

SIXTEEN

I was lucky. The bullet had passed clean through my arm and missed the bone. Despite the doctor's recommendation, I refused to stay in the hospital overnight. By the time they had finished with me, it was close to six and night was well under way. I called Minnie from the emergency room at Metropolitan and told her I was coming over.

"Good God," she said when she opened the door. "You look awful." She checked the hallway behind me and let me in.

"I'm alone." I let her help me take off a white medical jacket someone had given me in the hospital. It was little protection against the cold, but my jacket had been left at the comedy club and I needed something. Minnie disappeared into the second bedroom and returned with a hooded, zipper sweatshirt I keep there.

I let her help me into the sweatshirt and drank in the apartment, virtually a museum of the twenties. It was warm and inviting, which was just what I needed. There was Mahler on the stereo, something with onions on the stove, and two bottles—one of gin and one of tonic—out on the kitchen counter.

"Can you have that?" Minnie pointed to the gin as she led me into the kitchen, a huge room that was big enough to seat six as well as house a desk with a computer by the windows.

"I can. At least I think I can. Actually, I *want*, which outweighs can or cannot." With my left arm in the sling, my mobility was only somewhat hampered. My arm hurt like hell, but keeping it practically strapped to the front of my body seemed to lessen the pain. The doctor had administered a local anesthetic when she took the glass from my knees, so the pain there was still virtually nil. And once the fragments of glass were taken from my hands, it was as if I had nothing more than a dozen paper cuts there. I wouldn't want to make lemonade, but at least my hands were useful again.

Minnie went to the refrigerator and pulled out a small bottle of dry vermouth. "Make me a martini, would you, dear?"

I gingerly pulled a glass out from an overhead rack and poured a healthy shot of gin over ice for myself. I wanted to tell her what had happened, but the words stuck in my throat like the caster oil and orange juice combo my mom gave us as kids. I added tonic to my glass and took a long sip. When I had finished mixing her martini, I asked, "Did you know he called Nora?"

"Yes. He told me this morning." She took a chilled

martini glass out of the freezer and placed it on the counter. "Why don't we take those into the other room and you can tell me what happened."

Small brass lamps with green fringed shades lighted the living room along with a dozen or so candles. Minnie helped me get situated on the sofa. I propped a pillow under my knees and watched as she prepared to settle into her favorite chair, a rocker that had belonged to her mother. I felt like one of Minnie's more weary contemporaries, watching with a vague sense of envy as she seemed to float about the room, adjusting lamps, positioning coasters, and finally alighting gracefully onto the rocker.

"Did you learn much last night?" I skirted the real issue.

"Yes." She sipped her martini.

"What?"

She took a deep breath and studied the ceiling, the off-white surface with forest green molding in need of fresh paint. "I learned that I like David. I've always loved him, but, you know, ever since I can remember, he's made liking him difficult. Just like Juliet." She glanced at the picture of her parents on the table beside me. The silver frame contained a sepia-toned photograph of Juliet and James Sloane. He was a handsome man with soft, loving eyes who wore a full wiry beard, pince-nez, and stiff collar and tie. Her smile was almost pained, as if the camera frightened her, but she was beautiful, nonetheless. She had high cheekbones, delicate features, and thick dark hair piled up into a Gibson. "Mother couldn't stand the thought of getting too close with anyone, even her husband and children. I think she believed that if she remained distant, she wouldn't risk getting too hurt by loss or disappointment." She started rocking slowly back and forth. "David doesn't want anyone to get too close, either, but just for the opposite reason—because he's afraid he'll hurt others. Poor boy, he's invested so much time in deceiving people, I fear he's lost sight of who he is."

Silence filled the space between us. Finally, she asked, "Is he dead?"

It was several moments before I could answer. "Yes."

A faint sound escaped from Minnie's throat.

Neither of us moved. After a while, I remembered to breathe. Minnie's eyes were shut and her lips were moving as if in prayer. I tried to remember the last time I had prayed. I couldn't.

"Tell me what happened." She moved from her chair and sat beside me on the sofa. Half an hour and another drink later, Minnie knew the whole story.

"I told Gil that it wasn't either of our faults, but you know, Min, if I hadn't gone looking for him, chances are likely that David would still be alive. I didn't pull the trigger, but I killed him."

"You didn't kill him, darling, his work did." She placed her hand on my thigh and rubbed it gently. "David was a big boy and he made his own choices. Even as a child, he seemed to thrive on a sense of danger. You know after you left last night, he and I had a long talk. When I went to sleep this morning, I was happy for David, and do you know why?" She paused and I shook my head. "I was happy because he finally had a purpose in life. He really liked what he was doing, despite or maybe because of the danger." She stopped and smiled softly. "He said he never thought he'd get to be one of the good guys and it was important to him that we all knew it.

"So you mustn't hold yourself responsible for this, my dear. To feel guilty is really only egocentric. Besides,

David had a premonition that he was going to die. I think part of him actually wanted it." She held her glass out and toasted, "To David." She touched her glass to mine and drank.

The liquor was going to my head faster than I needed or wanted. We had dinner—a chicken cassoulet and arugula salad and sourdough bread—in the kitchen. I washed mine down with ice-cold milk, whereas Minnie chose a light chardonnay. By dessert, I was practically falling asleep in my tea.

"You'll sleep here tonight." Minnie led me to my room. I don't remember anything after brushing my teeth. As soon as my head hit the pillow, I must have been out like a light.

I slept late and when I awoke it felt as if my head and shoulder were directly connected with a pair of red-hot pincers. With the grace of a one-legged penguin, I was able to roll out of bed and into the shower. Between my knees and my shoulder, it took me more than an hour to shower and dress, but by 11:30 I was finally ready to face the world.

Minnie was puttering in the kitchen. Smudges of flour were on her cheeks, in her hair, and on the floor.

"How do you feel?" she asked absentmindedly.

"Wonderful," I lied.

"There's coffee over there." She pointed to the table, where there was not only a thermos of coffee but a pitcher of orange juice. "You want an egg or something?" she asked as she measured baking powder into a metal bowl.

"No thanks." I poured juice from the pitcher into a glass that had been placed beside it. "Maybe you should open a bed-and-breakfast," I suggested.

"Who has time for that?" She made an entry on her

small computer and then returned to the counter, where she sifted cornmeal into the same metal bowl.

"New recipe?"

"Mm-hm. New cookbook. Twenty romantic menus for couples on the go." She rolled her eyes. "I agreed to do it because I thought it would be a piece of cake." She snorted. "Boy, was I wrong!" She flapped her right hand at me and said, "Sit down and have a decent breakfast."

"This is fine." I stood as I drank the juice and poured some coffee. "I have a lot to do today."

"You should be resting today. I can't imagine you got any sleep making all the noise that you did."

"I made noise last night?"

"When you weren't thrashing around, you were crying."

"Well, I'm not surprised. Have you ever slept in that bed?"

She peered over her glasses and asked, "Would you like me to handle the arrangements for David's funeral?"

"No, thank you; that's something I have to do."

"Don't forget Nora."

"No, I won't forget Nora." I sighed. "But there are a few things I have to do first. May I use the phone in the bedroom?"

I called the office to listen to the messages and was surprised when Kerry answered.

"What are you doing there? It's Sunday."

"I left my telephone book here Friday and I needed it," she said shortly.

"What's wrong?"

"Where are you?"

"Minnie's. Why?"

"You must be stepping on toes. The office was broken into yesterday. The place is a mess. You want me to call the police?"

"No. I'll be right there. Have you started cleaning it?"

"Not yet. I've been trying to find you."

"I'll be right in. Don't touch anything, okay?"

Thanks to the fact that my body was a mess, it took longer to get there than usual, but within the hour I was standing in the doorway of our offices. Whoever had been here made a mess of the lock on my office door, as well as the frame. Don't these idiots know neatness counts?

"What happened to you?" Kerry came out of Max's office and pointed to my arm with a copy of the *Village Voice*.

"I found David yesterday."

"Oh my God, that's great!" She helped me slip off a jacket I had salvaged from Minnie's and asked quietly, "Did he do this to you?"

"No." I started moving through the chaos. Whoever was here had done a fine job of messing things up. Both of the file cabinets had been emptied onto the floor. "Can you tell if anything's missing?"

"No, but you should see your office."

My office looked virtually untouched until you got to the desk. The blotter had been pushed off to the side and on it there was a pile of ashes from a carefully burned set of files. Beside that, there was a slashed picture of Shelley and a yellowed copy of David's mug shot from the papers. Carved into the desktop was this message: "Leaf Me Alone." A common paring knife was jammed into the wood at the end of the note, like an exclamation mark. I ran my hand lightly over the scarred wood and felt a twinge of pain for the assault on this inanimate object I had come to love over the years. Adding insult to injury, they had broken the screen to my computer. Shit. Shit. Shit.

All in all, it looked like a bad cover to a Nero Wolfe novel.

"Weird, huh?" Kerry was standing right behind me.

"Well, Noah Alexander's dead, so this isn't his handiwork."

"David's dead?" Kerry touched my right arm. I nodded. "I'm so sorry, Sydney."

"Me, too, thanks." The pain in my arm was starting to act up again. I pulled out the vial of painkillers I had gotten at the hospital and took two with the dregs of cold coffee Kerry had brought in an hour earlier.

"I guess I'll call Gil. I doubt there are any prints, but I'd hate for him to think I was holding out on him."

"Use Max's office; it's clean."

"I'd say this has interfered enough with your day off. Why don't you do a half day tomorrow? I'll call that temp agency and have them send over someone to help you with this mess, okay?"

"Why don't I call them while you call Gil?"

"Thanks."

"Oh, I forgot, there was a message on the machine. From Jimmy, about the DNA. He said he'd call you later."

I called Gil, who, before I could utter a word, gave me the address of the morgue for the funeral parlor. I asked whether David could stay there for another day.

"He can stay in the cooler for as long as you need."

That was vaguely reassuring.

"I had a visitor yesterday," I said.

"What do you mean?"

"At my office. It looks like someone wanted me to think Noah Alexander wants me off the case." I gave him the details.

"I'll send someone over there for prints."

"I don't think you'll get any, but you can try."

"Can you guess who did this?"

"Nope."

"Sydney, I can't afford to lose another Sloane this week, you know what I mean?"

"I know, Gil."

"You want some protection?"

"No. Thanks anyway." It occurred to me that if Caleb had any more brothers, chances were likely that I could use some protection. The thought was chilling. "Listen, I've got to go. I'll talk to you later."

I went back to my office. The late-morning light warmed the room and actually made it feel safe, despite the knife protruding from my desk. I walked to the windows and looked out onto Broadway. So near to Zabar's, Conran's, and Shakespeare & Company, this stretch of block is almost always bustling on the weekends. I placed my hand on the window pane, almost expecting it to be warm because of the sun. It was cold and damp to the touch.

I went back to my desk and stared at the message. Whoever had done this had had the luxury of time, for each of the slanted letters was a good two inches high and dug at least a sixteenth of an inch into the wood.

And then it hit me.

I knew who I was looking for.

Kerry came into the office, smiling. "Talk about a fluke—there was actually someone there. They're going to send someone at ten tomorrow morning." The phone rang and she automatically reached for the receiver.

"CSI, may I help you? One moment, please." She put the caller on hold and told me that it was Eddie Phillips.

"Why don't you get out of here and enjoy what's left of the day?" I suggested before I took the call.

———

"Are you sure? I can easily change my plans, believe me."

"No, but thanks. Oh, and you can come in late or leave early tomorrow. It's up to you."

"I'll leave early. That way, if we're not finished, I can stay and hit you up for a full day off later." She winked. "If you need me tonight, just call, okay?"

I nodded and waited for her to close the door behind her. Then I picked up the phone.

"Eddie?"

"Sydney, are you all right?"

"Yeah, I'm fine. Why?"

"What do you mean why? I heard there was one hell of a shoot-out at that comedy club over on First and that Noah Alexander was one of the people killed. Was Alexander your brother?"

"Yes. What else did you hear?"

"There's a paragraph buried somewhere in the paper. Here, lemme read it. Let's see, blah, blah, blah, right, okay." He cleared his throat. " 'Four men, including Noah Alexander, were found dead at the scene. Alexander had been . . .' Blah, blah, blah, blah, blah, okay. 'Two others were injured in the shoot-out, an unidentified man, listed in stable but critical condition at Metropolitan Hospital, and Sydney Sloane, a private investigator who was treated and released.' " He stopped.

"When did that come out?"

"Last night."

I paused. "You busy this afternoon?"

"What do you have in mind?"

"How's about you and me making a little news?"

"I'm all yours. What do we do?"

I told Eddie what I needed. After our call, I unlocked the bottom drawer of my desk, removed the false bottom, and made sure my father's old Colt hadn't been touched.

The last thing I needed now was someone running around the city with a gun registered to me. Then I cleaned the one I had used the day before.

The phone rang and I monitored the answering machine. (Ain't modern gadgets great?) When I heard Leslie's voice, I stopped the recorder.

"I was just thinking about you." I cradled the receiver while I returned the Colt .38 to its hiding place.

"Are you all right? I just heard about yesterday."

"I'm fine."

"What does all this mean? Mom and I haven't heard boo from the police. Shouldn't they have contacted us or something?"

"Not necessarily." I slipped a new magazine into the Walther.

"Well, what did you find out? Was Alexander guilty or what? I mean, I have a few hundred questions I want to ask."

"Unfortunately, I can't answer any of them yet."

"What do you mean you can't answer?" There was an edge to her voice that could cut metal. "Let me get this right. I thought you and I had some kind of understanding. . . ."

"We do. But I told you before, that's all the more reason for you not to get involved." The painkiller finally started to kick in.

"But I am involved! Now, did Alexander kill my father or not?"

"No, he didn't."

"Then who did?"

"I don't know for sure."

"Well, what do you know?"

It was time to start sharing with Leslie.

"I know that Noah Alexander did not kill your father. I know this because before he was killed, we had a long conversation about what he did and did not see the day your father died. I know he saw your father after he had been killed but that another person was responsible for the executions." I paused. "I know, too, that Noah Alexander was actually my brother, David Sloane. That's all I know right now."

"He was your *brother?*"

"Yes."

"Did you know that all along?"

"I was working with that assumption."

She sighed loudly on the other end of the line. "I can't tell you how frustrating this is." She paused. "I'm sorry about your brother. But at the same time, I am so angry at you."

"Leslie, I promise you, I will get to the truth."

"For all *I* know, the truth could be that your brother *did* kill my father and you're trying to cover it up."

She had a point.

"You see, you're not the only one who wants the truth, Sydney."

Another point.

"Have you any idea how unfair it is that my mother and I are kept in the dark? I can't get a straight answer from anyone, not the cops, not the attorneys, not you. I guess I was mistaken to think I could expect more from you."

"Okay." I sighed. "Are you free after five today?" I suggested she give me the rest of the day and that at 5:15 we would meet at the Top of the Beekman for cocktails. At that time, I would give her a complete update. She agreed.

That gave Eddie and me less than four and a half hours to prove who had killed Jesse Washburn and Mildred Keller.

It looked like it was going to be another long day.

SEVENTEEN

When we were little, once a month my father would take us kids to the Beekman Towers for Shirley Temples and his favorite view of the city. Thirty years later, the view hadn't changed all that much. At five o'clock, I was the first customer, and I was enjoying the view of the United Nations, Queens, and the East River. I ordered a club soda.

As the waiter placed the drink before me, the elevator doors opened and Leslie Washburn stepped out wearing all black. It took her only a moment before she saw me sitting across the room. She started toward me just as the other elevator door opened.

Her cheeks were flushed and she smiled uncomfortably as she tossed her coat on the brass railing beside us. "Does it hurt?" She nodded at my arm.

"Not much." A lie. "You look great." The truth.

"Just shows you how deceptive looks can be. I'm a wreck." She squinted out at the panorama, took a deep breath, and sighed. "I don't know when I've ever been so tired. Or so wired. What are you drinking?"

I told her and she made a face.

"I need something a little more invigorating." She yawned.

People started straggling in and making beelines for the window tables. The sun was setting quickly and the sky was almost, though not quite, a pure midnight blue.

"How about an Irish coffee?" I suggested.

The waiter took Leslie's order and moved quickly from our table to the row of tables behind Leslie, briskly making his way up the aisle along the windows, taking orders at every table.

"So." She dropped her shoulders.

"So." I turned out from the table and crossed my legs.

"So you look great for a woman who's just been shot up." She plucked a pack of matches out of the ashtray and started bending the front row of cardboard sticks down over the flint strip.

"Thank you." The lights in the buildings and on the street seemed to shimmer in the distance. "Pretty, huh?" I nodded to the vista.

"Very." Her eyes hadn't moved off me.

"So." I took a small sip of soda.

"So." She smiled. "Sew your own socks. This conversation is definitely reminiscent of high school socials, know what I mean?" She tossed the matchbook, which now looked like Medusa's hair, back into the ashtray.

"I hated high school. I was too tall, too shy, and too self-conscious."

"Really? I loved it. There was so much drama, like every day was a matter of life and death." She waited while an Irish coffee was placed in front of her. "Life and death." She sighed. "I suppose I've had enough death to last me for quite a while." She stared at the peaks of whipped cream that covered the top of her glass.

"How's your mom?" I asked.

She shook her head. "God"—she sighed again—"I don't know. Who can get near her with Lloyd hovering over her? As far as I'm concerned, he only makes things worse when he tries to protect her. I mean, let's face it, my mother is not what you would call particularly fragile. Don't you agree?"

"Fragile? No."

Absentmindedly, she played with a string of pearls that hung over her black turtleneck. "Lloyd's like a mother hen. He has been ever since I can remember. Anyway"—she leveled her gaze at me—"you promised me information tonight." Her eyes were filled with brave apprehension. I wanted to reach out and reassure her, but instead I pushed her back farther into the chair.

"Lloyd spends an awful lot of time here, doesn't he? I thought he lived in Washington."

"He does, but he's pretty high-level at the company where he works. I suppose he has a lot of freedom, but I've never gotten involved in his work, so I don't really know." She tilted her head to the left and gave me a shy smile. "But we're not here to talk about Lloyd, are we?"

I shrugged.

"Tell me about yesterday." She rested her elbows on the tabletop and dipped a spoon into the whipped cream.

"Yesterday." It seemed like a million years ago and

I still hadn't started funeral arrangements. "Let's see, as I told you, Noah was my brother, David."

She stirred the whipped cream into the coffee.

"And he didn't kill your father."

"Who did?" She looked like a three-year-old who can't quite reach the doorknob.

"Hello, hello." Lloyd Washburn leaned over the brass railing next to his sister's coat and looked down at us.

"What are you doing here?" Leslie sounded both surprised and miffed.

"That's a nice greeting. I had time before my flight, and since you mentioned you were going to be here, I thought I'd join you. After all, I, too, have a vested interest in this, don't I, Leslie?" He addressed me. "You don't mind, do you, Sydney?"

"Lloyd, you might say I was counting on it."

"Were you, now?" His eyes narrowed and his smile was chilling. He pulled up a chair and snapped his fingers for the waiter.

"Don't snap your fingers. It's gross." Leslie tapped his leg.

"Yes, I was," I said as I watched him pull his chair into the aisle, becoming an impassable obstacle.

"Well, I wasn't," Leslie volunteered. "Well, as long as you're here, you should know we were talking about Daddy."

"I see you've made headway?" he asked softly as he glanced at my sling.

"You could say that."

"It hasn't been too painful, I hope."

"You know what they say, Lloyd, sometimes the truth hurts."

"Somehow you don't strike me as a woman who

would use clichés." He snapped his fingers again for the waiter.

"I suppose there's a lot about me that would surprise you."

"No doubt." He crossed his legs. "We read in the paper today that Alexander was killed yesterday. Good riddance, I'd say. I think it's a shame that this state, especially this state, doesn't have capital punishment. As far as I'm concerned, the bastard got what he deserved." He glowed.

"But he didn't kill your father."

"You still believe that?" He had a masterful sneer. "What about all that evidence against him?"

I shrugged my right shoulder. "He did, however, see the murderer."

"Why didn't you tell me that before?" Leslie asked.

Lloyd folded his hands in his lap and was playing war with his thumbs. "Really?"

"Who was it?" Leslie asked.

"You made one big mistake, Lloyd."

He forced his soft lips into a tight smile. "I'm afraid I don't know what you're talking about."

"Of course you do. Your mistake was that you called attention to yourself. Ego's amazing, it'll get you every time."

"Would somebody please tell me what we're talking about?" Leslie shifted uneasily in her seat.

"Murder," I said, never taking my eyes off Lloyd.

He let out a soft laugh. "Me? Don't make me laugh."

"Leslie, your brother was interested in my investigation not because he was afraid of slander but because he had something to hide. However, I didn't know *what* until this afternoon when I met a very nice woman with a fantastic memory." The sky had become black and our reflections in the window looked like three old friends having cocktails.

Lloyd played with his college ring.

I continued. "When I went to the office this morning, I found that I had had a visitor last night. First they did a pretty thorough job of trashing the place and then do you know what they did? They tried to point a finger at Noah Alexander." I leaned closer to Lloyd and said, "You would have been more subtle if you had used neon arrows."

His Adam's apple bobbed up and down as he swallowed. There was no smile now, no false display of courtesy. He stared at the tabletop.

"What's she talking about, Lloyd?" Leslie asked her brother.

He sniffed and glanced only briefly at her. "I don't know. It sounds as if your little friend is off her rocker."

I continued. "Well, I knew it couldn't have been Noah who'd left this little mess for me. He'd never been to my office and I had been with him when he was killed earlier in the day. Now there was another person who might have killed your father, but you blew it, Lloyd. If you had just left it alone, you would have been in the clear. You see, it would have been next to impossible to prove that this one man, who's now dead himself, had anything to do with your father's murder. However, the likelihood that he was connected to it was great, so chances are we would have gone on the assumption that he *had* killed your dad. But the mess in my office threw suspicion into a whole new direction. Someone, someone who didn't know that Alexander had been killed, did a very sloppy job of trying to frame him. You see, Lloyd, Noah—David was actually his real name—he was right-handed. He could barely open a door with his left hand." I glanced at his hands. "You're left-handed, aren't you?"

246

"Many people are left-handed." He chewed the inside of his cheek.

"Absolutely, which was why I went to the police with that information. I figured that was just enough tangible evidence for them to take another look at the files and see just where you were on the day of the murder. Between that and the help of a friend at the *News,* I do believe we have you backed against the wall."

Lloyd crossed his legs and pushed back into his chair. His eyes grew darker as he looked around the bar.

"Don't be stupid, Sydney," Leslie interjected. "Lloyd was in Washington when Dad was killed. I don't like what you're saying." Her face was flushed and she reached for her Irish coffee. The creamy liquid splashed over the rim of the glass onto her hand.

"Neither do I, but the fact is, Lloyd came into the city without telling anyone, didn't you, Lloyd?"

Three tables away, a foursome laughed loudly. Everything around us appeared so calm, whereas our little trio felt as if it were about to explode. I kept my eyes on his hands.

"I don't have to answer to you." He gripped the edge of the table until his manicured nails turned red.

"Were you in town that day, Lloyd?" Leslie's voice cracked.

"Don't be ridiculous," he scoffed. "For God's sake, Leslie, you were the one who picked me up at the airport that night."

I interrupted Leslie before she could answer. "That's right, Lloyd, it's all in the files. You were at a fund-raiser at nine o'clock when you got the call about your father and by nine-thirty you were on a shuttle flight here. Your second shuttle of the day. You left work at two o'clock, claiming that you had business in Georgetown. You told your date you would meet her at the fund-raiser at eight so that you'd have time to go home and shower. But you didn't really have business in Georgetown, did you?" I shook my head. "No, you had business right here at your father's liquor store. If you took the three-thirty shuttle into New York, you could have easily killed your father and been back in time for your eight o'clock date at the fund-raiser. You're a handsome man, Lloyd, a man most stewardesses would look at twice. And my friend at the *News* was able to find a stewardess who saw you that day, not on one shuttle flight but two."

Lloyd Washburn rubbed his jaw with his right hand and looked at Leslie, who was staring blindly out the window. "Well now, you're smarter than I would have thought, Ms. Sloane." His voice was calm. His slid his left hand into his jacket pocket. "You've placed me in a most uncomfortable position," he said clearly.

"Yes, I know." I sipped the club soda.

"Why, Lloyd?" Leslie asked. "How could you kill Dad?" Leslie spoke as if she were in a dream.

"He didn't leave me any choice, Leslie," Lloyd hissed at her.

"What are you talking about?" She spoke softly. Pain and confusion had darkened her face. She didn't take her eyes off her brother.

"For crying out loud"—he shifted in his seat like a fidgeting five-year-old on the brink of a tantrum—"that son of a bitch was killing Mom, him and that whore of his. Someone had to do something . . . and since none of you seemed to care, it had to be me. I'm the only one who really loves her."

"I can't believe you killed them." Her face was twisted with grief.

"Stop saying it like that!" He wiped his mouth. "Don't you understand? He never loved Mom. I watched the way he treated her, like a . . . like one of the guys—not

---

what she really is. She's more like a goddess, a very special woman who should be treated with respect and great love. Women like her are like . . . like rare jewels, and the men who are lucky enough to be their partners have an obligation to treat them with reverence." He was panting as he spoke, his hair damp against his forehead. "But no, not him, he had to go and ruin everything, just like I knew he always would. Ever since I was a kid I knew he'd ultimately try and cheapen Mom by screwing around with some piece of trash. And he did . . . oh boy, did he ever." His entire face was wet with perspiration and his eyes were glazed.

He laughed. "I couldn't believe how fucking blind you all were." He shook his head. "All my life, I hated that son of a bitch. It drove me crazy to think that someone like him was able to be intimate with Mom. Every night I'd lie in bed and listen to them talking or laughing or fighting or . . . God, on those endless nights when he'd . . ." His voice dropped to a whisper. ". . . when he'd make love to her; I wanted to die. I knew that nobody, nobody could love her the way I did, especially him." He swallowed several times as if trying to keep from being sick.

"I went to see him at the store once and that's when I first met Mildred." He said her name as if it tasted badly. "That stupid bastard thought I bought it when he introduced her as a regular, but I wasn't born yesterday—I knew what the story was. I sat on it for months and it was driving me crazy."

He took a deep breath. "In August, I came to town just to talk to him about his affair. But when I got there, I saw through the front window that she was there, too." Beads of sweat now dropped gently from his chin to his tie. His eyes looked deadened. "As it turns out, it was an unbelievable stroke of good luck. I went in through the back way so they wouldn't see me.

"They were standing at the counter when he turned and saw me. I'll never forget the look on his face. At first, he looked surprised and then he smiled." He snorted a laugh. "That's right, the son of a bitch smiled as if he was glad I'd caught him with his bimbo. Thank God I learned to carry a gun years ago. It was perfect." He exhaled a short laugh. "She actually wet herself when I made them go downstairs. Once we were down there, it was simple. I made them both lie down on the floor and then"—he shrugged—"that was that." His eyes were looking in my direction, but I don't think he was seeing anything. "What I did, I had to do. I had to protect my mother's honor."

Leslie stared at him.

"Your father never cheated on your mother, Lloyd." I said.

He snorted. "Yeah, yeah, I know, that's what *they* said, too. Sniveling cowards, begging for their lives and trying to convince me that I had it all wrong. Right, like they were nothing more than friends."

"So what do you plan on doing now?" Unstable people with guns always tends to put me a little on edge.

"Well now, you don't leave me much choice, do you, Detective?"

"And what about Leslie?"

"You're interfered in family matters enough, don't you think?"

"Lloyd, this is crazy." Leslie touched his knee.

"I don't think you understand, Leslie. Your little friend has become a liability to me."

"So you kill me, and then what?" I baited him. "Do you kill Leslie because she knows? And if Leslie knows, what about your mother, Lloyd? What are you going to do when Dorothy finds out what you've done? Do you think she'll be proud of her little boy? Why, maybe she'll just open her arms and—"

The sound that came from Lloyd sounded more like an animal than the word *no*. As he screamed, he pulled his hand from his jacket pocket and brought his fist—gun and all—across my left cheek. I saw it coming and was able to move fast enough to pull away from its full impact.

The glasses spilled, Leslie was yelling at Lloyd, and before you could blink, our waiter had Lloyd in a half nelson and a gun pressed to the side of Lloyd's neck, just under his ear. "Police. Drop it."

Lloyd struggled and the officer pressed the gun deeper into his neck. Pinned in my chair between the window and Lloyd, I was in no position to help. Five officers bolted over from various tables, at which point Lloyd took a deep breath and held open his hand. One of the officers grabbed his gun, a 9-mm Beretta that would probably match their father's murder weapon, and pulled him away from the table.

Leslie was standing with her back pressed against the window and her face streaked with tears. She watched as they dragged her brother to a nearby wall and frisked him.

I wanted to reach out to her, to somehow soften the blow she was suffering, but my good arm felt leadened.

Lloyd was now spread-eagle against a wall, being read his rights.

There was a muted din in the bar, almost like background music. I gathered all the strength I could find and walked to Leslie. I held my hand out to her. "Come on, you should sit down."

She looked at me as if she had forgotten I was there. Her face had been drained of all its color and her eyes were red. She opened and closed her mouth several times as if about to speak, but each time she pressed her lips shut. Finally, she gave up, clamped her lips together, and shook her head. She sank into her chair.

"Are you okay?" Gil, who had been sitting at the bar, touched my shoulder.

Okay? My brother was dead, her brother was a murderer, my arm felt as if it was on fire, and he wanted to know whether we were okay?

"Just great." I went to the bar and got a shot of brandy for Leslie.

I took Lloyd's seat and held the drink out to her. "Here, take a sip."

"I don't know how to tell her," she finally whispered to the drink.

"Do you want me to go with you?" I offered.

She blinked at me. "How long did you know?"

"Less than an hour."

"Did you know everything?" she practically whimpered.

"Only that he had been to New York earlier that day."

"So you didn't even know he had done it?"

"I had a hunch." I hadn't had a motive.

"This isn't what I expected. I don't know what to do." As her tears fell, I wished they could somehow wash away the pain.

I handed her a cocktail napkin. "I know," I sighed. "Leslie, I'm so sorry."

Half an hour later, we were on the street. Leslie hailed a taxi and got into the backseat without another word or glance in my direction. Her driver took off like a streak of light.

I walked a few blocks before I climbed into the back-seat of one of the last remaining Checker cabs.

We rode through the park and I stared up at the trees. They appeared so intricate and fragile as the moonlight shone through the twigs and branches.

Once home, I didn't bother to listen to the twelve messages on the machine. Instead, I unplugged the phone, turned the answering machine's volume down, and made myself a hot bath and a cup of herbal tea. Silence. The wind started rattling against the windows. I could picture David lying in the morgue. As sure as I knew my name (a name that David had given me as a child), I knew I was responsible for my brother's death. If I hadn't gone looking for him, maybe Caleb Simeon wouldn't have found him.

Feelings I had been successfully keeping at bay finally surfaced and undeniably clear sensations of loss and shame exploded inside me, dulling all of my other senses.

Later, when the bathwater had turned cold, my tears had run dry, and I was ready to get out and join the world of the living again, I redressed my arm and rummaged through the refrigerator.

After dinner of peanut butter, bean sprouts, and bologna on whole wheat, the doorbell rang. I debated whether or not to answer. Finally, on the third buzz, I did.

"Is that a trophy from your dinner date?" Max was leaning against the hallway wall, tanned, cheery, and wearing a down jacket with a huge hood. He pointed to my arm.

"Nah, a date with my brother."

"You don't look so good." He followed me into the kitchen.

"Thank you very much." I pulled a beer out of the fridge and tossed it to him. "You, on the other hand, look like an advertisement for tourism. Wait a minute—you're back early."

"Would you believe I was concerned about you?" He poured the beer into a glass.

"No." I filled a mug with hot water and a tea bag.

"Christ. Why is it you always want the truth?" He tossed his jacket onto the back of a chair.

"It's a quirk." A little lemon, a little honey. It still tasted like tea.

"Apparently, her husband didn't like her going off with other men." He shrugged.

"Husband?" I laughed.

"Ha-ha. I'm glad you think it's so funny." He carried his beer into the den. I followed.

"I guess he wasn't paying enough attention to her." Max continued courageously.

"I guess not." It felt good to laugh.

"Anyway, she thought a few weeks with me might rekindle his interest."

By now, I was laughing so hard, tears were streaming down my cheeks and I wasn't sure whether I was laughing or crying. Finally, I was able to ask, "Did it?"

"In a word, yes." Max chuckled. "Didn't know I doubled as a marriage counselor, did you?"

"No, but I'll keep it in mind."

"Don't bother." When he laughed, his deep brown eyes sparkled as if he had diamonds hidden there. "So, my friend, what have you been up to? A little scuffle, I see?"

It took me about an hour to give him all the details.

When I finished, he shook his head and sighed. "Wow."

I grunted.

We both stared at the phony log burning away in the fireplace.

"You need help with the funeral arrangements?" he asked.

"I think I need to do it alone, but thanks."

Max left the room and returned with two snifters of cognac. When he settled back on the sofa, he handed me a glass.

"You know, Syd, if you hadn't found him, you would never have resolved hating him. Here." He held up his glass. "To brotherly love, no matter how you find it." We drank.

"You have to admit that it's pretty funny he wound up being a hero." He took my left foot and gently started massaging.

"Who'da thunk?"

"You tell Nora yet?"

"After you do the right foot, I'll tell her." I leaned back into the pillows of the sofa and shut my eyes.

E P I L O G U E

David's funeral became a small, somewhat rowdy celebration of his life. As most of us had mourned his death thirteen years ago, the tone to his second passing was actually cheerful, to the point of being almost giddy. Even Nora came around and saw it as a time to celebrate David rather than focus on our loss.

Max had suggested that David died a hero. I suppose he did, but that doesn't stop the endless flow of questions I had hoped to leave at the cemetery. I tried to contact David's associates, ostensibly to tell them of his death. I guess what I really wanted was some verfication that what David had told me was the truth.

I never got that.

As I write this, Lloyd Washburn is undergoing psychiatric treatment and it doesn't look as if he'll ever have to stand trial for his father's murder.

Mrs. Gomes won't let me near Andrew, but her husband, Cal, has a soft heart. I have taken the money Caleb Simeon left with me and opened an account for Andrew's education. Hopefully, it's just a matter of time before I'll be able to participate in my nephew's life.

My knees are back to normal, but my arm is taking its time healing.

Someone stole my leather jacket from the comedy club. Ah well.

Maxo,

You were right, this was a great idea. Sunshine, anonymity, and solitude! No one bothers you here. May stay longer than planned if not needed at home. Will call later.

Love,
Syd

Congratulations, Nicotine-Free Gil!

You ought to try this. Sandy beaches, beautiful women, clear skies, and tropical breezes. I may just move down here and open a bar. Nah, on second thought, you'd miss me and my pahtner too much. Love to Jane.

Sydney

Dear Minnie,

Imagine that, Max actually had a good idea! Can't help thinking Caryn would love it here. Ah well, keep the home fires burning.

Love, Sydney

"Are you going to write postcards all day?"

I looked up and tried to shade the sun from my eyes. It was impossible.

"I mean, I've been sitting over there for the last hour waiting for you to stop. At the rate you're moving, I'll get sun poisoning."

She tossed her beach bag next to me and sat cross-legged beside it.

"What are you doing here?" I hid behind my sunglasses.

"I'm fine, Sydney, and you?" Leslie was wearing khaki shorts, a white sleeveless top, and a plain beige baseball cap. Her sunglasses dangled from a colorful cord around her neck. Her legs were longer than I had remembered.

"You surprised me." I felt exposed, sitting there in a revealing bathing suit Kerry had helped me choose. Somewhere in my bag, there was a large white shirt. Never taking my eyes off her, I felt around inside the bag: suntan lotion, chewing gum, car keys, a Margaret Atwood novel.

"Your friend Max told me where I could find you."

"Oh, yeah?" Sandals. Newspaper. Nail file. Room key.

"I'm sorry I didn't return your calls." She looked at my bag. "Did you lose something?"

"Lose? No, no, I didn't lose anything." Eureka. "I'm just hot, that's all. The sun, you know, it's . . . it's very hot." I slid the shirt over my head.

"I couldn't return your calls." She buried her hands in the sand.

"I understood. I wouldn't have wanted to talk to me." A hint of a breeze washed past us, bringing the sound of the surf with it.

"If you want, I can go. I mean, I can't believe I

actually came here." Leslie looked small and sad and beautiful. Her eyes were darker and her skin was pale. I reached out to her.

"Go? No, I'm glad you're here." I squeezed her hand. "Hell, we could both use a vacation. Right?"

She nodded.

"Do you have a place to stay?" I asked.

"I thought I'd play it by ear."

Dear Maxo,
     Staying longer than planned.

Love, Syd